DOCTOR WHO

SHAKEDOWN

The Doctor Who *Monster Collection*

THE MONSTER COLLECTION EDITION

SHAKEDOWN

TERRANCE DICKS

BOOKS

1 3 5 7 9 10 8 6 4 2

First published in 1995 by Virgin Publishing Ltd
This edition published in 2014 by BBC Books, an imprint of Ebury Publishing
A Random House Group Company

Doctor Who is a BBC Wales production for BBC One.
Executive producers: Steven Moffat and Brian Minchin

The Random House Group Limited Reg. No. 954009
Addresses for companies within the Random House Group
can be found at www.randomhouse.co.uk

A CIP catalogue record for this book is available from the British Library.

ISBN 978 1 849 90766 8

Editorial director: Albert DePetrillo
Series consultant: Justin Richards
Project editor: Steve Tribe
Cover design: Two Associates © Woodlands Books Ltd, 2014
Production: Alex Goddard

Printed and bound in the U.S.A.

To buy books by your favourite authors and register for offers,
visit www.randomhouse.co.uk

INTRODUCTION

I was very pleased to be asked to write an introduction to *Shakedown*, if only because *Shakedown* is a very unusual *Doctor Who* book.

Way back in the 1990s, I was approached by a group of *Doctor Who* fans with a mad scheme. You'll find them all credited in the lengthy dedication. They'd somehow got hold of the copyright to make use of the Sontarans – the brutal, potato-headed alien warriors from my time on *Who*. The Sontarans, or rather just a single Sontaran, first appeared in Bob Holmes's *The Time Warrior*, which was also Liz Sladen's first show.

These fans' mad scheme was to make and market a 50-minute video. Not a *Doctor Who* video, of course. They'd only got the rights to the alien monsters, the Sontarans – and heaven forbid they should infringe the BBC's sacred *Doctor Who* copyright. But, let's say, a *Who*-type video. They'd even got a basic plot idea – a space yacht on its shakedown cruise is taken over by the Sontarans for their own no doubt evil purposes.

That was all they'd got – Sontarans and the nub of a story. They wanted me to provide the rest and write the script.

Now it was, as I've said, a mad scheme. In my days on *Who*, we were always short of two things – Time and Money. This lot had even less of both. Their budget was totally inadequate, I had about two weeks to write the script, and the fee offered was a fraction of the television norm. Moreover, I had plenty of other work on hand.

The only sensible thing would have been to turn the whole thing down. But they were a likeable, enthusiastic bunch, particularly the proposed director, Kevin Davies, and the whole thing looked like fun. I found myself saying yes.

In the following weeks, we all worked like lunatics – well, I said it was a mad scheme. Somehow I delivered the script, and the show was eventually filmed on HMS *Belfast* – parts of which were disguised as the *Shakedown* space yacht, *Tiger Moth*. This time nobody could say the sets wobbled – the walls were made of three-foot thick steel! However, we hadn't realised that if moored battleships don't wobble they do bob up and down, and shooting was often delayed by various marine noises.

But we, or rather they, Kev and the others, did it! Thanks to a stalwart crew and a brilliant cast – including Jan Chappell, Brian Croucher, and old *Who* hands Michael Wisher, Carole Ann Ford and Sophie Aldred. Even the two leading Sontarans were real characters!

The show was eventually edited and sent out into the world – where it did amazingly well. There were good reviews, good sales and eventually, to my amazement, I received some modest royalties.

So much for *Shakedown* the video. What about the book? Don't worry, I'm coming to it…

Some time later – I really can't remember how long – I got a call from my editor at Virgin Books, then publishers of original *Doctor Who* novels. (By this time all the available *Doctor Who* scripts had been novelised, mostly by me!)

'We've seen *Shakedown*,' she said. 'It's very good. We want you to turn it into a *Doctor Who* novel.'

Now, I had then – still have, for that matter – the freelance mentality: never turn down a job.

'OK, fine,' I said. Then something struck me. 'There is one minor problem…'

'What?'

'The Doctor isn't in it!'

'So put him in it,' she said briskly and put down the phone.

So now I had a job – and a problem.

I could, I supposed, rewrite *Shakedown* and make the Doctor a major protagonist But it would be a hell of a job. And, I realised, I didn't really want to do it. I liked *Shakedown* as it was – a good tight little story that worked well in its own terms.

So I had to come up with a cunning plan. If *Shakedown* was to stay unchanged, the Doctor couldn't be on the space yacht, not at this point. But if he, like the Sontarans, was in pursuit of a Rutan spy with a tremendous secret – don't worry , it's all explained in the book – he could be desperately trying to board *Tiger Moth* – and just miss it! Then, since he knew its supposed destination , he could try to meet it on arrival…

So far, so good.

First, I did a straightforward novelisation of *Shakedown* – a pleasant and not unfamiliar exercise. Then I had to come up with the before and after sections.

Quite a lot more has to happen.

Kurt, tough ex-smuggler hero of *Shakedown*, meets the Doctor at a moment of supreme danger. Roz Forrester and Chris Cwej, two of the Doctor's companions at that stage in the universe of *Doctor Who* novels, pursue the shape-shifting, serial-killing Rutan spy through corrupt Megacity. (They encounter one of my favourites amongst my own characters, Garshak the suave, sophisticated Ogron.) They are reunited with the Doctor – just too late to board *Tiger Moth*. And Bernice Summerfield – the Doctor's other prose companion – pursues dangerous investigations on the Academic planet Sentarion.

It's all in the book ! I hope you enjoy reading it as much as I enjoyed writing it.

And it all started with *Shakedown* – a little group of *Doctor Who* fans with an impossible dream…

Terrance Dicks
October 2013

To:

Gary Leigh, Mark Ayres, Jason Haigh-Ellery
and Kevin Davies

Jan Chappell, Brian Croucher,
Carole Anne Ford, Sophie Aldred,
Rory O'Donnell, Toby Aspin, Tom Finnis
and
Michael Wisher,
Dave Hicks, Helly McGrother, Paige Bell
and
Ian Scoones

and to everyone who worked so incredibly hard in making
Shakedown – The Return of the Sontarans

'The merely difficult we do at once –
the impossible takes a little longer!'

PROLOGUE

Kurt was on the run.

He'd shaken off the customs-guards over by the landing bays. Now, almost invisible in black coveralls, he was slipping through the shadows, keeping to the darkness at the edge of the field.

The spaceport, such as it was, consisted of a flattened rock-plain, bordered by a high perimeter fence of rusting razor-wire. A group of low stone buildings huddled together at its centre. By night it was a bleak, unfriendly place. Black clouds obscured the planet's twin moons, and a cold wind howled between straggling rows of grounded space-freighters.

Kurt had been unlucky this trip, caught with a faked cargo manifest and a hold full of forbidden jekkarta weed. The newly colonised frontier planet was largely agricultural, and the ever-spreading jekkarta plant had long been the bane of its farmers.

Then some enterprising visitor discovered that, dried and smoked, jekkarta was a mild euphoric with almost no side-effects. The back-country farmers were astonished at the amount that off-planet traders would pay in good credits for the weeds they'd been raking out and burning at every harvest.

It surprised the Colony government too – but they soon recovered, slapped a massive duty on jekkarta weed and limited its export. Prices rose, the government, not the farmers, grew rich, and the smugglers moved in.

Most of them were small-timers, landing battered space-hoppers in remote valleys, doing petty, low-budget deals with nervous farmers. Kurt liked to operate with a little more class. He'd chartered an ancient but perfectly legitimate space-freighter and purchased a cargo of lenta, the tasteless but nutritious green bean that was the planet's main export.

With the help of a network of bribed spaceport loaders and officials, the cargo of lenta had magically become dried jekkarta – thousands of kilos of it, flown out under the nose of the customs, to a ready market on any one of a hundred planets.

At least, that was how it was supposed to be. The scam had already worked perfectly twice. This third and last cargo would fetch millions of credits – enough to bring Kurt the respectable trader's life he always claimed to crave.

Then it had all gone wrong. Just before blast-off an electrical fire in the power-room had spread to the cargo-hold. The thick, pungent smoke drifting out from the ship had produced some of the happiest cargo-loaders in the planet's history. An over-observant, and over-honest, young customs officer had done the rest.

Kurt wasn't too worried. He was heading for a service-gate in the perimeter fence, left open by a friendly, well-bribed cargo-loader. The profits from the first two trips were safely banked in a coded account on Algol III – except for a substantial slice in the money-belt beneath his coveralls. He'd lie low for a few days in the back-alleys of Port City. It was pretty much of a hell-hole, but anywhere was tolerable with enough credits and he could do with a rest. Then he'd buy a new identity and a passage off-planet. If things calmed down enough, he might even manage to bribe his freighter and his cargo free again.

At least, that was how it was supposed to be. But as Kurt headed for the gate and freedom, disaster dropped out of the sky.

With a roar of retro-rockets a shuttle craft landed directly ahead of him. With astonishing speed a door opened, a ramp slid down and squat figures in space armour descended and fanned out. To his amazement, Kurt saw that other craft were landing all over the field, each one spewing out its quota of stocky figures, all armed with a variety of unpleasant-looking weapons.

Whatever was happening, Kurt decided, he wanted no part of it. But he had hesitated too long. A beam of light caught and held him and a voice blared, 'Stop! Do not move or you will be killed.'

Wearily Kurt held up his hands. 'All right, all right, no need to get nasty. Go ahead with your invasion, it's nothing to do with me. I don't even live here. I'm just a peaceful off-planet trader on his way home to bed.'

'You are our prisoner,' said the guttural voice. 'You will come with us.'

Kurt lay on the cell's hard wooden bunk for what felt like for ever, listening to the confused sounds drifting in from outside. There were a few shouts, the odd crackle of blaster-fire, occasionally the boom of some heavy weapon. Then silence.

The bit of the invasion he'd actually witnessed had been carried out with ruthless military efficiency. The Colony militia wouldn't stand up to that sort of thing for very long. By now, guessed Kurt, the invaders must have taken over the spaceport, and presumably most of the planet as well. As far as Kurt was concerned they were welcome to it. He just wanted to establish his status as not-so-innocent bystander and clear out. After a while he drifted into sleep.

When he awoke it was morning and he had company.

A smallish man in a crumpled white suit and a battered hat was perched on the end of the bunk.

'Morning,' said the newcomer politely.

Kurt grunted. 'Is it?'

'Not at your best before breakfast?' said the little man sympathetically. 'I know how you feel. Never mind, I'm sure it's on the way. Coffee, toast and marmalade, bacon and eggs and a spot of kedgeree and you'll feel a new man.'

Kurt rose and stretched. 'What do you think this is, the Intergalactic Hilton? We'll be lucky if they feed us at all.'

'Surely we get the traditional hearty breakfast?'

'Traditional for who?'

'Condemned men?'

There was a clanking in the corridor outside the cell and the door was unlocked from outside. An armed guard pulled open the door and stepped aside. An enormous anthropoid creature entered, stooping to get through the entrance. It was carrying an iron bucket in each hand. The left-hand bucket was filled with green sludge from which projected the handle of a ladle. The right-hand one held wooden bowls and wooden spoons.

Kurt studied the creature with mild interest. He'd never seen one so close before. It was a Jekkari, the native species of the planet. The Jekkari lived in the forests that covered most of the planet's surface – the forests the colonists were clearing for their crops. Most of the dispossessed Jekkari simply retreated into the forests. Some, however, seemed fascinated by the colonists, hanging around their farms and camps.

The colonists had shot quite a few of them before realising they were completely harmless. Now they used them as low-grade servants. The tame Jekkari were incredibly strong, and they could easily be trained to perform simple tasks. Best of all they worked for nothing.

The creature set the buckets on the floor, took two empty bowls from the right-hand bucket and put two wooden spoons beside them. It used the ladle from the left-hand bucket to fill the two bowls with sludge. All the while it was looking at Kurt's companion, a strange intensity in its great dark eyes.

To Kurt's astonishment, the little man reached out and took the Jekkari's giant hand. His fingers drummed on the black and velvety palm in a complex tattoo.

The guard appeared in the doorway. 'C'mon, hurry it up, boy.'

The Doctor had already released the Jekkari's hand. It picked up the buckets and left the cell.

'Eat hearty,' said the guard. 'Trial's starting before very long.' He turned to go.

'Hey, listen,' yelled Kurt. 'What the hell's going on? How can you have a trial in the middle of an invasion?'

'Invasion's over,' said the guard. 'We've gotta new government, very keen on law and order. They'll sort you two out all right.' He slammed the cell door and locked it.

Kurt looked curiously at his companion. 'What was all that business—'

The little man shook his head, putting a finger to his lips.

Kurt shrugged, and picked up his bowl of sludge and his wooden spoon. He sipped the sludge. 'Lenta stew. Contains all the elements of nutrition necessary for health – so they say.'

His companion did the same and shuddered. 'And absolutely none of the ones necessary for pleasure.'

'You get used to it,' said Kurt indifferently. 'Cheap,

nutritious, with a mild sedative effect. Standard fare in a lot of jails.'

'You seem to know all about it.'

'I've been in a lot of jails.' Kurt looked after the departed guard. 'That guy must have changed sides pretty quickly.'

'If you spend your life locking people up, I don't suppose it matters too much who you're locking them up for. Besides, the Sontarans have very efficient methods of recruiting local help.'

'Such as?'

'You work for them or they kill you.'

'Who did you say they were?'

'The Sontarans. Best summed up by the philosopher Hobbes's description of the Life of Man – nasty, brutish and short. They're an intensely militaristic species – they live for war. They reproduce by cloning, a million warriors at a time.'

Kurt remembered the stocky armoured figures, swarming out of their battlecraft and spreading out with deadly efficiency.

'You'd think the galaxy would be overrun with them.'

'They're tied up in a war with their old enemies the Rutans.'

'So what do the Sontarans want with this planet?'

'I rather think they must be setting up a *cordon sanitaire* around their home world.'

'A what?'

'A protective zone. If they're attacked they'll fight the war here, and on other planets like it. The planets in the zone will be devastated but the home world will stay secure.'

Kurt nodded, absorbing the information.

After a moment his companion went on, 'I don't want to pry, but what brings you to this delightful spot?'

'I'm a smuggler,' said Kurt cheerfully. He explained about the ill-fated cargo of jekkarta weed. 'And you?'

'Just a wandering scholar, interested in other life-forms. I'd been out in the forests, living with the Jekkari. When I came back to Port City, the planet had changed hands.'

'You were *living* with the Jekkari?'

The other nodded.

'But they're just animals – apes,' protested Kurt. 'They don't even talk.'

'Silence doesn't always imply stupidity, you know,' said his companion sharply. 'Sometimes just the opposite. The Jekkari live in houses in the trees, whole villages of them. They're vegetarians, they don't like killing and they hate machines. They have an excellent civilisation of their own, one that suits them, and suits the planet. Or at least, they used to—'

'— until the colonists came,' said Kurt. 'And now the Sontarans. Looks like your Jekkari have had it, one way or another.'

'Not necessarily,' said the little man mysteriously. 'Sometimes two wrongs can add up to a right.'

Kurt gave him a baffled look. 'OK, so you've been living up a tree with the Jekkari. How come you ended up in jail?'

'According to the Sontarans, I'm a spy.'

'And are you?'

'Who, me? Do I look like a spy? I'm a simple scholar, spending my life in the search for knowledge.'

'Sure you are. And I'm a humble trader, in search of an honest credit. Nothing like getting your story straight.'

They came for Kurt and his companion shortly afterwards, a human guard backed up by two Sontaran troopers.

They were marched across the landing-field to the central administration buildings.

Apart from the one wrecked outbuilding and a toppled space-freighter there were few signs of battle. Kurt saw his own freighter, still unharmed, at the edge of the field. Unharmed, and, presumably, still fully loaded.

Kurt shook his head, thinking sadly about wasted profits. If the Sontarans had invaded a day later, they could have had the planet and welcome to it.

The spaceport's main conference room had been transformed into a court. A flag, presumably that of the Sontaran Empire, was draped over the rear wall, flanked by two Sontaran troopers.

A table stood before the flag with an empty chair behind it. Kurt and his companion were taken to a spot directly in front of the table and left to wait. A huddle of spaceport officials stood under guard at the back of the room.

After what seemed a very long time, the door behind the table opened and a Sontaran came through it. The Sontaran guards stiffened in salute, arms across their chests.

The Sontaran officer walked to the chair and sat down. He removed his helmet, placing it on the table beside him.

For the first time, Kurt looked into the face of a Sontaran. It was a moment he was never to forget.

The Sontaran's huge round head seemed to emerge directly from the massive shoulders. The hairless, strangely ridged skull was covered with leathery greenish-brown skin. The nose was a pig-like snout, the cruel mouth long and lipless. But the worst thing of all was the eyes. Small and red, they glowered out from beneath bony ridges, like savage fires burning deep in a cave.

Kurt had seen many aliens in his time, and done business with most kinds. He had traded smuggled goods with everything from arachnoids to octopods. He liked to say any conceivable body shape, any assortment of eyes, claws and limbs, was fine by him – as long as the credit rating was sound...

But never before had he met an alien life-form that conveyed such an immediate chill of fear. It was a primitive, atavistic sensation, and suddenly Kurt realised its origin.

Kurt had grown up in the back-alleys of his native planet's Port City. He had been brought up, more or less, by a kind-hearted, slatternly woman who kept a back-street tavern. At bedtime she had told him gruesome fairy-tales from a score of planets.

The Sontaran, Kurt realised, came straight out of his childhood nightmares. It was the monster in the woods, in the cupboard, under the bed. It was the bogeyman that would get you if you were a bad boy.

Kurt had been a very bad boy indeed in his time. Now the bogeyman had got him.

The Sontaran raised his burning gaze and stared into Kurt's face. 'I am Commander Steg, commander of the Sontaran Expeditionary Force, currently in charge of this newly constituted Sontaran outpost. First case.'

The voice was harsh and guttural.

A white-faced spaceport official came reluctantly forward. 'Who are you?' barked Steg.

'I am the Prosecuting Officer of the Jekkar Spaceport Authority.'

'Continue.'

'This man is known only as Kurt. He has a long criminal record and is a known smuggler and arms runner. He has also been accused of space-piracy, although charges were never proved—'

Steg cut across him. 'His criminal past does not concern

me. What crimes has he committed *here*, on Sontaran territory?'

'He was caught attempting to smuggle jekkarta weed immediately before your – arrival.'

In a trembling voice, the official gave details of Kurt's offences against Colony law. They were many and complicated.

Steg listened impassively. He considered for a moment or two.

'Guilty!'

'Now hang on a minute!' shouted Kurt.

The Sontaran trooper raised his blaster.

Commander Steg held up his hand. 'Sontaran justice is renowned galaxy-wide. The prisoner may speak.'

'Ah, well,' said Kurt, rubbing his stubble of beard and struggling to rally his thoughts. Then, as so often in a crisis, his mind went into overdrive and inspiration came.

'Even if I did commit this smuggling offence – and I'm not saying I did, mind you – what do you Sontarans care? What's it got to do with you?'

Commander Steg frowned. 'That is your defence?'

'Yes, it is,' said Kurt defiantly. 'The crime – the alleged crime – took place when this planet was an Earth colony. It is now a Sontaran outpost. Do the Sontarans have any laws concerning the export of jekkarta weed? I very much doubt it.' He folded his arms triumphantly. 'I rest my case!'

The Sontaran's thin lips twitched in what might almost have been a smile. 'Ingenious. Most ingenious. However, it is the policy of the glorious Sontaran Empire to uphold the laws of such territories as it may acquire – except when such laws conflict with the guiding principles of the Sontaran military code.'

'Which are?'

'Anything not expressly permitted is forbidden.' Steg slammed a three-digited hand down on the table. 'The prisoner is found guilty. He will be shot at dawn.'

'Shot for smuggling?' Kurt was outraged. 'I thought you were committed to upholding Colony laws.'

'That is so.'

'Well, the most they'd have given me for smuggling is a fine. How can you justify the death penalty?'

'It is quite simple,' said Steg patiently. 'You were found guilty under Colony law, but you will be punished under the Sontaran Military Code, where the death sentence is mandatory.'

'For *smuggling*?'

'For everything. Next case.'

Kurt was dragged back and the other prisoner shoved forward.

This time a Sontaran officer came forward to give evidence.

'The accused, who gives his name as Smith, was found without permission on Sontaran territory. He is charged with spying.'

Steg nodded. 'Has the prisoner Smith anything to say?'

'I most certainly have,' said the prisoner Smith indignantly. 'I am a harmless and innocent scholar, studying the native life-forms. When I left Port City this planet was an Earth Colony.'

'When you returned it was Sontaran territory,' Steg pointed out. 'Since you are undoubtedly here, you are undoubtedly, technically speaking, a spy.' His hand slammed the table once more. 'Guilty. To be shot at dawn.'

The prisoner Smith was also inclined to protest. 'That's outrageous! What am I supposed to have been spying on?

11

There's nothing of interest on this planet but anthropoids in trees!'

'They are now Sontaran anthropoids in Sontaran trees,' explained Commander Steg. 'Everything inside Sontaran territory is automatically classified as top secret.'

'But they weren't Sontaran anthropoids when I was studying them. Nor are they now. The Jekkari are a free people.'

'Not any longer,' said Commander Steg. He rose and studied the two prisoners. 'You may consider your sentences harsh. In a sense, they are. But that is for a very good reason.'

'That's nice to know,' said Kurt, who reckoned he had nothing to lose. 'Are we allowed to know what it is?'

'This planet is now a Sontaran military outpost. Its laws must be scrupulously obeyed. Your deaths will serve as an immediate and dramatic example to others. Insignificant as you are, you give your lives for the glorious Sontaran Empire. I trust you appreciate the privilege.'

'It's a great consolation,' said the prisoner Smith politely.

'Puts the whole thing in an entirely new light,' said Kurt.

Commander Steg turned and stalked from the room. Two troopers bustled Kurt and the prisoner called Smith away.

As they crossed the landing field they passed close to a couple of Jekkari, who were clearing rubble from the wrecked building under the supervision of a colony guard.

Smith stumbled and fell against the nearest Jekkari. As he gripped a massive hairy arm to save himself, Kurt saw his nimble fingers beating a swift tattoo. One of the troopers dragged Smith free and shoved him onwards.

Back in their cell, Kurt marched up and down cursing the

Sontarans and all their works. 'Pot-bellied, potato-headed, murderers. Call that justice!'

Smith perched cross-legged on the bunk, listening with mild amusement. 'You should be grateful for at least one Sontaran characteristic.'

'Which is?'

'Their strong sense of military tradition. For some reason prisoners are always shot at dawn. If they ever sentenced people to be shot at tea-time we'd be in trouble.'

'You mean we're not?' said Kurt bitterly. 'I must say, Smith, you're taking all this very calmly.'

'Not so much of the Smith, if you don't mind,' said the little man with dignity. 'I'll have you know you are in the presence of General Smith of the Jekkari Liberation Army.'

Kurt gaped at him.

Smith leaned forward. 'I originally came to this planet because I didn't like the way the colonists were treating the Jekkari. I didn't bargain for the Sontaran invasion, though. Maybe I can kill two oppressors with one revolution.'

'Those Jekkari,' said Kurt slowly. 'All that tapping business… You were communicating with them.'

Smith nodded. 'The Jekkari don't speak because they have no vocal cords. They communicate by a very complex system of signing.'

'But if the Jekkari are as intelligent as you say – why do they hang round doing dirty jobs for the colonists…' Kurt saw the answer as soon as he asked the question. 'Yes, of course…'

'That's right,' said Smith. 'Intelligence agents. Spies if you like. It cost them quite a few lives at first, but as soon as the colonists became convinced they were dim and harmless, the Jekkari could come and go as they liked. They were studying the colonists to discover their weaknesses. They completely fooled the colonists. With luck, they'll fool the Sontarans too.'

Kurt was only concerned with his own survival. 'Will they help us to escape?'

'They'll help me,' said Smith. 'And you might as well come along – if nothing else, it'll annoy the Sontarans.'

'Thanks a lot. So what do we do now?'

'We wait till dark.'

As the shadows of night spread across the little cell, there came a muffled thumping from the corridor outside. The heavy metal door of the cell began to creak and groan and vibrate. With a shriek of metal it disappeared – ripped from its hinges from outside.

Smith and Kurt moved out into the dark corridor. They could just make out the massive shape of a Jekkari crouched over the prone body of a guard. It was rocking mournfully, to and fro.

'He's upset because he killed the guard by mistake,' whispered Smith. 'They hate killing.'

He drummed rapidly on the Jekkari's shoulder, and the giant anthropoid rose and led them down the corridor.

Another guard came round the corner, saw them and said, 'Hey—'

It was all he said because the edge of Kurt's hand took him across the throat. Kurt drew back his arm for the second, killing blow, but Smith caught his wrist in a surprisingly powerful grip.

'No! I hate killing too.'

Smith's fingers gripped the still-choking guard's neck, and the man went limp. Kurt caught him and lowered him to the ground. He rubbed his wrist. Little Smith was stronger than he looked.

They moved across the dark, silent landing field until they reached Kurt's freighter.

'Can you pilot that thing by yourself?' asked Smith.

Kurt nodded. 'I had it adapted for solo use. Partners cut down profits.'

'Then I'd get on board and blast off. I don't think the Sontarans will follow you. Most of them are out subduing Port City. The ones left here are due for some unexpected trouble at their command centre. The Sontarans won't find this planet as easy to hold as they think.'

As if to belie his words, a harsh voice croaked, 'Halt!'

Kurt, Smith and the Jekkari all froze, as a Sontaran trooper stepped from the shadows, covering them with his blaster.

'You are all my prisoners. Return to the command post. Resist and you will be killed.'

Kurt decided that he couldn't face losing his freedom now. He tensed himself for a suicidal attack. If he could get his hands on that blaster –

Smith put a restraining hand on his arm.

A huge dark shape materialised behind the Sontaran trooper. Giant hands seized him, raised him high in the air – then dashed him head-first to the stony ground with such shattering force that they heard the skull shatter and the thick neck-bones snap.

Kurt let out a long shuddering sigh. 'I thought you said they didn't like to kill.'

'They don't. But they can do it now, if they must. It's something I had to teach them,' said Smith sadly.

Kurt swung the metal wheel that opened the entry-hatch.

'Come with me. I'll take you anywhere you like.' Sudden, overwhelming gratitude pushed Kurt into utter recklessness. 'Hell, I'll even give you half my profits on this trip – well, a third, anyway…'

Smith smiled and shook his head. 'Keep your profits, Kurt. If they're big enough, you could even turn honest.'

'How are you going to get away from here"

'I've got my own transportation, hidden in the forest. Besides, I'm not leaving yet. I've got unfinished business here.'

Kurt opened the hatch. 'Suit yourself.' He paused, looking at the strange little man, flanked by his two giant allies.

'I owe you, Smith, I owe you big. I'm an honest criminal, I always pay my debts. Anything I can do, anywhere, any time.' He grinned. 'John Smith! I don't even know your real name.'

'Few people do. Why don't you just call me the Doctor?'

The Doctor turned and vanished into the darkness.

Kurt scrambled inside the hatch, closed it behind him, and climbed the ladder to the control room, praying that the ancient engines would fire first time.

Just for once they did. Smuggler's luck, thought Kurt, as the old freighter lumbered into the sky. Well, he was due for some.

He set the course on automatic pilot, took a bottle of Jekkar brandy from a locker and took a long, long swig straight from the bottle.

As the comforting warmth seeped through his veins, he started thinking about the Doctor, wondering if the odd little man would survive.

After a while he gave up on that and started working out the profits from the trip. They should run into millions. He decided that he might even be able to afford to go straight as the Doctor suggested. He wondered if he'd like it. What would he do for excitement? He'd have to take up some upper-class sport – like solar yacht racing.

On the edge of the forest, the Doctor paused to study the skies and raise a hand in farewell. Nice fellow, Kurt.

It was curious, thought the Doctor, how he'd always got on better with rogues and riff-raff than with field-marshals, high officials and other top people. If it wasn't for that he might still be Lord President of Gallifrey.

Thanking fate for less than respectable tastes, the Doctor looked up at the towering forms of his two gorilla-like friends.

'Me Doctor, you Jekkari,' he said. 'I wonder if I'd look good in a loin-cloth?'

The two Jekkari looked politely puzzled.

Smiling, the Doctor followed them into the dark forest.

BOOK ONE
BEGINNINGS

1
RIPPER

All over Megacity, the word was out.

From the penthouses where the fat cats lived, high above the stench and filth of the smoggy streets, in mid-town bars where the wheelers and dealers connived and plotted, down to the sleazy dives of a thriving criminal underworld.

Someone was asking questions. Two someones to be precise. Humans, or at least humanoid; a big fair-haired man and a small dark woman. They'd arrived from somewhere off-planet and they were on someone's trail. Somebody big.

The rumours grew in the telling. Those with something to hide – practically everybody – were getting nervous. One ambition united crooked politicians in their office suites and muggers in back alleyways. To find out what the newcomers wanted and make sure that they didn't get it. Not without paying a very high price – like their lives.

Lingering over an over-priced breakfast in a hideously over-decorated and expensive hotel, Roz Forrester thought that Megacity was an Adjudicator's nightmare. She was used to corruption. It had caused her to quit her job with the Adjudication Service – a job that had been her entire life. But at least that had been a case of corruption within a reasonably honest system.

Here in Megacity, corruption *was* the system.

Megacity covered most of a planet called Megerra – as unattractive a planet as you could wish to avoid. A rock-ball in space – but a rock-ball of incredible value. Megerra was mineral-rich to an amazing degree, with vast deposits of gold, silver, iron, nickel and uranium.

The planet was carved up between Earth's major mining corporations – who were ripping the guts out of it.

Megerra was covered with mines, factories and workshops – and with Megacity, where its inhabitants lived, worked, played and very frequently died. Megacity was a very dangerous place.

The race to rip out the minerals promoted a boom economy. Miners and engineers flocked in from all over the galaxy. The money they made attracted gamblers, whores, drug-dealers and just plain thieves, dedicated to taking that money away from them.

Megerra was a planet where you came to get rich quick and move out. But while you were there, you had to eat and drink and enjoy yourself. Megacity catered for every imaginable taste, all round the clock. Just about everything went in Megacity – as long as it didn't cut mining profits or slow down production.

Which gave rise to Megerra's other industry – tourism. The businessmen on the Planetary Council ran Megerra as one big open city. The freewheeling entertainment facilities, originally designed for the miners and engineers, appealed to others as well. Word spread that Megacity was the place for a wild time with very few questions asked. Tourists flocked in from more primitive, or more respectable, planets.

In Megacity, everyone was on the make.

Roz had to bribe the hotel-clerk to honour their reservations, bribe her way from a room over the noisy main drag to a quiet one at the back. Everything for a price, she thought sourly.

She looked up as a handsome blond-haired blue-eyed

giant made his way over to her table. Normally, Chris Cwej, her fellow ex-Adjudicator and current companion, professionally speaking only, whatever he might hope, looked offensively happy and healthy, especially first thing in the morning. Today, Roz noted with malicious satisfaction, there were black rings under his blue eyes and the fair skin had an undoubtedly greenish tinge.

Chris nodded carefully, and sat down beside her. The chair, like most chairs, was too small for him.

It had taken Roz ten minutes of scowling, snarling and table-thumping to attract the attention of the long-legged, short-skirted, big-haired, big-bosomed waitress, but suddenly here she was at Chris's side, leaning over his table and threatening to poke his blurred blue eyes out.

'Full breakfast, sir?' she purred. 'A man your size needs to keep his strength up.'

'Try the mixed sea-food platter,' suggested Roz callously. 'Baby sand-lizards, squid, honey-covered sea-slugs and deep-fried eels.'

Chris shuddered and shook his head. Looking up at the waitress, then hurriedly raising his eyes to her face, he said desperately, 'Just tea. Do you have any herb tea?'

'I'll bring you some *materra*,' cooed the waitress seductively. 'Specially imported from Rigel IV. They say it has aphrodisiac properties.'

'Don't waste your time, sister,' said Roz. 'To do him, or you, any good it'd need to have corpse-raising properties.' The waitress gave her a murderous smile and flounced away. Roz sat back and surveyed her unhappy partner.

'Now, what do we do during our first few days on a strange planet?' she said in schoolmarmish tones. 'We have our shots, we swallow our pills, we eat bland foods till our system settles down and acclimatises.'

'Give me a break,' said Chris feebly.

Remorselessly Roz went on, 'We do *not* make our way to the only remaining ethnic restaurant in town and blow ourselves out on Fugora-fish stew.'

'It's the planet's speciality,' pleaded Chris. 'You can only get it here on Megerra. Since the original population became extinct, hardly anyone knows how to make it.'

'Fugora-fish stew is probably *why* the original population became extinct. You look pretty extinct yourself.'

'I'm all right,' insisted Chris. 'The pills are working.'

The waitress brought him a tall glass of herb tea and a dazzling smile. Cautiously, Chris sipped the straw-coloured liquid.

'I don't know what's going to do you in first,' said Roz wearily. 'Alien cuisine or the Doctor's mad schemes.' She sighed. 'I suppose we'd better hit the streets again. Though what good it will do…'

They had already spent several days checking the mean streets of Megacity for traces of their quarry. It was, thought Roz, an almost impossible task. Good police work was essentially local. You had to know the turf, the snitches, the players and the patterns of crime. A new city was bad enough, but a new city covering most of a new planet was almost impossible.

'Never despair,' said Chris. 'I think I've got a lead. Picked it up on the morning newscast.'

'Already? Doesn't waste any time killing again, does he?'

Chris shrugged. 'By now he needs cash, a new identity, a place to stay. He only knows one way of getting them. I guess that's why the Doctor wants us to catch him.'

'The Doctor wants us to find him,' corrected Roz. 'Find him and follow him, without upsetting his delicate sensibilities. We're not doing too well, are we?'

'We nearly had him on Formalhaute Four.'

'We nearly had him on lots of planets. But we always end up following a trail of corpses.'

'We'll get him this time,' said Chris confidently.

Ah, youth! thought Roz. She threw a small fortune on the table and stood up. 'Well, let's get started.'

Megacity was a planet of perpetual night – or rather, of perpetual artificial day. The planetary sun was feeble enough to begin with and the smog layer never let you see it anyway. All over the city the shop-windows, the ever-changing light-ads and the bar and casino signs blazed brightly all around the clock. The miners worked ever-changing shift-systems, and they needed to be able to eat, drink and play at any hour of the day and night.

Roz and Chris stood looking up and down the busy street. Rickety twin walkways on either side of the road carried a variety of pedestrians. The road between them was rutted and potholed. Civic maintenance seemed to be a low priority in Megacity. Most of the miners were humanoid, with a marked tendency towards the squat and powerful. With their broad shoulders, bow-legs and pitted faces, they looked, thought Roz, like dwarves or trolls.

There were quite a few non-humans mingling with the miners. Roz saw Arcturans, Alpha Centaurians, Falardi and Foamasi. There were also surprising numbers of a barrel-chested Ursine species resembling teddy-bears with a bad attitude.

She nudged Chris in the ribs as one of them shouldered his way towards them. 'You spent a fortune trying to look like that!'

Chris nodded sadly, regretting his vanished fur. The

result of an expensive body-bepple, it had literally gone up in smoke.

The Ursine seemed to resent their interest. It lurched to a halt in front of them. 'Something funny about the way I look?'

'No indeed, sir,' said Chris politely. 'We were just admiring the splendour of your appearance.'

Enviously he stroked a thick-furred arm.

The Ursine snatched it away and brandished a massive claw under Chris's nose. 'Don't get funny with me,' it growled.

Suddenly another Ursine appeared. In what was clearly a practised move, the two backed Roz and Chris into a recess beside the hotel doorway.

'What's going on?' growled the second. Its fur was black, and it looked even bigger and meaner than the first.

'Lousy tourists insulted me,' snarled the first one. It jerked a paw at Chris. 'This one even made a pass at me.'

'Please, sir,' said Chris, 'I assure you, I had no such thing in mind. You simply misinterpreted a friendly gesture.'

The Ursine ignored him. 'Goddam off-world pervies, coming here insulting honest citizens. We oughta rip 'em up.'

'Maybe we could just fine them,' suggested the second. It glared menacingly at Roz and Chris, who had been listening to this well-rehearsed routine with calm professional interest.

The Ursine waved a massive paw under their noses. 'Well, what's it gonna be? Your credits or your hide? Pay or bleed?'

Chris looked at Roz. 'What do you think?'

'You handle it. I didn't get much sleep.'

Chris stepped forward and hit the astonished Ursine

beneath the breastbone. It was a beautiful punch, a low left hook, delivered with Chris's considerable body weight, and a spiralling motion that drove his fist deep into the Ursine's thick-set body.

The Ursine said 'Oof!' and sat down hard on the pavement. It breathed, or tried to breathe, in a series of deep choking coughs.

The black-furred Ursine lunged forward – and stopped when it felt something cold and hard jammed up one flaring nostril.

It was the nozzle of the pocket blaster in Roz's hand.

The attacker stood very still, paws raised. 'Sorry, lady, just trying to raise a few credits for a drink.'

Chris looked at Roz. 'Should I call the police?'

'No, please, not the police,' begged the black-haired Ursine. 'I'd sooner you blasted us down right now.'

'I don't think we can spare the time to fill out police reports,' said Roz. She pulled back her blaster, and wiped the nozzle on the Ursine's chest fur. 'Beat it!' She pointed to its still-whooping companion on the pavement. 'Take your friend with you. And pass the word. If anyone else bothers us, we may have to be unpleasant about it.'

They watched as one Ursine dragged the other away. None of the passers-by took the slightest notice.

Chris rubbed his fist. 'Trouble with non-humans, you never know where to aim for. Solar plexus is usually best – if they've *got* a solar plexus. I broke my hand on an Androgum's chin.'

Roz put away her blaster. 'We'd better get a cab.'

They shoved their way to the kerb and tried to hail a hovercab. After three drivers had sped past them with a sneer, Chris stopped the next by the simple expedient of stepping in front of it, arms outspread, so it had to stop or run him down. The rodent driver, who looked like a giant rat in a leather jerkin, decided to stop – but only at the last possible second.

Chris yanked open the door, handed Roz inside, climbed in himself and said, '2003 Spaceport Boulevard.'

'You like tour of Megacity, hit all the high-spots?' squeaked the driver. 'You want vraxoin, crackerjack, jekkarta weed?'

He continued offering them strange sights, illicit substances and opportunities to indulge in a variety of exotic perversions, until Chris reached forward and clamped a hand on his skinny neck, squeezing hard enough to produce an anguished squeal.

'2003 Spaceport Boulevard, please,' said Chris politely. 'Nowhere else, nothing else, and take the most direct route. I know the city well.'

The last bit was bluff, but he reckoned it was worth a try.

Spaceport Boulevard, as its name implied, ringed Megacity's main spaceport. It was lined with tourist shops, fast-food joints, night – or rather day-and-night – clubs, casinos and bars, for the benefit of impatient tourists who couldn't wait to get downtown to be swindled and robbed. Money-changing bureaux were everywhere offering to turn any currency in the galaxy into the mandatory Megacity credits at exorbitant rates of exchange.

The hovercab sighed to a halt outside Number 2003 and dropped to the ground with a bone-jarring thud. The driver-rat demanded triple fare, and pulled a vibroknife when Chris refused.

Chris took it away from him and threatened to return it somewhere he wouldn't like. They compromised on double fare and the driver went away happy, after pressing a plastic ident-disc into Chris's hand. 'You need cab, you call me,' he squeaked. 'I show you good time!'

'Here,' said Chris. 'You want your vibroknife back?'

'Keep it!' said the driver, with a sharp-toothed grin. 'Come in useful.' He produced another, larger knife. 'I got plenty more!' The cab lurched into the air and sped away.

2003 was a long thin room, its front open to the street. It was lined with booths, all fronted with blast-proof glass except for a thin slit at the bottom. Through the gaps, clerks were accepting bundles of exotic currency and returning thin sheaves of Megacity credits. Computerised credit wasn't much used in Megacity. After suffering a number of highly ingenious hi-tech swindles, most honest merchants preferred old-fashioned cash in hand. The dishonest ones insisted on it.

Ignoring the change-booths, Roz and Chris strode down the room to an unmarked door at the end. Roz hammered on it authoritatively. 'Open up!'

An eye-level hatch slid back, revealing a long, sharp nose and two watery suspicious eyes. A reedy voice said, 'Yes?'

'A few more questions about the murder,' said Roz gruffly. 'Do you open up, or do we kick it down?'

The door opened to reveal a tall skinny humanoid in dusty high-collared black robes. He had a long thin face and a high-domed skull with a few strands of greying hair plastered across. He led them into a bare and shabby office. It held a desk, an ancient computer terminal and an enormous safe, now open and empty.

'Real hi-tech set-up,' grunted Roz. 'You the boss now?'

The skinny man went and sat behind the desk. 'I suppose so. I'm Relk, the chief clerk. Some syndicate runs the exchange bureau. I'm just keeping things going till I hear from them.'

Roz leaned over the desk, staring into his eyes. 'Knock the old guy off to get the job, did you? Pocket full of cash and a nice promotion?'

The clerk recoiled from her dark, angry face. 'No! All I did was find the body.'

She grabbed him by the collar and heaved him across the desk.

'Come on, confess, save us all some time.'

Chris reached out and grabbed her shoulder. 'Give the poor guy a break, boss. At least let him tell us what happened.'

Roz shoved the flustered clerk back into his chair. 'Right, let's go through it all again. From the beginning.'

'But I've already made a statement.'

'Make it again. Don't miss anything out, or you'll be sorry.'

Relk gave her a terrified look, too frightened to speak. Chris patted him reassuringly on a bony shoulder. 'Just take your time. All we want are the facts.'

In a trembling voice, Relk told his story.

'A customer came in yesterday night… He had a bundle of cash, mixed currencies, wanted to change the lot into Megacity credits. The amount was way over the booth limit, so I sent him in to see Mr Sakis, the boss.'

'This customer,' snapped Roz. 'What did he look like?'

'Shortish, fattish, black hair. Expensive clothes, looked very prosperous. Might have been a banker, something like that.'

Roz and Chris exchanged glances. The description matched the mutilated body they'd seen on Lorelei.

Hanno Seth had indeed been a banker. Soon after he'd been found dead in his office, a duplicate Seth had taken passage on a passenger-shuttle to Megerra – with Roz and

30

Chris, as usual, one jump behind.

'Go on,' said Chris encouragingly.

'They were in there quite a while. Then Mr Sakis came out, carrying this big plastic sack. Said he'd got to go out somewhere on important business, I was to look after things till he got back.'

'How did he look, when he was talking to you?' asked Roz.

'Weird. He didn't look at me and his voice was sort of flat.'

Roz nodded. The clerk went on with his story.

'Anyway, off he went and after a while I realised I hadn't seen the customer leave. There's only one way out of the office, and it wasn't like the boss to leave anyone alone in there. So I thought I'd better check. He'd locked the door but I've got a code-card for emergencies, so I opened it and went in…'

He broke down, his voice quivering.

'Take it slowly,' said Chris gently.

'Sakis was lying in the middle of the floor,' said Relk. 'Even though I'd just seen him go out. His body was all cut up…'

'You mean stabbed? Slashed and hacked about?'

Relk shook his head. 'It was neater than that – tidier. Bits of his insides were – arranged beside the body.'

Roz looked across at Chris. 'Could just be an organ-legger. We don't want to waste our time.' She turned back to the clerk. 'Any bits missing? Heart, lungs, liver?'

'How the hell would I know?' said Relk, showing sudden signs of spirit. 'I'm an accountant not a medic. I didn't take an inventory of his guts. I don't know what's supposed to be in there in the first place!'

'All right,' said Chris soothingly. 'Then what?'

31

'Then I called the police, of course,' said Relk. 'They turned up in their own good time, made me tell the story ten times over, took the body away and told me not to leave town.'

'I take it the safe was emptied as well?' asked Roz.

Relk nodded. 'Two days' takings – nearly fifty thousand credits.'

'Was it broken into?'

'No, just opened. He must have made the boss do it before…'

Chris looked meaningfully at Roz. Hanno Seth's vault had been opened and emptied too.

'It's him,' said Chris quietly.

Roz nodded. 'Looks like it.'

'You mean something like this has happened before?' asked Relk excitedly. 'The guy's a serial killer, right? Is there a reward? I could identify him!'

'I'd keep quiet about that if I were you,' warned Roz. 'He might come back and rearrange your innards too. What did your boss look like?'

'What do you care, he's dead. Why don't you go down to the city morgue and take a good look if you're so interested?'

Roz reached out and grabbed him by the collar, her knuckles digging into his skinny neck. 'Just answer the question!'

The clerk croaked something indistinguishable, and Roz squeezed harder. 'Speak up!'

Gently Chris moved her hands away. 'He can't talk while you're choking him.' He turned to Relk who was massaging his neck and gasping for breath. 'Please answer the question, sir. I assure you that it's in your own best interests to assist us with our enquiries.'

'What question?' croaked Relk.

'The same one,' snarled Roz. 'What did your boss look like?'

'He was tall,' croaked Relk. 'Very tall with silver hair, always wore it long. He had this natty little pointed beard and he always wore the best, silk robes mostly.'

'That's more like it. Clear off!'

'Thank you for your co-operation, sir,' said Chris.

Relk sneered at him and hurried away.

Roz looked at Chris. 'Now what?'

'We go on looking.'

'How?' demanded Roz. 'Where? He's got more credits and a new appearance.'

'We've got the new description.'

'What's the point? We won't find a trace of him until there's another killing – and another and another. Until he gets tired of this planet and moves on to—'

'Fresh fields and slaughters new,' said Chris poetically.

'With us panting behind like a pair of worn-out Vrangian tracker-pigs. I'm getting pretty tired of it, Chris.'

Suddenly they heard the roar of ground-car rocket motors, hoarse angry shouts and the tramp of booted feet. Three enormous figures burst into the room. Bigger even than Chris, they wore jackboots, leather trousers and leather jerkins. They had massive skulls, brutal underhung jaws and high-domed foreheads fringed with matted hair. They carried big old-fashioned blasters, all trained on Roz and Chris.

Roz knew a gang of Ogron bandits when she saw one. She turned to Relk, who could be seen hovering behind the three giant newcomers. 'Don't just stand there, call the police,' she yelled.

She was reaching for her blaster when Chris's hand gripped her arm. 'No use calling the police. They are the police!' He pointed to the rusty badge pinned to the leading giant's jerkin.

The Ogron stepped forward. 'You come with us!' it roared. 'You under arrest!'

2
CHIEF

'I don't think you quite understand,' said Chris. 'You see we're private investigators engaged on a legitimate—'

'You under arrest! You come with us!'

Chris reached in his pocket for his credentials and was immediately grabbed by a pair of huge hairy hands.

Strong as he was, Chris knew better than to wrestle with an Ogron.

'Tell you what,' he said. 'Why don't I just come with you?'

Chris and Roz were grabbed, roughly searched, and relieved of their weapons. They were dragged out of the office, through the change bureau and thrown into the back of an armoured hover-wagon, already occupied by two burly miners and a deeply depressed Alpha Centaurian.

The latter was so overcome by the shame of arrest that he sat huddled in the corner with his head in his tentacles.

The miners were still fighting drunk. Chris had to bang their heads together to ensure a peaceful journey.

He then had to spend some time pacifying Roz, though rather more gently. She'd scooped up many a suspect herself, but she didn't much care for being on the other end of the process.

'Try and see it as a new perspective on law-enforcement,' urged Chris.

Roz told him where to put his perspective.

After what seemed like a very long ride, the wagon screeched to a halt and they were all decanted in a cobbled yard behind a high wall. Their fellow passengers were hustled away towards a low stone cell-block. Chris and Roz were taken into the main building, marched up a grimy stone staircase, and thrown into a holding cell, a barred recess in a long corridor. The building was dark and dank and gloomy, like some medieval castle. The stone walls seemed soaked in the pain and suffering of the prisoners who had passed through here. Somehow you felt there were dungeons and torture chambers down below.

Chris looked around, sniffed deeply and smiled happily.

'What are you looking so cheerful about?' snarled Roz.

'Oh, I don't know... It's all so familiar somehow. I mean, a station house is a station house any planet you go to. They're all more alike than they're different. They even smell the same.'

'I hate to spoil this orgy of nostalgia, but we happen to be on the wrong side of the bars here.'

'It's probably all a mistake,' said Chris optimistically.

'You think so? What kind of administration uses Ogrons for police work?'

'No wonder those furry muggers pleaded with us not to call the police,' said Chris. 'At least there seems to be some respect for the forces of Law and Order here.'

'Law and Order? In Megacity?' snarled Roz. 'Don't make me laugh. The Chief of Police is probably a Dalek!'

After the usual interminable wait, another feature of station houses everywhere, an Ogron policeman appeared, opened the cell, and motioned them out with a blaster. They were herded along a stone corridor and shown into an enormous office.

The guard shoved them into the centre of the room and stepped back, standing sentinel at the door.

Chris and Roz looked around them in amazement.

The vast room was lavishly carpeted, its walls lined with gorgeous hangings and colourful holographs. Comfortable-looking chairs and elegantly designed tables were scattered about. Sculptures, depicting a variety of exotic life-forms, stood around the room.

On the far side of the room, a massive figure sat behind an enormous desk. It was another Ogron, the biggest, most brutal-looking Roz had ever seen. It wore a luxurious version of the usual Ogron dress. The shirt appeared to be silk rather than sack-cloth, and the jerkin was made of finely embroidered calfskin.

Most surprisingly of all, the Ogron was jabbing at the keyboard of an antiquated computer terminal with its long hairy fingers.

Well, an Ogron in silk was still an Ogron, thought Roz. The only way to deal with Ogrons was to dominate them – if you lived long enough. A low-ranking species, mostly used as guards, bodyguards and jailers, they were used to obeying the voice of authority, if it was loud enough. She took a deep breath.

'Why you bring us here?' she shouted. 'We good people, we not do bad things.'

The Ogron rose and bowed. 'My dear lady, I'm sure you wouldn't dream of doing bad things. Do forgive me for keeping you waiting. Pressure of work, you know. Megacity is such a *busy* place. Allow me to introduce myself. I am Garshak, Chief of Police of Megacity.'

It was a rich, resonant, almost plummy voice and Chris and Roz stood listening to it in silent astonishment.

Garshak waved at the Ogron by the door. 'Chairs for our guests, you oaf. And fetch some refreshment.'

The guard picked up a massive armchair in each hand and slammed both chairs down before the desk. It retreated through the door and returned with a loaded tray which it placed carefully on the desk. It returned to its position by the door.

Roz saw that the tray contained a tall slender teapot surrounded by delicate cups. A number of plates held an assortment of elaborate little cakes and pastries.

Garshak reached for the teapot with a massive hairy hand.

'Shall I be mother? Isn't that what you say on Earth?'

Roz had never said any such thing, and didn't intend to. Dumbly she accepted a cup of herbal tea, and a plate of little cakes. She made a desperate attempt to regain the initiative.

'I insist on knowing why we have been brought here,' she repeated. 'What are the charges?'

Garshak took a delicate sip of tea and glanced at the monitor screen of the desk-computer. 'Oh, I don't know. How about "Impersonating a police officer" for a start? According to the deposition of Mr Relk…'

Chris swallowed a little cake and said indistinctly, 'Not guilty, we never said we were police officers.'

'Of course not,' agreed Garshak. 'You merely forced your way in, threatened and bullied the poor little fellow, and asked him a number of questions about matters that were none of your business. Naturally he *assumed* you were the police.'

'Can't help what people assume,' said Roz smugly.

'Come now,' said Garshak. 'Isn't that being rather pedantic? We must obey the spirit, not just the letter of the law. Surely you are both guilty of *Suppressio veri et suggestio falsi*?' He saw Chris's baffled face and said, 'Suppressing the truth—'

'And suggesting a falsehood,' completed Roz, thankful

she'd remembered the scrap of Old Earth legal jargon from some long ago course in the Adjudicator's Academy.

'Exactly,' beamed Garshak. 'So refreshing to deal with a being of education.'

Roz bowed her head, accepting the compliment. 'All the same, Chief, surely the law is pedantic? It means what it says. Did we actually claim to be police? No, we didn't. Case dismissed.'

'Generally speaking, your argument would be irrefutable. However, here in Megacity the law is rather more flexible. It means what I say it means.' Garshak leaned forward. 'I don't give a Drashig's fart about the charge,' he roared. 'What I want to know is, *why have you two been going around Megacity asking questions?*'

'Why is it such a big deal?' asked Chris innocently.

'Because a lot of very important people in Megacity have something to hide. Quite a few somethings, most of them. Stock deals, share manipulations, irregular sources of income, involvement in organised crime…'

Roz frowned. 'If you know so much about these people, why don't you do something about it?'

'Why should I? It's not my job.'

'Then what do they pay you for? What *is* your job?'

'To keep reasonable order on the streets, not to mention the bars and dives, to lock up drunken miners, to see tourists aren't robbed more than is reasonable, or murdered unless absolutely necessary – and to manage Megacity so that the rich who run it keep getting richer.' Garshak smiled, showing long, yellow fangs. 'It's the job of the police in most big cities actually. We're just a little more open about it here. Oh, and they don't pay me by the way. Not a single credit.'

Roz smiled. She and Chris weren't paid either, not as

such. She remembered asking the Doctor if they drew a salary.

Chris looked at the richly dressed figure and glanced around the luxuriously furnished room. 'Then how...'

'The job is self-financing,' explained Garshak. 'How do you think we arrived so quickly at the change bureau? The late proprietor paid a regular fee for quick service in case of trouble. So does every bar, club and casino in town, incidentally. Then there are our criminal clients – like your fellow passengers.'

'What happens to them?'

'The two miners will be released as soon as they've sobered up and paid a small fine. Usually the mining corporation pays it, and docks it from their wages.'

'What about the other one?'

'The Alpha Centaurian?' Garshak beamed. 'Now he really is worth something. He'll have to pay a very large fine.'

'Why does he have to pay more than the others?'

Garshak looked at him in surprise. 'Because he's *got* more. They're poor miners, he's a prosperous merchant. Surely that's only fair? Besides, Alpha Centaurians hate scandal, so he'll pay extra for a quick release and no publicity.'

Roz gave him a disgusted look. 'Wall to wall corruption. Quite a system you've got here.'

'Thank you,' said Garshak. 'I'm only a poor corrupt police official but I do my best. But we seem to be straying from the point. You still haven't told me the purpose of your activities here.'

'Can't we just pay a fine and leave?' asked Chris.

Garshak shook his head. 'Unless you're a little more frank with me, you won't be leaving at all.'

'You can't do that,' said Roz indignantly. 'What about our rights?'

'You haven't any,' said Garshak simply. 'I can lock you in a cell in the sub-basement and forget about you. They're so inefficient down there, they'll probably forget to feed you.'

Chris looked enquiringly at Roz. 'Looks like we don't have any choice.'

It was time for the cover story. Roz leaned forward and her face took on the expression of transparent honesty that always meant she was lying. 'Well, to tell you the truth, Chief – we're P.I.s – operatives for Pinkerton Intergalactic.' She indicated her breast pocket. 'May I?'

Garshak nodded.

Taking care to move slowly, Roz produced a silver badge in a black leather holder and held it out. The badge showed an open eye in a silver circle.

Even Garshak was impressed. 'Pinks!'

The Pinkerton Agency – The Eye That Never Sleeps – had started on Earth, back in the mists of history, a spy service in some long forgotten civil war. It had flourished as far back as the nineteenth and twentieth centuries, and when men had gone to the stars the Agency had soon followed.

Public justice and public policing were often erratic on far-flung worlds, and the demand for the private kind grew ever stronger. In their hundreds of years of existence the Pinks had acquired legendary status. Stars of innumerable holovid series, agents of interplanetary justice, invisible and invincible, they were everywhere, and they never gave up. Whatever the obstacles, whatever the odds, they always got their sentient life-form.

Garshak studied the badge. 'Pinks in Megacity – this is not going to reassure the bosses. Who are you after?'

Roz put the badge away. 'No one they need worry about. Someone from off-planet, like us.'

'We're chasing a serial killer,' said Chris. 'We call him the Ripper and we've tracked him from planet to planet.'

'What made you pick up on the change bureau job?'

'Typical Ripper MO,' said Roz. 'We think he spends most of his loot on space-liner fares – he always travels as far as he can. He's broke when he arrives, so his first job is done to raise petty cash, often somewhere near the spaceport.'

'What does he do next?'

'He usually does a few more jobs, until he's raised enough finance to feel secure. Then he digs in, gets to know the score, picks a victim, does one last big job and moves on.'

'Anything else?'

'Usually – not always, but usually – he partially dissects his victims. And he steals their identity as well.'

Garshak looked puzzled. 'He does what?'

'He nearly always impersonates his victim after the murder,' explained Chris. 'That's how he makes his getaway. He did it again today.'

Garshak sat back considering all they'd told him, balancing profit and loss for himself and the tycoons who ruled Megacity.

'It doesn't seem like this new arrival is going to be much of an asset for my masters on the City Council.'

'They might find him a downright liability,' said Roz. 'They sound just like the sort of people he'd go for.'

'How come?'

'The Ripper doesn't like to use credit, leaves too much of a trail. So he tends to go for people who have large sums in easily realisable assets – credit bills, bearer-bonds and so on. And who keeps large sums of untraceable cash around?

Top-level crooks.' She smiled sweetly at Garshak. 'Sounds just like your City Councillors to me!'

Chris gave him a sincere look. 'So you see, Chief, it can only be to their advantage, and yours, to co-operate with us.'

Garshak seemed to be thinking hard. 'Who's actually after this Ripper?'

'We are,' said Chris innocently.

'Who's paying the bills?'

'He killed a multi-millionaire banker back on Earth,' said Roz. 'The family want him caught – whatever it costs.'

Garshak was still searching for an angle. 'Is there a reward?'

Roz shook her head. 'The Agency advised against it. Big rewards bring big publicity. We don't want every bounty hunter in the galaxy muddying the trail and scaring off our Ripper.'

Garshak looked dejected. 'Pity.'

He cheered up when Roz went on, 'There is, however, a substantial contingency fund. We are authorised to make discretionary payments to anyone who is of real help to us.'

Garshak held out an enormous hand, palm-upwards.

'To anyone who is of real help,' repeated Roz.

'Letting you go is a real help, isn't it? You won't do much investigating from inside a cell.'

'Good point.' Roz produced a sheaf of Megacity credit notes and began dealing them one by one into the leathery palm.

When she stopped, Garshak said, 'Don't forget your fines.' She dealt more notes.

'And the voluntary contribution to the Police Benevolent Fund?'

'What benevolence?' said Roz, putting the notes away. 'I haven't seen any. Forget it!'

43

'Ah well,' said Garshak. He closed his palm and the notes disappeared inside his jerkin.

'Now start earning it,' said Roz, a snap in her voice. She stood up, leaning over the desk, glaring into the astonished Ogron's face. 'I want a list of the biggest and richest crooks in town, and the names of all the joints they own or where they hang out.'

Garshak looked horrified. 'I can't let you have a list like that! It's more than my job's worth.'

'Call it a list of civic benefactors and their favourite beauty spots if you like,' snarled Roz. 'I need names and places and I need them now! Oh, and put out a full description of the murdered manager of the change bureau.'

It was Roz at her most forceful, and there was no resisting her. Garshak's long, hairy fingers stabbed at the desk-computer console. There was a whirring and chuntering and an ancient printer ground out a long strip of coarse paper bearing a list of names and addresses in blurred type.

Garshak handed it over. 'Don't leave it lying about.'

'If there's an emergency, my partner will eat it,' promised Roz. 'Get the description of the murdered change-bureau manager on the most-wanted list right away.'

'But he's dead!' protested Garshak.

'Only after a fashion,' said Roz. 'There's a good chance the Ripper may still be using his appearance. And tell your beat patrols to be on the look-out for unexplained strangers with money, bizarre or violent behaviour, all the usual stuff.

'In Megacity,' said Garshak, 'bizarre and violent behaviour is pretty much the norm. But I'll do my best for you.'

'Right, that's it, for the moment,' said Roz. 'If we could have our property back?'

Garshak opened a drawer and produced a small slim-line blaster, a much larger one, a neuronic stun-sap, and the hovercraft driver's vibroknife, laying them on the desk.

Roz picked up the slim blaster and tucked it back into its underarm holster. She looked at the other assorted armaments for a moment. She'd carried a vibroknife herself for a while but she didn't like to any more.

She turned to Chris who was finishing off the last of the cakes. 'Come on, pick up your toys and let's get going. We've got work to do!'

Chris got up, went over to the desk and collected his various weapons, stowing them away about his person. He paused for a moment, looking curiously at Garshak. 'Forgive me if I'm being too personal – but you're not exactly a typical Ogron, are you?'

'I'm an experiment,' said Garshak. 'A freak.'

'I'm sorry, I didn't mean to pry.'

'Not at all,' said Garshak expansively. 'I quite like telling the story.' He leaned back in his chair. 'A scientist came to our planet with a plan for brain augmentation. It was a scheme to turn what he called lower species, like ours, into more useful servants, capable of a greater range of tasks. He paid a local chief handsomely to volunteer a group of us. The scientist experimented on us with drugs, with brain surgery, with neurological stimulation.'

'What happened?'

'Half of his subjects went mad and died. A few others recovered, with their intelligence very slightly improved. The rest of the survivors were unchanged. In only one case was the experiment completely successful.'

'You?'

'Me.'

'What happened to the scientist?'

'When he realised he'd succeeded, even once, he was eager to buy more subjects and go on with his experiments. I was fully recovered by then. I persuaded him to change his plans.'

'How?' asked Roz. Somehow she already knew the answer.

'I killed him,' said Garshak. 'I killed the chief who'd sold us as well. Then I stole the scientist's ship and took the other survivors off with me. I felt responsible for them somehow.'

He shrugged massive shoulders. 'We became mercenaries, bodyguards, the usual sort of thing. We ended up here at the time the job of Police Chief became vacant. They'd been having rather a high turnover in police chiefs in Megacity.'

'And they gave you the job?'

'There was one other candidate, a Martian Ice Warrior, but I persuaded him to withdraw.'

Roz held up her hand. 'I won't even ask... Come on Chris. Goodbye, Chief.'

'Justice by your side,' said Garshak.

'Fairness be your friend,' chorused Roz and Chris automatically. They looked at each other in consternation.

Garshak smiled. 'Adjudicators. I thought so.'

'Ex-Adjudicators,' corrected Roz coldly.

'I didn't know there were any.'

'Only us,' said Chris.

'It must be rather lonely.'

'Like being an intelligent Ogron,' said Roz. She turned and marched from the room. Chris nodded to Garshak and followed.

*

As they descended the stone staircase Chris said, 'Interesting character.'

Roz snorted.

They went outside and stood on the steps of the police barracks, looking up and down the long rutted road for hovercabs. There weren't any.

Chris saw a com-unit by the door and slotted in the hovercab driver's disc. After a moment a voice said, 'Hovercab seventy-nine. Wa' you wan'?'

'Pick-up outside police HQ, two passengers back downtown,' said Chris. 'Triple fare if you get here right away.'

'Thass me you see pulling up,' said the voice. There was a crackle and the disc popped out of the com. Chris pocketed it and grinned at Roz. 'Better the devil you know!'

They stood waiting, trying to breathe as little of the warm polluted air as possible.

On the flat roof of the police barracks opposite' a wiry cloaked figure checked the sights on a laser-rifle and levelled it, using the low parapet as a rest.

A white spot appeared above the door of the police building. It drifted downwards towards Roz and Chris.

3

SENTARION

Bernice Summerfield stood outside the hot and dusty little spaceport and stared at the towers and spires and turrets of Sentarion City. They gleamed in the desert sunlight, huge birds wheeling around them.

Even a cynic like Bernice Summerfield couldn't help being impressed.

Sentarion, the university planet, the greatest concentration of scholars and scholarship in the known galaxy. A place where nothing mattered but the accumulation of knowledge and the cultivation of wisdom, where the only passions were the passions of the mind.

It was the academic dream that Bernice Summerfield, planet-wise, widely experienced and totally unqualified archaeologist, had aspired to all her life.

It felt like coming home.

True, her impressive credentials were forged, her research project was a cover story, and she was once again a pawn in the Doctor's dark and devious schemes – but why let a few inconvenient facts spoil things?

Bernice Summerfield felt terrific. Despite the long journey in the primitive planet-hopper that had deposited her on Sentarion and immediately blasted off again, she felt fresh, alert and alive.

She knew why, of course. 'You'll like Sentarion,' the Doctor had told her, sounding like a Gaztak trying to sell you a second-hand spaceship. 'Quite apart from the academic side, it's a low-gravity, high-oxygen planet. Takes years off you. Last time I was there, I felt like a lad of a hundred.'

Bernice drew a deep breath of the clear, dry air. Air like wine, she thought. No, more like Eridanean brandy. I wonder if there's anywhere I can get a drink? She looked at the gleaming spires. I wonder how the hell I get to the University?

Sentarion was a desert planet, very largely uninhabited. Its sun, bigger and closer than that of Earth, shone fiercely in a clear blue sky. The complex, crystalline spires of Sentarion City gleamed across the rocky desert, from somewhere in the distance. Bernice suspected that it was further away than it looked. Its relative closeness was an optical illusion, produced by the clean, clear desert air.

The odd thing was that there was no road. Nothing, not even a track. Just the spaceport and the city, out here in the desert.

Logic told Bernice that the problem must have a solution. The University had visitors, somehow they had to be able to reach it. There was no one to ask, the spaceport was shut up and deserted. Her planet-hopper was the only arrival of the day.

Maybe it's a test, she thought. You march across the desert to prove your dedication, and the survivors get to study.

She glared at the gleaming spires, so near and yet so far, irritation rapidly replacing admiration. So how am I supposed to get there? Fly?

That was when she saw the big bird. It appeared out of the heat haze and flew clumsily towards her, huge wings beating slowly up and down.

Then she saw it wasn't a bird at all. It was a flying craft, with wings that flapped up and down like those of a bird. What was the word? An ornithopter, that was it!

Bernice watched as the strange craft thumped to the ground just in front of her. There was someone – something – in the cockpit, a stubby creature with a shiny black carapace. It looked like a giant beetle.

'Professor Summerfield?' it squeaked. 'For University?'

'Er – yes,' said Bernice. 'For University.'

'Please to mount.'

Bernice hesitated. She'd never really liked flying, even in spaceships where you couldn't usually see where you were going. The thought of trusting herself to this rickety contraption terrified her.

'Please to hurry!' rasped the pilot.

Bernice remembered a film about man's early attempts at flight that the Doctor had once shown her. This craft looked very like the primitive planes in the film – the ones that crashed.

Telling herself the alternative was a march across the desert, Bernice lifted her pack, and climbed into the passenger seat behind the pilot.

The wings began flapping again and the ornithopter lurched back into the air. Whatever the power-source was, it was completely silent – electricity perhaps. The only sound came from the creaking of the wings.

I bet there's no in-flight drinks service, she thought, and fished a flask of Eridanean brandy from a pocket of her pack.

It was all quite logical, Bernice told herself as she sipped the brandy. This contraption would never have got off the ground on Earth, but here on this low-gravity planet it was perfectly practical.

That's why there were no roads, they'd developed simple

51

flying craft instead of ground cars. The things she'd taken for birds flying around the city were actually traffic.

As for the pilot, that was understandable too.

'Insects are the dominant life-form on Sentarion,' the Doctor had told her.

Bernice had shuddered. Bugs and creepy-crawlies had never been favourites of hers, though she'd been ashamed to say so to the Doctor, who seemed to find all life-forms equally fascinating.

She hadn't been much reassured when the Doctor went on, 'Very large insects as a matter of fact. The low gravity supports their exoskeletons, enables them to grow bigger and live longer. They've developed a very interesting civilisation.'

She saw another ornithopter, a sleeker-looking model, flapping towards them from the city. It seemed to be heading for the spaceport. Idly, Bernice wondered why, since hers had been the only landing of the day. Could be a spaceport official, she told herself. Could be a hundred reasons.

Suddenly she realised that they were heading directly away from the city.

She leaned forward and shouted, 'I want to go to the University please. The University!'

'That is correct,' said the pilot. 'University!'

Bernice drew a deep breath. 'I want to go to the main University,' she shouted. 'The one in the City. I have to report to the Chancellor.'

The pilot ignored her. The ornithopter headed off into the desert, leaving the gleaming spires of the city behind.

'Hey, you!' yelled Bernice. She leaned forward and rapped the pilot hard on his shiny black back.

'Desist!' said the pilot. 'Do not cause problems!'

Bernice rapped again, harder. 'Take me where I want to go!'

The pilot swung completely round. Small eyes glittered in a narrow face. Suddenly a long needle-like spike shot out from its proboscis.

'Please do not be troublesome,' it squeaked. 'It is not seemly to kill you in flight. Wait until we have landed, and I will drink your life with the proper rituals. You will accept your death with dignity.'

'The hell I will,' said Bernice Summerfield, and smashed the heavy brandy flask down on the creature's head. It shrieked and fell backwards, green ichor oozing from a large crack.

The ornithopter lurched and headed towards the ground.

Bernice scrambled forwards and struggled to reach the controls. But the pilot's body was wedged into the cockpit, blocking her access. She heaved desperately at the body, trying to pull it free, but the squat insectoid form was incredibly heavy and somehow she just couldn't get a proper grip.

All the time the ornithopter went on plunging downwards. The wings were moving much slower now, and the craft was going into a spin. She looked round for some kind of parachute, but there was nothing to be seen. Perhaps they hadn't been invented here.

Down, down, down spiralled the ornithopter, while Bernice wrestled desperately with the body of the pilot, which obstinately refused to move. If she had any sense she'd have waited to clobber him until they were on the ground. If she had any sense she wouldn't be here at all, she told herself. She wouldn't have listened to the Doctor's blandishments.

'Just a spot of simple research on a project I'm toying with,' he'd said. 'Bit of a sideshow, I suspect, but it's worth a try. I've already got Roz and Chris working on the more practical end. This bit's ideal for you, you've got such a talent for research. Nobody else could do it half so well – except me, of course, and I'm a bit tied up just now. You'll love Sentarion – it's so peaceful. I'm sure you'll find it's your spiritual home.'

Well, it was going to be her final home, thought Bernice. She'd really excelled herself this trip. Off the shuttle, into this weird flying machine – dead.

She was letting the Doctor down, thought Bernice, as she tugged desperately at the obstinately unmoving pilot. Somehow that was the most annoying thing of all.

In the middle of these bitter reflections, the ornithopter slammed into the ground. Bernice realised with some indignation that she was still alive. She was jarred, bruised and shaken, but she definitely wasn't dead.

It must be the low gravity she told herself, as she scrambled out of the wrecked craft. Or maybe the flapping wings had some kind of parachute effect themselves, slowing down the rate of fall. Whatever the reason, she seemed to have survived the crash.

She grabbed her pack and scrambled out of the wreck, afraid that it might blow up, as they did in the holovids.

The ornithopter, however, simply flapped its wings feebly a few more times and then collapsed in on itself.

Bernice drew a long shuddering breath. She still had her flask in her hand – it was dented but not broken – and she took a quick restorative swig.

She looked around, assessing her situation. The gleaming spires of the city seemed further away than ever.

Looks like the long hike after all, Benny, she told herself.

There wasn't much brandy left. What she really needed was water.

Then she saw the second ornithopter, the sleeker one, flapping towards her. Maybe it was the local equivalent of the Red Cross. Or maybe someone was coming to finish the job.

Bernice started rummaging in her pack. After much scrabbling – inevitably what she was looking for was right at the bottom – she pulled out a blaster. A voice inside her head said, 'Standard issue, power-pack in the butt, Setting One delivers a solid punch, Setting Two disables, Setting Three kills.'

'All right, Ace, all right,' she muttered out loud. 'Where are you and your portable armoury when I need you?'

Setting the blaster on Two she straightened up, just as the second ornithopter landed close by.

A tall green figure unfolded itself from the cockpit and came stalking towards her. A good three metres tall, it had huge glowing eyes surmounted by long, thin antennae, two pairs of forelegs, and a huge pair of back legs, with reversed knee-joints. It looked very much like a giant grasshopper. A gold cloak was draped about its body.

Bernice raised the blaster. 'That's close enough.'

The creature bowed stiffly. 'Professor Summerfield?' it said in a high, reedy voice. 'For the University? Please to mount!'

Bernice gestured towards the wrecked ornithopter and its dead pilot. 'That's exactly what he said. It didn't work out too well for either of us – especially him. Don't make the same mistake.'

'There can be no comparison. I am Hapiir, your appointed mentor. I am official of the University, Grade Five.'

'And who was he?'

'One of the Harrubtii – bandit scum, from the outer desert. They prey on unwary travellers. You have been very rash, Professor.'

'I've been rash?' said Bernice indignantly. 'I arrive here an accredited guest of the University, that murderous – thing there picks me up and threatens to drink my blood and I have to fight for my life and nearly get killed in a crash and *I've* been rash?'

Hapiir waited until she ran out of breath and said reprovingly, 'Did you not read the notice warning against boarding unlicensed 'thopters? See, my own bears the University mark.' Hapiir gestured towards the row of gold-painted symbols on the side of his craft. He looked scornfully at the shabby unmarked wreck. 'How could you mount such a vehicle as that? Have you never left your home planet before? Have you no experience of the perils of travel? Had you been killed it would have caused the University a great deal of trouble.'

'Sorry, I'm sure,' said Bernice icily.

'Your apology is accepted. Now, please mount so that we may avoid further delay.'

'Just a minute,' said Bernice. 'Do you have any identification?'

Hapiir produced an ornate gold badge from beneath his cloak. 'My seal of office.'

It could have been a merit badge from the Sentarion Scout Troop as far as Bernice was concerned, but she was too tired to argue. Reaction had set in and she felt suddenly exhausted. If the bugs that lived on this planet were so determined to knock her off, let them. Just so long as they let her have some food and a drink first.

Wearily she climbed into the passenger seat of the second ornithopter. She waved the blaster.

'All right then, home, James. Take the direct route, not the pretty way.'

In a dignified silence, Hapiir climbed into the pilot seat. The wings flapped gently, and the ornithopter glided smoothly upwards. Bernice held on to her blaster – and her brandy-flask – until it was clear that the ornithopter was heading for the city.

Then she put both away and leaned forward to speak to Hapiir.

'How come you turned up to the rescue?'

'I was assigned to meet you and take you to the city. Unfortunately, I was slightly delayed. I arrived in time to see you leaving in another 'thopter. I was concerned and I followed.'

Bernice considered. 'You say these bandits prey on passing travellers?'

'Regrettably, that is so.'

'They can't make much of a living.'

'I do not follow the logic of your argument.'

'One landing a day? And today, only one traveller? Not what I'd call rich pickings.'

Hapiir gave a high-pitched whistle of exasperation.

'This is a quiet time. When full term begins, there will be many landings and many travellers.'

'And another thing,' said Bernice. 'That bandit knew my name. He wasn't just some casual airway robber, he was waiting for me.'

This time there was a little silence before Hapiir replied.

Then he said reluctantly, 'It is feared that there are those on the University staff who sell information. If the bandits learn of the arrival of a distinguished visitor they set an ambush. You are an archaeologist, are you not? No doubt the bandit hoped you were carrying valuable alien artifacts. He planned to take you to the inner desert and rob you.'

'That sounds like a hell of a well-organised operation,' said Bernice. 'I thought this place was a haven of peace and scholarship. It's beginning to sound more like good old Chicago. Do any of your visitors make it back home alive?'

'Thousands of scholars visit Sentarion every year,' said Hapiir. 'Most of them enjoy a happy and rewarding stay. Please do not judge us by this one unfortunate incident. Now, if you will forgive me, I must concentrate on piloting the 'thopter. You would not wish to experience two crash landings in one day.'

Hapiir's jaws closed with an audible click and Bernice sat back in her seat, allowing him the last word. It was all plausible enough, she thought. But was it true?

They were high over the city by now, and Bernice studied it in fascination. Incredibly, it all seemed to be one huge building, stretching as far as she could see. Or rather a series of buildings linked by passages and walkways at every level. The buildings resembled fantastic castles, decorated with towers and turrets and battlements and spires. They were constructed from some gleaming white crystalline substance, shot through with occasional flares of colour. In between the castles were squares with fountains and patches of vivid green that looked like parks and gardens.

Far below her, tiny figures scurried across the walkways, moving from one building to another. Ornithopters of all colours, shapes and sizes fluttered between the towers like giant moths.

Bernice leaned forward. 'It's beautiful,' she said.

'It is the City,' said Hapiir proudly. 'Once it was a handful of buildings in an oasis, the home of a few poor scholars. Gradually it grew. Room after room was added, dwelling after dwelling, libraries, dormitories, laboratories... Now it is as you see.'

The ornithopter swooped down between the buildings and glided to land on a ramp that projected from one of the towers. Spindly green figures hurried out and secured it with ropes, dragging it into a huge airy chamber. Bernice climbed down and looked around. There were rows and rows of ornithopters with folded wings. Even as she watched, one moved towards the ramp.

Reflecting that a car park was a car park anywhere in the cosmos, Bernice turned and saw that Hapiir was bowing formally.

'Welcome to Sentarion, Domina,' he said. 'I hope you will forget the unfortunate incident of your arrival and enjoy a fruitful and rewarding stay with us.'

'What did you call me?' asked Bernice curiously.

'Domina. It is the customary term of address for distinguished female scholars.' Hapiir looked anxiously at Bernice, taking in her dusty jeans, worn field-boots and many-pocketed safari-jacket. 'You are a female? My experience with alien species is rather limited.'

'Don't worry, you got it right,' said Bernice.

'Our current Chancellor is a historian and the universities of Old Earth are his special field. We have adopted many of their customs and practices. He is looking forward to meeting you.'

'Not like this,' said Bernice firmly. 'First I need to clean up and change.'

'If you will follow me, I will take you to your quarters.'

Clad in the gorgeous scarlet robes of a Master of Arts of the University of Antares, Bernice followed Hapiir along a wide crystal colonnade that ran along the outside of the tower.

(Her quarters had turned out to be a bare cell-like room with a bunk bed, a table, a chair and some simple sanitary arrangements. It was evident that Sentarion was a place for plain living and high thinking.)

Other life-forms strolled along the lofty colonnade, some human or humanoid, others not. Many were insectoid, like Hapiir, though with an astonishing number of variations in basic size and shape. Quite a number wore the same odd-looking head-dress, a round cap surmounted with a square board, with an ornamental tassel in the centre.

As they passed Bernice, these head-dresses were solemnly raised. Equally solemnly, Bernice inclined her head inside her scarlet hood.

Considering that they'd originally been made for the Doctor, the robes fitted her surprisingly well. The Doctor, as he modestly said, was a Doctor of practically everything. With so many degrees, he could easily spare one for her.

Some day, vowed Bernice, she'd go to university, complete her studies and become a real professor not a fake one. Some day…

They turned off the colonnade, went down a short corridor hung with rich tapestries, and halted outside a set of double doors. The doors swung open, and Hapiir waved Bernice inside. The doors closed behind her.

She found herself in a big comfortable study, its walls lined with books – not discs or tapes or holovid reels but actual books! A richly coloured carpet covered the floor, there were massive leather armchairs, polished mahogany tables, old pictures on the walls in massive gold frames.

Behind the huge leather-topped desk on the other side of the room, a towering figure rose and came forward to greet her.

Bernice found she could take the Lord Chancellor's

appearance in her stride. An outsize beetle had tried to assassinate her and she'd been given a big grasshopper for her guide.

Why shouldn't the Lord Chancellor be a giant soldier ant?

The Chancellor's shiny black segmented body was wrapped in a long black academic gown and one of the strange hats was perched on his narrow insectoid head. Glowing black eyes, ablaze with intelligence, studied her intently, and a fore-claw reached up and raised the incongruous academic hat. 'Greetings, Domina.'

The voice was deep and mellow.

Bernice bowed low. 'Greetings, my Lord Chancellor.'

The deep voice went on, 'You come to us, recommended not only by your own most excellent qualifications' – a claw gestured towards her academic robes and Bernice felt a twinge of shame – 'but also by your association with our old friend the Doctor.'

Does the Doctor have well-placed and influential friends *everywhere* in the cosmos? thought Bernice. Yes, he probably does.

'For the Doctor's sake, I pledge the University's aid,' said the Chancellor. 'How may we assist you?'

'I am conducting research into the Rutan-Sontaran conflict.'

There was a moment of silence.

'I could wish you had chosen some other subject,' said the Chancellor regretfully. 'But a pledge is a pledge, and I owe the Doctor much.' He paused. 'Both for his sake and yours, I must warn you to proceed with discretion. Both races are secretive and suspicious – paranoid even. Your researches may be resented, perhaps opposed. Sentarion is not always as safe as it may seem.'

'I've discovered that for myself,' said Bernice deliberately. 'I ran into a specimen of your local bandits as soon as I arrived. One of the Harrubtii…'

She gave him a brief account of events at the spaceport.

The Chancellor listened with absorbed interest. When she had finished he said, 'My most profound apologies for your unhappy experience. However, you seem to have coped with it most resourcefully.' He paused for a moment. 'Who told you the Harrubtii were robbers?'

'My assigned mentor, Hapiir.'

'Strange that he should make such an elementary mistake.'

'I don't understand, Lord Chancellor.'

'The Harrubtii would think robbery beneath them. One could scarcely call them bandits.'

'What are they then?'

'They are assassins.'

'Why should they want to kill me?'

'Why indeed? Usually, the Harrubtii only kill each other; they engage in endless blood-feuds. Occasionally, however, for an important customer and for a very high fee, they will hire out their services.' The Chancellor settled back in his chair, folding his six legs. 'I regret to say, Domina Bernice, that someone very rich and very powerful desires your death.'

'But that's impossible,' said Bernice. 'Why should anyone want to kill me? I accept what you say about my research, but surely no one would kill me to stop me doing it?'

'Perhaps there may be some other reason,' said the Chancellor. 'Strangely enough, given their profession, the Harrubtii are also our greatest religious zealots. If they thought you intended to pry into matters of religion, they would be totally ruthless. Possibly someone has misinformed them as to the purpose of your visit?'

Possibly someone has, thought Bernice. If, as the Lord Chancellor had suggested, someone wanted her dead, putting the local religious fanatics on her trail would be a very good way to achieve it.

That someone must know of her mission and be ready to go to any lengths to stop her succeeding. Which meant that there was something on Sentarion for her to find out.

Maybe her trip to Sentarion wasn't such a sideshow after all.

4
BLASPHEMER

Bernice Summerfield was silent and thoughtful as she made her way back along the endless colonnade.

Her guide Hapiir gave her a worried look.

'You seem preoccupied, Domina. Your interview with the Chancellor did not go well?'

'Perfectly well, thank you. The Chancellor was most charming.'

'Yet you seem concerned. Is something troubling you?'

'Yes. You are, actually.'

'But in what way, Domina?'

'I was wondering why you told me the Harrubtii were simply bandits. Your Chancellor says they are assassins. He said they were religious zealots as well. He seemed to think that someone might have told them I intended to pry into their religious secrets. Why didn't you tell me any of this?'

Hapiir glanced round, lowering his voice to make sure they were not overheard. 'I was ashamed, Domina, afraid that you would think we were barbarians on Sentarion. Also, I wished to spare you alarm.'

'How do you mean?'

'To be attacked by casual bandits is bad enough. But to be the target of the Harrubtii – they are relentless fanatics.'

'Wouldn't it have been better to tell me the truth? If I know the real danger, I have a better chance of dealing with it.'

'That may well be so, Domina. My intentions were for the best. If I was in error, I am very sorry.'

Hapiir sounded sincere enough, thought Bernice. All the same, he was one of the few to know the time of her arrival.

He hadn't turned up to the rescue until she had dealt with things herself.

And not telling her of her real danger made her an easier target for any future attack.

Hapiir had tried to play down the assassination attempt from the beginning. Perhaps he was just concerned to keep up the good name of the University, as he claimed. Or perhaps he had other motives.

They turned off the colonnade and walked along the narrow corridor that led to her quarters.

Hapiir paused by her door. 'Dinner will be served in the Great Hall very soon, Domina. You will hear the bell. You can find your way by following the others. I will meet you tomorrow morning in the Main Library at the beginning of the First Quarter. Anyone will tell you the way.'

Inclining his tall spindly body in a bow, Hapiir turned and scuttled away with unseemly haste, as if anxious to avoid more awkward questions. Or perhaps he was just embarrassed. There was just no way of knowing who you could trust.

Telling herself she was rapidly becoming paranoid, Bernice pushed open her door – and found the contents of her pack scattered all over the room.

It had been tipped out and the contents thoroughly searched. It could hardly have been Hapiir, he'd been with her – except when she'd been in the Lord Chancellor's study. Would he have had time? Of course, there was no reason to assume he was working alone. He could have tipped off an accomplice that she was out of her room.

Even if Hapiir was innocent, it was quite possible that

her mysterious enemies – the Harrubtii perhaps, or whoever was behind them – would have agents amongst the University staff and servants.

Cursing silently to herself, Bernice took off her scarlet robes, changed into dark trousers and tunic, and set about tidying away her things into the built-in shelves and cupboards provided. At first she thought nothing had actually been stolen. Then she realised – her blaster had gone.

By the time she finished her task the clamour of a great bell was echoing along the corridors.

Draining the last of her Eridanean brandy to give herself courage, Bernice went out into the corridor and joined the stream of hungry scholars heading for dinner.

The Great Hall was a huge cathedral-like space, with an elaborately decorated arched roof. It was filled with row upon row of stone tables and stone benches, arranged on two levels. The lower level filled the body of the hall. At the back of the hall, a smaller number of tables ran along a raised dais.

The lower tables were mostly unoccupied and Bernice realised that this was because term hadn't started yet. Only the staff of the University and visiting scholars, like herself, were in residence.

Unsure of her place in the academic scheme of things, Bernice found a seat at one of the smaller tables on the dais, already half-filled by an assortment of human, humanoid and non-human scholars.

Scurrying beetle-like servants hurried about the hall, carrying steaming tureens of soup, loaves of coarse bread, great bowls of fruit and salad, and earthenware jugs.

As soon as Bernice sat down, one of them poured her a bowl of soup. Another poured a glass of sparkling green liquid from a jug. She swigged it down and grimaced. It was fruit juice.

'If you were hoping for champagne, or even a simple *vin de* planet, you're out of luck,' said a voice from the other side of the table.

Bernice looked up and saw a large, plump, red-faced, white-bearded man in an embroidered tunic. He had a sunburned bald head, sparkling blue eyes, and the broken-veined nose of a dedicated drinker.

'The Sentarrii believe that alcohol clouds the intellect and blurs reality,' he went on.

'Well, of course it does,' said Bernice. 'Otherwise there'd be no point in drinking.'

He held out his hand. 'Professor Lazio Zemar. Xenosociology.'

'Professor Bernice Summerfield. History and Archaeology.'

They shook hands.

'I hope they haven't passed a Prohibition law,' said Bernice. 'I once visited a town where they tried that. It didn't work.'

'Prohibition only applies on University premises,' said Zemar. 'There are a few low dives scattered around the University, mostly in Old Town. They cater for the alien element – meaning us! I think I can claim to know them all.'

Bernice looked hard at him. He looked amiable and harmless – and she had to start finding her way around sooner or later.

'You wouldn't care to show a newcomer around, would you?'

He bowed his head. 'I should be most happy to give you a guided tour.'

Bernice finished her vegetable soup and helped herself to a bowl of chopped green salad.

'You're on! All this healthy living is getting me down.'

While they ate, Zemar gave her a quick run-down on Sentarion society. 'There are an infinite number of variations, but just three main divisions. The smaller black ones are the workers, the builders, the cleaners and servants – like the excellent creatures looking after us now. They work hard, speak little and never complain. The green ones are civil servants and functionaries. They are meticulous and pedantic, obsessed with rules and correct behaviour. You'll be assigned one as a mentor.'

Bernice selected a peach-like fruit from the bowl on the table. 'I've already got him. His name's Hapiir.'

'An excellent fellow,' said Zemar. 'You couldn't do better. Where was I? Finally we have the dominant species, the Sentarrii themselves. Highly evolved, dispassionately intelligent, devoted to scholarship in all its forms. A most mysterious species.'

'Mysterious how?'

'The Sentarrii evolved from soldier-ants – one of the most implacably ferocious life-forms in the universe. Yet at some stage in their history they underwent a kind of mass conversion, and dedicated themselves to non-violence and to scholarship. At the same time their technology made a kind of quantum leap.'

'How do you mean?'

Like most academics, Zemar couldn't resist the temptation to lecture. 'Most technological civilisations evolve in much the same way. Fossil fuels, steam-power, the internal combustion engine – and then atomics. It's only when they've already polluted most of their planet that people start looking for something better. But the

Sentarrii bypassed all that and went straight for electricity – with solar power as their prime energy source.'

Apparently the crystalline rock of which all the buildings were built actually stored solar energy. Entire buildings acted as giant storage units.

'The ornithopters are solar-powered as well,' Zemar explained. 'There are solar panels on the wings – they replenish their energy as they fly. So, no roads, no rail, no ships, no hovercraft – and no pollution. The 'thopters take care of all transport. They're not fast but they're cheap, and they keep going for ever.'

'What about space travel?'

'They don't bother with it. They let the cosmos come to them!'

'Does it work?'

Zemar beamed. 'Obviously. After all, here we are!'

'So we are,' said Bernice. 'How about that drink?'

Zemar led her out of the University complex and into the warm twilight. The twisting alleyways of Old Town were lit with myriad softly glowing lights, filled with a variety of strolling life-forms, most of them alien visitors of one kind or another.

The indigenous insectoids, explained Zemar, didn't socialise much. They disappeared into homes or nests or hives every evening and reappeared next day.

Bernice was still hungry after her healthy meal, and they stopped at a street stall, run by a large and furry arachnid, for grilled desert-lizard kebab, and flagons of fizzy local beer.

'That's more like it,' said Bernice, wiping her lips. 'Lots of mind-blurring alcohol and lovely cholesterol. Where next?'

Next was a long, low underground bar. It was much favoured by students in term-time, said Zemar, though few students were up at the moment. They sat in a wooden booth and a squat beetle-like waiter came to take their order. Bernice asked Zemar's advice, and he stroked his beard judiciously.

'Well, you've tried the beer – it's wet and warm and there's not much more to be said for it. They've got two kinds of wine, red or white. The red tastes like vinegar, the white like battery acid. If I were you, I'd stick to *rekkar* with a beer chaser.'

Rekkar turned out to be that basic form of booze available in most cultures on most planets – distilled white spirit, tasteless, colourless with a kick like a Soggorian swamp-elephant. It was served in small thick glasses. You banged them on the table to make them fizz, swallowed the contents straight down with a ritual cry of 'Hey!' and grabbed for your beer to stop the back of your throat burning out. Bernice soon got the hang of it. Several 'Heys!' later, she was feeling no pain, and she and Zemar were the best of friends.

But the feeling of benevolence didn't seem to be universal.

At a nearby table, shiny-backed worker beetles tossed back straight *rekkar* with no visible effect at all. Suddenly a fight broke out. It spread with amazing speed, until they were surrounded by jostling shiny-backed figures, chittering shrilly and locked in some mysterious struggle.

Bernice grabbed Lazlo's arm. 'What are they fighting about?'

'Some minor point of religious lore, probably,' said Zemar. 'They take their religion very seriously on Sentarion. We'd better get out of here.'

Lumbering to his feet he shoved a path through the battling crowd, like a tugboat through stormy seas. Bernice followed in his wake, still clutching her half-full beer mug.

Suddenly a voice behind her hissed, 'Your time has come. I shall drink your life!'

Bernice whirled round. There close behind her was a black figure, not one of the squat worker beetles but one of the desert Harrubtii, wrapped in a swirling black cloak.

Its killing-spike flashed out and it lunged towards her. Without hesitation, Bernice smashed the heavy stone beer-mug down on its head. It shrieked and dropped to the floor, to be immediately trampled by the legs of the fighting insects.

Zemar was still forging ahead, apparently quite oblivious of what had happened. Dropping the shattered remains of the mug, Bernice hurried after him.

'Sorry about that,' he said, once they were outside. 'Bit of a tough joint actually, no place to take a lady.'

Not unless you want to get her killed, thought Bernice. It was perfect for that. It had been a classic set-up. Brawl breaks out in low bar and rash tourist, who shouldn't have been there anyway, gets accidentally killed.

Zemar had made her acquaintance in the Great Hall, and Zemar had taken her to that particular bar.

On the other hand she'd chosen to sit at his table in Hall, she'd asked to go on a bar crawl and there were only a handful of joints for them to visit.

Hapiir all over again, thought Benny. All she could do was to keep an eye on them – and on everyone else.

One consolation, she thought, since someone's so keen to kill me, I must be getting somewhere – and I haven't even started yet!

They moved on to a smoky club where a centipede harpist played strange alien harmonies.

As a drinking companion, Zemar turned out to be something of a disappointment. Cheerful and amusing to begin with, he became, like so many drinkers, both gloomier and more garrulous as the evening wore on. He told Bernice how he'd never been appreciated, how his assistant at his home university plotted against him, and how the only girl he had ever loved had left him for a curly-haired space pilot on the Mars-Venus run.

'All teeth and curls he was,' he said gloomily. 'Can't see what she saw in him.'

Bernice, who had a much harder head, and was pacing herself by now, listened abstractedly to his ramblings, and made the appropriate sympathetic noises from time to time.

They ended up on the terrace of a restaurant at the edge of town, eating a savoury pile of stir-fried chopped-up meat and vegetables, washed down with chilled flagons of a distinctly superior beer.

From the terrace they looked out over the desert, its crystalline rocks catching the light of a faintly glimmering moon.

By now Zemar's mood had turned from gloomy to vainglorious. He began hinting about some great discovery he'd made, or was on the verge of making. Something that would make all those people who'd scorned and neglected him realise how wrong they'd been. 'I'll be famous,' he boasted. 'The best-known xenosociologist in the galaxy. The one who solved the mystery of the Sentarrii.' He leaned forward across the table, planting an elbow in his supper. 'Remember what I was telling you earlier, at University, over supper? 'Bout Sentarrii an' Great Leap Forward?'

Bernice nodded, wondering how she was going to get him back to the University. She stared out over the desert. Was something moving, out there in the shadows?

'Norralorra people know this,' said Zemar. 'Marrerrafac, *nobody* knows but me!'

'Knows what?'

'It's all tied up,' whispered Zemar. 'Conversion to peace and scholarship, technological breakthrough, all tied up with *religion*. Nobody thought Sentarrii had a religion. Supreme rationalists of the cosmos, right? Religion just for the lower classes, worker beetles, officials and so on. But I knew better. Every culture gorra have a religion!'

'Seems an odd mixture,' said Bernice, her interest aroused. 'All right, it would explain the pacifism. But religion tends to hold hack science more often than not.'

'Aha!' said Zemar mysteriously. 'Worrabout "Chariots of the Gods" syndrome?'

'Come again?'

'Folk myth on every planet,' said Zemar. 'Even had it on Old Earth. Aliens come from the stars, bringing peace and wisdom.'

'An advanced alien civilisation, interfering with a primitive culture, accelerating its development? You hear stories, but I've never seen any proof.'

'Precishely! But suppose it really happened, right here on Sentarion?' His voice rose excitedly. '*Suppose it's still going on?* There's a secret temple, somewhere in the heart of the city. At certain times, the Sentarrii go there, to worship the Shining Ones—'

The desert darkness became solid and flowed over the railing that bordered the terrace, knocking over their table and hurling both Zemar and Bernice to the ground.

The darkness divided itself into several shapes, dreadful shiny-backed black shapes that clustered around Zemar's body. He let out one terrible choking scream that died quickly away. It was succeeded by a ghastly sucking sound.

Bernice scrambled to her feet and hurled her flagon at the nearest shape. The crystal shattered on the armoured carapace.

The creature swung round and glared at her red-eyed. It was a Harrubti, like the one that had just tried to kill her. The same long spike projected from its proboscis. This time the spike was dripping blood.

Shouts and screams were coming from within the restaurant. Suddenly all the Harrubtii flowed back over the terrace rail, disappearing into the darkness of the desert.

They left behind the crumpled shape that had been Lazio Zemar. The embroidered shirt had been ripped open and there were great blood-filled holes, puncture wounds, on his neck and on his torso. The body looked hollow, unreal, like a grotesque model made of papier mâché. It was as though not only the blood but the very life-essence had been sucked from the body.

Bernice turned and saw a fearful group huddled by the doorway between restaurant and terrace. She recognised the beetle-waiter who'd served them, and beckoned him forward.

Reluctantly he advanced.

'One of your customers has been murdered,' she said. 'Hadn't you better tell someone?'

'There is nothing to be done,' whispered the waiter. 'He blasphemed, and the Harrubtii came for him. They have drunk his life!'

5

MEETINGS

It was a sea of ice, glittering under bright, fierce moonlight. The sea was not frozen solid, but made up of myriad jagged, free-floating ice fragments. White mists floated eerily above the constantly moving ice-field.

Here and there great ice floes arose like islands. On one of them, larger and flatter than the others, something strange occurred. With a weird, wheezing, groaning sound, a blue box materialised out of the thin, cold air.

It sat there on the ice floe for several minutes, the light on its top flashing on and off. The light stopped flashing, the door opened, and something very like a Yeti in a battered hat emerged and stood shivering on the ice floe.

Huddled inside his huge fur coat, the Doctor stood surveying the bleak beauty of the icescape. He wondered how long it would take his unwilling hosts to realise that they had a visitor.

Not very long, he thought.

He would have to do some fast effective talking to succeed in his mission – or even to stay alive.

After a brief, cold wait, the Doctor became aware of a disturbance in the frozen sea just ahead of him. A huge glowing sphere rose out of the icy depths, not floating but hovering just above the ice-pack.

It hung there like a huge glass nest, fiery veins of electricity flickering beneath the opaque surface.

It looked like some incredible, mythic sea beast, and it

was, thought the Doctor, quite beautiful.

He stood quietly waiting.

After a moment an aperture opened in the side of the ship and it extruded part of itself to form a ramp. A glowing sphere, trailing glowing tentacles, floated down the ramp and came to rest before him.

A cold, faintly burbling voice said, 'Why are you here?'

The Doctor drew a deep breath. 'I come to help you. I come as your friend.'

'You are not our friend, Doctor. You killed us, long ago, on a place called Fang Rock on a primitive planet called Earth.'

(A bad start, Doctor.)

'I was responsible for the destruction of a Rutan,' admitted the Doctor. 'A Rutan who was trying to kill my companion and myself. I regret the necessity, but I plead self-defence.'

'We are Rutan, we are one,' said the cold, unearthly voice. 'To harm one is to harm all.'

(Think fast, Doctor.)

'Regrettable as it was, it was an isolated incident,' said the Doctor. 'I have clashed far more frequently with your old enemies, the Sontarans. I have fought them and defeated them many times.'

'What is that to us?'

'There is a saying on Earth – "My enemy's enemy is my friend."'

There was a long pause as the Rutan digested the data. Then they said again, 'Why are you here?'

'On a matter that concerns Rutan security – a threat from the Sontaran Empire.'

'What is this threat?'

'It's rather a long story.'

Silence.

Deciding that the chances of being invited on board for a nice cup of tea or a drink were minimal, the Doctor launched into his narrative.

'Some time ago I became interested in the affairs of a planet called Jekkar, on the far edge of Sontaran space. The planet was first colonised by humans, and later invaded by the Sontarans. I worked with the native resistance movement that eventually drove the Sontarans from the planet.'

More silence.

'When the Sontarans finally left the planet, they destroyed and abandoned their command post,' the Doctor went on. 'The intelligence data-banks had been blown up, but I was able to reconstruct traces of a secret correspondence with Sontaran Command HQ. It concerned some great Rutan secret.'

'What secret?'

'I don't know – the files were largely destroyed. As far as I could gather, the Sontarans had stumbled on the secret's existence by accident. But they were confident that they could use it to achieve a final, crushing victory. They also feared that an agent of yours, someone they called Karne, knew that they knew about the secret, and would try to warn you.'

(It's hopelessly vague, but it's all I've got to go on – until Roz and Cwej or Bernice come up with something.)

Another silence.

'Why do you tell us this?'

'To help you. Whatever this precious secret of yours is, the Sontarans are on its trail. You need to protect yourself.'

'Why should you wish to help us?'

Now it was the Doctor's turn to pause. He decided to be openly Machiavellian – to fall back on absolute honesty.

DOCTOR WHO

'Because you are the only force that can contain the Sontarans. If you are ever totally defeated, they'll turn their attentions to the rest of the galaxy.'

There was another long silence. At last the icy voice said, 'What you suggest is impossible. No such secret exists. The Sontarans can never defeat us. It is we who will win.'

'Please, you must listen—'

The hovering shape of the Rutan pulsated with light.

'Go, Doctor. Whatever your motives, you have tried to serve our cause. We shall allow this to cancel out our death on Fang Rock. We shall allow you to live. Do not interfere further in our affairs. If you do, you will die.'

The Rutan floated back up the ramp and vanished inside the ship. The ramp retracted, the aperture closed and the Rutan ship sank slowly beneath the icy waves.

The Doctor turned and went back inside the TARDIS, his mind full of 'if onlys'.

If only Roz and Cwej had succeeded in finding Karne, he could have used the Rutan spy to confirm the truth of his story.

If only Bernice had found some clue as to the great secret, he could use the information to force the Rutans to be more frank with him.

But they hadn't, not yet, and the Doctor had decided it was worth trying to convince the Rutans of their danger on his own. There was no telling if he'd done any good. Still it had been worth a try – and at least he was still alive.

He wondered how Roz and Chris and Bernice were getting on. Surely he would hear from them soon.

Provided, of course, that *they* were still alive.

The Doctor set the controls for dematerialisation, and the time-rotor began its steady rise and fall. Hands spread flat on the console, eyes staring blankly ahead through space and time, the Doctor pondered his next move.

Inside the Rutan ship, in a crystal chamber with gently glowing translucent walls, the Rutan captain held counsel with their crew – or rather, with the other embodied aspects of their Rutan self.

Close together in the familiar atmosphere of the ship, their minds were as one, the flashing thoughts accessible to all. 'Does the Doctor know the secret?'

'That is not possible.'

'If he does, he must die.'

Then the captain. 'He does not know the secret. He knows only that it exists. We believe he spoke the truth.'

There was a silence, heavy with concentrated thought. 'Perhaps we should close the Way.'

'The Way has served us as safeguard for generations. We need it still.'

'An associate of the Doctor is on Sentarion. She seeks to discover the secret.'

'She will find nothing. Our servants will deal with her.'

'The Doctor is cunning. He may still discover the secret of the Gateway. He may lead the Sontarans to it.'

'If there is danger of this, the Doctor must die.'

'Safer to kill him now.'

'No. He may yet be of use to us. We will observe, and wait.'

'He spoke of Karne.'

'Karne died long ago.'

The captain's mind again. 'We did not sense his going from us.'

'Karne lived too long amongst aliens – as an alien. His links with us were weakened, his mind corrupted.'

'Karne endangered his Rutan soul to serve our cause. He was the greatest of all our spies.'

'Karne is dead.'

A surge of hope flooded the Rutan mind. 'No. We believe that the Doctor spoke truth. Karne lives!'

On the Sontaran War Wheel, a planning conference was about to begin. It was to be presided over by Admiral Sarg, commander of the Special Expeditionary Force.

To be present at the conference, to be on board the War Wheel at all, was a signal honour.

This was the most important military expedition in Sontaran history. The force that was to defeat the Rutans for ever.

Commander Steg looked round the dark and gloomy conference room. It was a massive hexagonal chamber, stark, metallic and functional.

High-ranking Sontaran officers, each accompanied by staff and aides, sat straight-backed on metal benches, grouped in a semicircle around Admiral Sarg's command chair.

Despite his comparatively low rank, Steg occupied a place of honour in the front row. He was acting as the Admiral's aide. For his own aide he had a certain Lieutenant Vorn – a mixed blessing since Vorn's intelligence failed to match his undoubted enthusiasm.

Vorn, thought Steg cynically, was lucky to be here. He owed his place on the expedition to his membership of the influential Gunnar Clan. Such factors were supposed to be of no account in Sontaran society, but clan influence carried weight. It always had, and it always would.

Not, reflected Steg, that he had any right to be critical. He was lucky to be here himself – after Jekkar.

After years of glorious and successful service, Commander Steg had been placed in command of the force sent to take over a primitive agricultural planet on the far edge of Sontaran space. The planet, it was felt, might make a useful advanced command post, one of the wide ring of disposable buffer planets surrounding the Sontaran home world.

It had begun as a model operation. Steg's main force had captured the spaceport and its adjoining town, while smaller forces took over the handful of scattered human colonies.

The conquest of the planet had gone according to plan.

Nothing else had.

The human colonists presented no problem. A few exemplary executions had soon ensured their co-operation. Trouble came from a totally unexpected source.

According to the information provided by Intelligence, the planet's nearest approach to an intelligent life-form was a primitive species of giant anthropoids called Jekkari. They were timid, non-technological and presented no danger whatsoever.

As Steg had pointed out in a series of increasingly acrimonious complaints to Intelligence, he had been seriously misinformed about the Jekkari.

Far from being timid, they were cunning and ruthless guerrilla fighters. They raided Sontaran bases, ambushed land convoys and brought the occupation of the planet to a grinding halt.

Their attack methods, if primitive, were ruthlessly effective. Falling trees and hidden mud-pits disposed of Sontaran ground-cars and their occupants. And if the Jekkari had no technology of their own, they proved appallingly capable of handling stolen Sontaran weapons.

It was an uncomfortable experience, Steg discovered, being bombarded in your besieged base by your own stolen field-cannon.

After every raid, the Jekkari disappeared into their endless forests. The Sontaran patrols that went in after them never came out again. As soldiers do, Steg began to get the feel of the mind that opposed him. He was convinced that the Jekkari were being *led* – by a guerrilla general of genius.

He assumed at first that the Jekkari themselves had thrown up this unknown leader. But rumours filtered back of someone human, or humanoid, fighting with the Jekkari guerrillas. Interrogated colonists came up with the matching description of an eccentric wandering scholar called Smith who had been studying the indigenous life-forms.

Steg remembered a couple of insignificant fugitives, captured on the first night of the invasion. He checked up on the details of their execution, and discovered that it had never taken place. They had escaped. He had held the enemy in his grip – and lost him.

The guerrilla attacks went on. Steg fought back with savage efficiency, but his resources were limited and he was overstretched. His invasion force decimated, he sent for reinforcements.

Reinforcements were refused.

Instead it was decided that perhaps, after all, the planet was too far from the home world to make an effective advance base. Another would be found. The High Command ordered not a retreat – the word did not exist in Sontaran military vocabulary – but a strategic redeployment of resources.

In practice, this meant that Steg blasted off with his few

surviving troopers in his few still-unsabotaged spaceships. It was the smallest of incidents in the unending Sontaran-Rutan war, but it was a blemish on his record all the same.

For this reason Steg had fought desperately to be included on this expedition. He owed his place to the fact that Admiral Sarg still had faith in him. They had served together when Steg was a young lieutenant, and Sarg still a commander.

Something of a link, almost a friendship, had grown up between the future admiral and his lieutenant. Perhaps it was because they shared, unlike most Sontarans, a dangerously individual cast of mind.

Commander Steg's reflections were interrupted by the arrival of Admiral Sarg. The ranks of Sontaran officers rose as one, arms across their chests in salute.

Admiral Sarg waved them to be seated and sank, a little stiffly, into his command chair. Steg studied his old commander keenly. Sarg's skull-wrinkles had deepened with age, and his eyebrow-bristles and vestigial Sontaran beard were now pure white. But the fierce red eyes that swept round the group of high-ranking officers were alive as ever.

The admiral's deep, rasping voice rolled around the conference chamber. 'This expedition, as you know, has been a long time in preparation. Some of you at least may be surprised by the suddenness with which it was actually mounted.'

Most of the Sontaran officers present stared blankly at him. It would not have occurred to them to question their orders. They simply obeyed. Up to a certain point this is an excellent attitude in a soldier. But in the highest ranks, where independent thought is not only desirable but necessary, it can be a positive disadvantage. Even the

Sontarans were slowly coming to realise this. It accounted for the unofficial tolerance towards such mavericks as Admiral Sarg.

Steg had noticed the discrepancy to which the admiral referred. It had long been rumoured that the High Command were preparing some devastating stroke against the Rutan enemy, some hammer-blow that would end the war altogether.

Yet the expedition itself had been mounted in a kind of scrambling haste. The War Wheel had been assembled, its crew of troopers and officers recruited at top speed, as if some last-minute crisis had occurred.

'For security reasons, what I can tell you is limited,' Sarg continued. 'But you must know this. For some time we have suspected the existence of a secret weakness in the Rutan defences. Our task has been to find it and exploit it. That task is *almost* complete. However, there is one other important factor. It is vital that we know the Rutan secret – but it is equally vital that they do not know that we know.'

Admiral Sarg surveyed the largely blank faces of his officers and sighed. 'Let me put it another way. You are attacking a heavily defended enemy base. Word reaches you that a door has been left open. You plan to find that door and press home your attack. But what happens if, *before* you find the door, your enemy discovers that you are looking for it?'

No one answered, and Sarg snapped, 'Commander Steg?'

'The enemy find the door themselves and shut it.'

'Precisely. They shut the door!' Sarg slammed a three-digited hand on the arm of his chair. 'Now listen carefully – this data will not be repeated. As you all know, amongst the many disgusting characteristics of our Rutan enemy is the ability to mimic the appearance of other life-forms. They can even take on the form of Sontarans. One particularly skilful Rutan spy assumed the identity of a Sontaran officer called Karne, and maintained it for a considerable period of time.'

A shocked murmur spread through the conference chamber, and one or two officers began glaring suspiciously around them.

'Do not concern yourselves,' said Sarg drily. 'You will recall that you were subjected to an extensive scanning process before boarding. I can assure you that no Sontaran officer in this chamber is really a Rutan.'

Admiral Sarg's thin lipless mouth twitched at the corner. He glanced at Steg and saw an answering twitch. Everyone else looked appalled at the very idea.

'Until recently we believed this false Karne to be dead,' Sarg went on. 'Reports have now reached us that he lives. Worse still, it seems possible that he has learned that we suspect the Rutan secret, and is returning to his home planet to warn them. If he succeeds, our mission will fail before it has begun.'

He glared around the room. 'Priority One – Karne must be found and killed before he can deliver his warning. Our agents are on his track. As soon as he can be located, we shall destroy him.'

An angry growl of agreement filled the conference chamber.

Sarg held up his hand for silence. 'Since troubles never come singly, we have another old enemy to contend with. There is a renegade Time Lord known as the Doctor.'

There was another fierce, angry mutter. The Doctor's name had long been hated amongst the Sontarans.

'The Doctor's people claim that he is a rebel and an outcast,' Sarg went on. 'We suspect that this may be a cover for the fact that he sometimes acts as their agent. The Doctor has frustrated our plans in the past. It seems likely that he is meddling in our affairs again. He has been in contact with the Rutans, and there is evidence that he too is seeking Karne, both personally and through agents of his own. His intentions are unknown but they are unlikely to be of benefit to us. Priority Two! The Doctor and his agents must be found and destroyed.'

Sarg paused. 'Until both priorities are dealt with, we dare not strike. The search for all our enemies is in the hands of our security service and their agents.' He glanced at a silver-collared officer in the front row. 'I am assured that successful results are imminent.' There was an edge of irony in Sarg's voice.

'Meanwhile,' he continued, 'the War Wheel will proceed as if on routine patrol, moving steadily but circuitously towards Rutan territory. As yet we do not wish to alarm the enemy.' He rose abruptly. 'That is all. You may go. Commander Steg, you will remain.'

The Sontaran officers rose, saluted and marched from the room. Steg remained, standing stiffly to attention.

Sarg scowled at him for a moment and then growled, 'Sit, Commander, sit!'

He waved towards a chair beside the command desk. Steg sat, though he still sat to attention. Sarg opened a drawer in the desk and produced two silver goblets and a stone bottle of the fiery liquor called *vragg*. Filling both goblets, he passed one of them to Steg. Steg took a cautious sip, gasped and put the goblet carefully down on the desk. You had to be careful not to spill *vragg*. It was reputed to be able to eat through a battle-cruiser's hull.

Admiral Sarg drained his goblet and poured himself another.

'Do you know what the High Council of Admiralty think of this operation, Commander Steg?'

'No, sir.'

'They think it is the last mad scheme of a senile old fool. When it fails, as they are sure it will, it will give them the excuse they need to replace me.'

Steg said nothing. He knew that no answer was called for.

'Do you know the main strength of our Rutan enemies?' Sarg went on. 'They are single-minded. Indeed, they are a single mind. They think, they move, they strike as one. And how do we counter them? We become like them. We too become single-minded, monolithic. Right, Commander?'

Again Steg made no reply. It seemed safer.

'Wrong!' roared Sarg. 'As long as we think like the Rutans, we can never defeat them. Look at the history of this war. A battle won, a battle lost, another fought to a draw. A planet conquered, a planet lost. The battle line wavers to and fro and nothing changes. Nothing! I tell you it needs original thinking to win this war. A single bold stroke – like this one! That is why I chose you to help me, Steg. If we succeed we shall be immortal. If we fail, we may well be executed – by our own side!'

Sarg poured them both more *vragg*.

'You had a certain amount of trouble on Jekkar, Commander, with a guerrilla leader called Smith?'

'Yes, Admiral.'

'You actually had him in your hands, but he escaped?'

'That is so, Admiral,' said Steg woodenly.

Sarg smiled. 'I thought it might interest you to know that the name "Smith" is a frequent alias of our enemy the Doctor.'

Steg thought of the scruffy little man with his querulous protests. The man who had fooled and defeated him.

'So that was the Doctor.'

'Since the Doctor is known to be concerned in this operation, it may be that your paths will cross once more.'

Steg's eyes burned red. 'I hope so, Admiral. I should very much enjoy meeting the Doctor again.'

6
TRACKDOWN

Roz Forrester glanced impatiently down the long road. 'So where is he?'

Chris shaded his eyes with his hand. 'He's coming. Isn't that a dust-cloud in the distance?'

'No,' said Roz bluntly. 'Let's go back to Garshak and insist on a ride in a police wagon – I gave him a big enough bribe to buy one! The Ogrons brought us here, they can take us back.'

Chris grinned down at her – and saw the white spot poised just over her heart.

Chris's thought processes were sometimes a bit slow, but there was nothing wrong with his reflexes. He swept Roz out of the way with one arm, drawing his blaster at the same time. A chunk of stonework exploded into dust, just where she'd been standing. Chris fired at the cloaked figure on the parapet and missed.

Another chunk of stonework exploded inches from his ear.

'Back inside!' yelled Roz, her own blaster in her hand. 'He's out of our range but we're not out of his!' Despite her words, she couldn't resist snapping off a quick blast herself. A window several feet below the parapet exploded in a shower of plasti-glass.

A massive hand closed over her arm. 'Do be careful, that building is police property,' said Garshak protestingly.

'Someone up there's trying to kill us,' yelled Roz.

'Don't worry, it's all being taken care of.'

Garshak pointed upwards, and they saw a number of massive figures closing in on their attacker.

'I spotted him from my window and sent a message across to the barracks,' said Garshak. 'They'll take care of him.'

Roz started to say, 'Tell them we want him—'

Even as she spoke, the figure on the roof scuttled along the parapet – straight into the arms of an Ogron policeman, who swung it high in the air, and hurled it straight over the edge.

'– alive,' concluded Roz as the body plummeted down towards them. 'Ah well!'

The assassin landed with an unpleasant crunching sound, twitched briefly and lay still.

'Sorry,' said Garshak apologetically. 'They tend to get carried away.' He walked over to the shattered body and turned it over with his foot. They saw a long-muzzled, fur-covered face with needle-sharp teeth bared in a death snarl.

'Wolverine,' said Garshak briefly. 'One of Megacity's more vicious street gangs. Robbery and extortion mostly, but they do the odd contract killing if the price is right. They don't work cheap, though.' He smiled at them, revealing his own yellow fangs. 'Looks as if someone very rich and powerful wants you dead.'

'You wouldn't have any idea who?' asked Chris.

'This Ripper you're trying to catch?'

'No,' said Roz. 'Not his style, he's too much of a loner. He does his own killing. What about these worried fat cats of yours?'

Garshak shrugged. 'It's possible. I was offered a handsome bribe to make sure you died in police custody. People do.'

'Why didn't you take the bribe?'

'I did – but it wasn't as big as yours. I'll pass the word that you're harmless – to the Megacity élite anyway. That may help take some heat off. But I'd advise you to watch your backs all the same.'

'We'll be watching all around us,' said Roz.

A hovercab came speeding down the road and slammed to the ground in a cloud of dust. A rat-like face appeared out of the front window. 'Downtown? Less go!' The driver noticed the shattered body in the road. Bright black eyes looked up at Garshak, and a long muzzle twitched. ''Nother suicide, Chief?' He turned to Roz and Chris. 'Don' worry, happens all the time. Prisoners in here seem to get very depressed. Any time you drive past Police HQ, you gotta zig-zag to dodge falling bodies.'

Garshak reached out for him with a massive hairy arm, but Chris stepped in the way.

'Let him live, Chief, we need the ride.'

Roz and Chris climbed into the battered hovercab.

'Good luck with your enquiries,' said Garshak. 'Do let me know if I can be of any more help.'

'I don't think I can afford it,' said Roz.

The hovercab's motors roared, it rose a few feet in the air and sped away in a cloud of dust.

Thoughtfully Garshak watched it go. An unusual pair, and they'd told him a fascinating story. He didn't believe a word of it. He wondered what they were really up to. It might be very interesting, and very profitable, to find out.

In a part of town so disreputable that the Ogron police avoided it, and even the muggers worked in pairs, Lieutenant Gorsk of Sontaran Intelligence had set up his base in the cellar of a ruined building. With a com-unit and a field generator he could be self-sufficient for a very long time.

The cellar was in the basement of a burnt-out bar whose owner hadn't kept up his protection payments. It was dank and gloomy, with green mould growing on the walls. Gorsk felt quite at home there.

The Sontarans had come to realise that once seen they were seldom forgotten – a natural consequence, no doubt, of their striking and distinguished appearance. However, it was something of a disadvantage in intelligence work. Wherever possible they preferred to remain undercover, working through local intermediaries.

Gorsk's hand moved towards his blaster as he heard scuttling sounds in the rubble outside his cellar. He relaxed as a sinuous fur-covered shape, wrapped in a dark cloak and hood, appeared in the cellar doorway.

'Well?' he demanded.

'We failed. We attempted to kill them outside Police HQ but the Ogrons intervened.'

'It was not, perhaps, the wisest place to choose.'

'Your orders were to lose no time,' snarled the Wolverine. 'We shall kill them at their hotel; it will be easy there. I shall bribe the hotel staff and set up an ambush in their rooms.'

'No,' said Gorsk. 'There is a change of plan.'

'You no longer wish their deaths?'

'Not yet. We both hunt the same quarry – and they are trained investigators. I shall let them lead me to the one I seek – then we shall kill them all. Until then, I want them followed at all times. See to it.'

'As you wish. But they have caused the death of one of my pack-brothers. When the time comes, we shall rip out their throats and drink their blood.'

*

Chris and Roz spent the next few days in a prolonged pub, club, beer-hall and bar crawl. As Chris said, it was a tough job but someone had to do it.

They visited big flashy casinos where hundreds of punters threw their money away in well-rigged games of chance, or rather of no chance.

They spent hours and credits in over-priced underground bars where they could hardly see each other, let alone their quarry.

They were offered a wide variety of strange drinks and drugs, and the opportunity to indulge in a wide variety of perverted pastimes, some of which made even Roz Forrester blush.

It soon became clear that, despite any reassurances Garshak might have given, their presence in Megacity was still far from welcome. Heavy hints had been dropped that travel would be good for their health. Generous offers had been made to cover their travelling expenses to the distant planet of their choice.

The general opinion seemed to be that they would, in any case, be leaving Megacity soon, by space shuttle or by body-bag.

Other kinds of persuasion had been tried as well. They were checking out a beer-hall in one of the poorer quarters when four burly miners swaggered in. They spotted Roz and Chris drinking quietly at a corner table, bought themselves beers, and went into a prolonged huddle.

'Over there, by the door,' said Roz quietly.

Chris glanced up. 'Half-drunk. Looking for trouble.'

'Looking for us,' corrected Roz.

Chris yawned. 'Same thing. Want another beer?'

'Why not?'

When Chris went up to the bar to fetch more beer, the

miners moved close to Roz's table. They began a loud conversation about the depraved sexual habits of off-planet tourists, who only came to Megacity to meet virile miners who knew what a woman needed.

'Ain't that so, sweetie,' said the biggest. Suddenly he grabbed Roz's arm and pulled her to her feet. He looked across at Chris. 'I reckon sonny-boy over there's outgrown his strength. Or did you wear him out?'

'Why don't you ask him?' said Roz sweetly.

'Sooner find out for myself,' he said, pulling her closer.

Roz brought up her knee hard and he screamed and doubled up, no longer much interested in anyone's sex life, even his own.

Two of the remaining miners made a grab for Roz, and suddenly felt Chris's big hands gripping the backs of their necks.

'Really, gentlemen,' he said reprovingly, and slammed their heads together with a clunk that echoed through the bar.

Dropping the limp bodies, he turned to the fourth and last miner, but he was already half-way to the door, with Roz's victim hobbling painfully after him.

Chris went back to the bar, returned with two beer-mugs and sat down. He glanced down at the two remaining miners, both still unconscious. 'Who do you think set these clowns on to us?'

'Who knows? One of Garshak's worried fat-cats probably.'

'I thought Garshak was going to tell them they needn't worry about us?'

'You think they trust Garshak? An endorsement from him's probably as good as a death sentence.'

'Shall we wake them up and ask a few questions?'

'Why bother? They're strictly small fry – and so is anyone who'd employ them.'

Chris nodded and took a swig of beer. 'Might as well move on when we've finished these beers. This isn't the Ripper's kind of joint anyway.'

This, however, definitely was, thought Roz Forrester, later that night. She was sitting in yet another sleazy joint, sipping yet another filthy cocktail, and thinking that all nightclubs everywhere were pretty much the same.

The same surly, but bribable, heavies on the door, the same steep, smelly stairs leading up, or down, to the same hot, smoky, dimly lit room. The same overpriced booze and filthy food, the same fools throwing their hard-earned credits away, and the same smooth operators raking them in. The same crowded floor and the same tiny stage displaying some sordid attraction.

True, the drinks, the drugs, the games and the life-forms varied from planet to planet. All the same, nightclubs were like police stations, more alike than they were different.

Roz turned to communicate this amazing insight to her partner Chris. He was sipping happily from a tall glass of clear green fluid in which a number of minute alien creatures were swimming, and watching the gyrations of an over-endowed exotic dancer with an expression of childlike enjoyment.

Telling herself that even idiots deserved their moments of pleasure, Roz went back to scanning the crowd – which was supposed to be why they were here.

All they had to go on was the Ripper's established pattern. He'd already committed his first more or less routine murder to give him operating credits. Next he'd be going for the big score, the one that would get him off-planet and on the way to wherever he was heading.

The nightclub proprietor, a smarmy little butterball in an expensive white silk dinner-suit, was one of the most likely candidates. He caught her eye and came over, bowing and smiling and rubbing his hands.

'Everything all right, sir, madam? You enjoy your evening?'

His name was Raggor, and he was reputed to control a major slice of the drugs and gambling in Megacity. He was also a ruthless killer, who had personally garrotted several rivals with the white silk handkerchief overflowing his breast pocket. Most important of all, he dealt largely in cash and was rumoured to keep vast sums in his office safe.

'Everything's fine,' said Roz. 'Isn't it, Chris?'

Chris dragged his attention away from the dancer. 'Oh, yes indeed. Most entertaining!'

'I send you over nice bottle of wine, compliments of house.' He lowered his voice. 'Any friend of Chief Garshak, hey?' He hurried away to greet some newly arriving customers.

If they had no luck here, thought Roz, there were only a couple more places to try. She knew that it was long odds against their being in the right place at the right time. But it was all they could do.

If it didn't work they'd have to wait for the next crime to be committed, and set off yet again on an already-cold trail.

A flurry of movement at the door caught her eye and she saw a distinguished-looking humanoid coming into the club. He was very tall with long silver hair and a neat pointed beard, and he wore expensive-looking silk robes.

He was obviously a valued customer. The proprietor was baring rows of shining teeth in welcome, bowing and rubbing his hands and showing the newcomer to a reserved table close to the stage.

Foaming wine was poured into a tall crystal goblet by an obsequious rodent-like waiter, and scantily clad humanoid hostesses hurried to the table.

Roz studied the newcomer with fascination. She had never seen him before, but she was familiar with every detail of his appearance. He wore the shape of the late Mr Sakis, murdered proprietor of a change bureau on Spaceport Boulevard.

In reality he was Karne, the Ripper, the quarry they had sought for so long.

She gave Chris an elbow in the ribs that made him choke on his drink. Spitting out a small, still-wriggling worm he said indignantly, 'Hey!'

She glanced briefly across the room.

Chris, who was efficient enough once his attention was engaged, looked hard and then gasped. 'It's him.'

'Yes,' said Roz. 'It's him.'

'After all this time,' breathed Chris. He started to rise, reaching for his blaster.

Roz grabbed his arm to restrain him. 'Wait.'

'But this is the closest we've ever been. Let's take him now, before he moves on.'

'No.'

'Why not?'

'We don't take him, remember, not to begin with. We follow him, make contact without alarming him and offer him our help. We escort him off the planet, protect him, pay his fare to wherever he wants to go – as long as he agrees to talk to the Doctor first. If he doesn't agree, *then* we take him in – if we can.'

Chris looked at her in consternation. He'd forgotten the Doctor's original instructions in the excitement of the hunt. 'But he's a killer.'

'That's not our concern. We're not Adjudicators any more. The Doctor wants us to bring him back alive, so that's what we do.'

The visitor and the manager were deep in conversation. After a final warm handshake, the manager turned away and disappeared through an inconspicuous door on the other side of the room.

Chris was slumped sulkily into his seat, glaring angrily across the room.

'Stop staring at him like that,' hissed Roz. 'Keep it down to the occasional glance, just to make sure he's still there. When he leaves we'll follow.'

The silver-haired man stayed at the table for some time, drinking, watching the dancers, chatting to the hostesses. To Roz, he looked like a ghastly parody of life, an automaton with jerky movements and frozen smile, having a ghastly parody of a good time. How could anyone think he was really human, really alive?

The hostesses seemed happy enough. Maybe if you spread enough credits around, no one cared if you were a zombie.

'He's leaving,' said Chris.

The tall silver-haired man had risen and was leaving his table. He headed not towards the exit but towards the door at the back of the room.

As he reached the door, a massive Ogron bodyguard loomed up to bar his way. The silver-haired man spoke briefly, the guard stepped aside and the man went on through the door.

'Got an appointment with the boss,' said Roz. She sat waiting for a moment, and then rose. 'Come on.'

'I thought you said—'

'Never mind what I said. Remember the change bureau?'

Threading their way between the tables they made for the little door. As they reached it, the Ogron bodyguard appeared, barring their way.

Arguing with Ogrons is a lengthy process at best, and Roz felt that she just didn't have the time. She delivered a ferocious elbow-strike to the Ogron's midriff. The blow would have paralysed most humanoids for several hours. The Ogron just grunted and doubled over a little.

Chris slammed it behind the ear with his blaster, using all his strength. The Ogron's eyes glazed and it staggered back against the wall. Roz and Chris caught the massive body between them and lowered it gently to the ground.

Roz opened the door and went inside, and found a scene of nightmarish horror.

The manager was spread-eagled on his back on the floor, eyes staring blankly at the ceiling. A glowing shape crouched over him. Even as they watched, a thin fiery tentacle extruded itself, and sliced the tubby little man open down the middle like a surgeon's laser-scalpel, spilling out his intestines in a welter of blood, turning the white silk suit scarlet, and splitting open the breastbone to reveal the still-beating heart.

7
SLAUGHTER

'No!' shouted Chris. He raised his blaster and fired.

The glowing shape seemed to repel the energy blast in a brief crackle of electricity, and then flowed swiftly towards them.

Roz flung herself back and down. Swinging her legs round in a semicircle, she swept Chris's ankles from under him, bringing him crashing to the ground.

The glowing sphere flashed over their heads and out into the big, crowded room beyond. Crackling fiercely, it hurtled through the nightclub like a fireball, flinging aside everyone in its way through the sheer power of its energy.

Those who were brushed by its passing were thrown back shocked and burned. People screamed as their clothes burst into flames.

There was, not surprisingly, a panic-stricken rush for the exit.

Roz and Chris scrambled to their feet and saw the glowing sphere trying to force its way free of the crowded room. The way out was already blocked by a terrified crowd of patrons, all trying to leave at once by the same narrow stairway.

Some tried to fight back. Many of the nightclub's patrons were armed, and the room echoed with the fierce crackle of blaster fire.

The sphere glowed brighter, seeming to repel the blasts. At the same time it reacted angrily to the attacks. Long fiery tentacles lashed out from the central shape, slicing through whatever they touched.

Roz saw a severed arm, the hand still clutching a blaster, fly through the air, while its owner stared unbelievingly down at the stump.

She saw a headless Ogron bodyguard take several stumbling steps as its still-snarling head rolled away across the nightclub floor.

The room seemed drenched in blood and the air was filled with the shouts and screams of the wounded and dying. It was as if someone had fired off a rocket-projectile in a crowded room.

By now people were desperately hurling themselves away from the glowing sphere and a path through the packed crowd opened magically before it. The glowing shape moved swiftly across the room and floated up the staircase.

Forcing their way through the bloody shambles left by its passing, Roz and Chris hurried after it.

As they burst out of the door at the top of the stairs, they saw the hovering sphere surrounded by a semicircle of cloaked and hooded figures. Fierce red eyes glowed beneath the hoods and they saw long muzzles and the flash of sharp white fangs.

'Wolverines!' whispered Roz.

Laser carbines appeared from beneath the cloaks, all trained on the glowing shape that hovered before them. Laser-fire crackled from a dozen carbines. Sizzling with energy, the glowing sphere grew larger, brighter. It whirled into the semicircle of Wolverines like a wheel of knives, the deadly tentacles lashing out and cutting them to pieces. Arms and legs flew in all directions, and they saw one Wolverine sliced totally in half.

Leaving dead and dying Wolverines in its wake, the sphere vanished down the alley in a storm of energy.

Silence fell on the alleyway, though you could still hear muffled screams and shouts from the nightclub below. Half a dozen Wolverines were still alive and on their feet – and their laser carbines were trained on Roz and Chris.

'One has escaped us, but we can still carry out two-thirds of our contract,' snarled their leader. 'Kill them.'

Roz glanced quickly at Chris. They had blasters in their hands but they were seriously outnumbered. They'd take a few Wolverines with them, but they'd be lucky to survive.

There was a sudden fierce crackle of blaster-fire – but it came from *behind* Roz and Chris – behind them and over their heads. One of the Wolverines staggered and fell. Chris and Roz – who managed to shoot straight for once – shot down two more. The three survivors turned and fled down the alleyway – only to find it blocked by an Ogron police patrol.

Two of the Wolverines opened fire and were immediately shot down. The third, their leader, veered to the left, ran straight up a rough stone wall, and disappeared over the top.

Roz and Chris swung round to look at their unknown rescuer. To their astonishment it was the Ogron they'd knocked out and left by the door.

'Thanks,' said Roz. 'We don't deserve it, but thanks.' She turned to Chris. 'Come on, we've got to get after Karne.'

The blaster in the Ogron's hand swung to cover them. 'No. You stay.'

'But we must go—'

'On the contrary, dear lady, you must stay,' said a familiar voice behind them. 'You're both under arrest. Good work, Murkar.'

They turned and saw the approaching police squad was led by Garshak himself.

'Well, well, quite a night out,' said Garshak.

It was some time later and they were back in his office, only this time there were no tea and cakes.

'A nightclub wrecked, half a dozen dead citizens, a dozen more shocked, seared and wounded and poor old Raggor gutted like a Fugora-fish. Oh, and about a dozen dead Wolverines, though they're no loss. What have you got to say?'

'Not guilty,' said Roz.

'That's right,' said Chris 'We didn't commit any crimes, we were trying to prevent one.'

'There's always assault on the police,' said Garshak. 'You two laid out one of my officers.'

'We didn't know he was one of your officers when we laid him out,' said Chris. 'What was he doing there anyway?'

'Looking for this criminal of yours. I put someone in all the places on that list I gave you. Apparently Sakis – or whatever that thing was that looked like Sakis – started coming to the club a few nights ago, spread a lot of credits around, and convinced Raggor that he had some shady scheme that was going to make them both rich. He had an appointment to discuss it tonight.'

'The only scheme was the one he used in the change bureau,' said Roz. 'To get into his office and rob him.'

'Old Raggor had plenty too,' said Garshak. 'Richest crook in Megacity. No use to him now, with all his insides outside.'

'Listen,' said Roz urgently. 'You've got to let us get after him. We stopped him from robbing the nightclub manager, so his resources are limited, and he won't have changed his disguise. It's the best chance of catching him we've ever had.'

'I'm afraid you're already too late,' said Garshak. 'I checked. Someone answering Sakis's description turned up at the spaceport right after that business at the club. They noticed him because he looked odd. He booked passage off-planet on the first ship that was leaving. Didn't seem to care where it was going.'

'Where was it going?' asked Chris.

'Place called Space Station Alpha. It's a way-station somewhere out in deep space. Transit point for a lot of the transgalactic lines.'

Roz groaned. 'He could go anywhere from there.' She looked appealingly at Garshak. 'Please, you've got to let us go after him.' She hesitated. 'I imagine you realise we haven't been telling you the whole truth about all this.'

Garshak gave her an impassive look. 'The thought had occurred to me.'

'Well, I still can't – and even if I could, you probably wouldn't believe me. But if we don't find Karne the consequences will be terrible. Not just more killings, but a war that could devastate all the galaxy – this planet included.'

Garshak sat for a moment, drumming his long hairy fingers on his desk. Then he looked up. 'I'm going to do something very stupid. I suppose that's what you'd expect from an Ogron. I'm going to believe you, and let you go. But I want you off this planet – and don't come back.'

'Don't worry,' said Chris.

Garshak smiled. 'There's another shuttle for Station Alpha leaving late tonight. I imagine you'll want to be on it. I've laid on transport to take you straight to the spaceport. Your luggage is being sent from the hotel.'

'You're in a great hurry to be rid of us,' said Chris.

'I've a great deal of investigation to do,' said Garshak blandly. 'That terrible business at poor Raggor's club. All his loot stolen by some interplanetary criminal—'

'But Karne didn't get hold of the money this time,' protested Chris. 'We stopped—' He broke off with a grunt as Roz's elbow took him in the ribs.

She stood up. 'We'll be on our way, then. I hope you manage to get your hands on those missing credits.'

Garshak rose as well. 'I shall do my best,' he assured her.

Chris got up too. He opened his mouth, caught Roz's eye, and then closed it again.

'Goodbye then – and thanks,' said Roz.

Garshak bowed. 'A pleasure to meet you, dear lady,' he said.

Roz had a strange feeling that he meant it.

The Ogron at the door opened it and stood aside.

Chris and Roz went out, leaving Garshak standing alone in the incongruous luxury of his office.

Roz and Chris were driven to the spaceport in a sleek police hovercar, presumably the property of Garshak himself.

The driver was Murkar, the Ogron who had posed as a bodyguard in the club. He parked outside the main entrance and led them into the vast metallic dome of the space terminal, where a port official was waiting with their travelpacks.

Murkar stood by while they bought shuttle tickets for Station Alpha and saw them to the landing bay. With an Ogron policeman for escort, service was excellent. There were no delays, no customs examinations, no formalities.

Roz was quite glad of the Ogron's presence. She'd noticed one or two cloaked figures lurking in the spaceport's dark shadows.

Murkar was still with them as they stood by the entry ramp to the shuttle, waiting for the barrier to open.

'I get the impression Garshak ordered him to make sure we really go,' said Chris.

'Garshak good Chief,' rumbled Murkar.

Roz looked up at him in surprise. It was rare to hear an Ogron speak. She wondered if he was one of the partial successes in the experiment that had produced Garshak.

'Not much law in Megacity,' growled Murkar. 'What there is – us!' He tapped his chest. 'Ogrons do good – get respect. All because of Garshak.'

'Well, they say every city gets the police it deserves,' said Roz. The barrier rose and she held out her hand. 'Goodbye. Thanks for saving our lives.'

Murkar's great paw took her hand with surprising gentleness.

Chris held out his hand as well. Murkar took it in a bone-crushing grip that Chris did his best to match.

Murkar bared long yellow fangs in a grin. 'Strong!' he said approvingly. He rubbed his own skull. 'Hit hard! You get tired of Pinks I give you job with us.'

'There's a career opportunity,' said Roz.

They picked up their packs and filed on board the shuttle. It was bare and functional, half-filled with weary engineers and technicians, going back to work on Station Alpha after a spell of debauchery in Megacity.

When they were settled in their seats, Roz produced a small crystal cube and spoke quietly into it.

'This is Roz. Positive ID Karne, now heading for Space Station Alpha. In pursuit. Ends.'

The cube glowed for a second then disappeared from the palm of her hand.

'What the hell was that?' demanded Chris.

'T-mail. Time Lord technology. The information goes into the space-time continuum and reappears in the TARDIS data-banks.'

Chris nodded. 'Let's hope the Doctor keeps up with his T-mail.'

Lieutenant Gorsk listened impassively as the Wolverine leader came to the end of his account. 'Total disaster, in fact. Is it too much to hope that you know where they are now?'

'We have watchers at the spaceport,' growled the Wolverine. 'The ones you seek – and the one *they* seek – took the shuttle for Space Station Alpha.'

'And is that all you have for me?' said Gorsk angrily. 'One small nugget of information in all the dross of failure!'

Actually Gorsk was quite pleased. This one piece of vital information was all that he needed.

'Now it is finished for us,' growled the Wolverine leader. 'You must pay.'

'Pay for what? I ordered you to kill these people and they still live. I asked you to follow them, and they got away. You've done nothing, achieved nothing.'

'You must pay as you promised,' said the Wolverine menacingly. 'I have lost many pack-brothers. The failure was not our fault. The police interfered.'

'The police interfered!'

Although he was quite adequately funded, Gorsk was proceeding according to another aspect of Sontaran policy. Not only did you employ alien species to do your dirty work, you cheated them, lied to them and betrayed them whenever possible. Just because the necessities of Intelligence work forced you to associate with inferior species, there was no need to treat them fairly.

'We made a contract,' growled the Wolverine. 'Do not try to cheat us. If you do, you will not leave this planet alive.'

In Gorsk's mind the threat justified the course of action he planned to follow anyway.

'Of course I won't cheat you,' said Gorsk indignantly. 'I am a Sontaran officer. I give you my word of honour. You shall have everything you deserve. I have your payment here.'

He turned to a fieldpack in the corner of the cellar, straightened up with a blaster in his hand and shot the Wolverine dead.

Booting the still-twitching body into a corner, Gorsk powered up the generator and sent a brief message via sub-space radio.

'All Targets currently in transit Space Station Alpha. Mission here finished. Request pick-up soonest. Gorsk out.'

Taking advantage of the fact that the generator was operational, Gorsk plugged the feeder-hose into his probic vent and allowed himself the exquisite pleasure-pain of an energy burn. Dreamily he wondered if he had been rash in killing the Wolverine leader. Perhaps. But what did it matter, after all? If he ever returned to this miserably polluted planet it would be as part of a conquering Sontaran army – once the Rutans had been destroyed.

It is during the brief period of an energy-burn that a Sontaran is at his most vulnerable.

It was extremely unfortunate for Gorsk that in the middle of his dreams of conquest a pack of Wolverines swarmed into his cellar. They saw the body of their dead leader and ripped Gorsk to pieces and ate him before he could disconnect himself.

But at least he died happy.

8
DISCOVERY

Bernice Summerfield glared at the oval screen set into the crystal panel before her.

Fizzing with rage and frustration, she sat back in her chair and tried to think calmly.

She had been working in the Great Library for several days now, researching the Rutan-Sontaran war.

The library itself was a vast, cool, circular chamber, ringed with tier upon tier of stone galleries, each gallery divided into innumerable booths, each booth holding a computer terminal.

Bernice's research was running into problems. Considering how long the Rutan-Sontaran conflict had been going on, she'd expected the files to be loaded with information. Up to a point, they were. But the coverage was curiously one-sided.

There was an enormous amount of information about the Sontarans.

By now Bernice knew all their complex clan structure and their early history of internecine warfare.

She had studied the period in which the battle-hardened survivors of the endless civil wars had at last united, turning their now ingrained aggression onto other species.

She knew about their discovery and eventual adoption of clone reproduction, about the incubation complexes that could reproduce a million hatchlings in a matter of minutes.

She knew of their weapons, their tactics, their endless drive for conquest, the civilisations they had destroyed, the planets they had overrun.

Even their involvement with the Doctor was documented, the attacks on Earth, the abortive invasion of Gallifrey.

As far as the Sontarans were concerned, Bernice felt like the little boy who complained that his book about penguins told him more than he wanted to know.

About the Rutans, on the other hand, there was almost no information at all.

Very little about their culture – though it *was* recorded that all Rutans were united, bonded almost, to an incredibly high degree. So much so that they saw themselves not only as one race but as one personality.

But there was nothing about their shape-shifting abilities, their military capacity, their total ruthlessness when threatened. Nor was there any hint that they bore any share of responsibility for the long conflict with the Sontarans.

The Rutans appeared only as the pacific, almost saintly victims of Sontaran aggression.

Bernice Summerfield didn't believe a word of it. She knew she was reading a thoroughly slanted version of history. But why?

Her mind went back to her conversation with the Doctor.

'The Rutans have a secret weakness,' he'd said. 'Something the Sontarans could use to destroy them. But they either don't know, or won't admit, that the weakness exists – and until *I* know what it is, I can't help them. There may be some kind of clue buried in the history of the Rutan-Sontaran war. Go and find it for me!' So far Bernice had found nothing. But suppose the Doctor was wrong?

Suppose there was nothing to be found – at least, not where she was looking.

What if the clue was to be found, not in the history of the Rutans' war with the Sontarans, but in that of the Sentarrii? What if Lazio Zemar had stumbled on the secret the Doctor sought?

Her mind went back to Zemar's horrifying death. Sobered by shock, she had hurried back to the University to report it. Nobody wanted to know. Neither officials nor faculty members were available at such a late hour, and she could get no sense out of the beetle-like servants.

Next morning she'd kept her appointment with Hapiir in the Great Library and reported it to him.

Hapiir didn't want to know either.

'Please, Domina,' he hissed agitatedly. 'Such matters are not to be discussed!'

'Oh yes they are!' said Bernice. 'The Harrubtii tried to kill me as soon as I arrived, and now they've actually murdered a visiting scholar. You can't expect to be allowed to ignore something like that.'

But that was exactly what Hapiir did expect.

Bernice told him of Zemar's ramblings just before his death. Hapiir quivered with horror. 'Do not speak of such things, Domina,' he begged. 'Do not even think of them. Otherwise Lazio Zemar's fate will be yours.'

He told her that on Sentarion all religious matters were utterly taboo. The Harrubtii, religious zealots, as well as assassins, had constituted themselves the guardians of the true faith. They dealt ruthlessly with blasphemers – and apparently any stranger showing interest in the secrets of Sentarion religion was automatically a blasphemer.

Hapiir's long green body was quivering with nervousness.

'I beg of you, Domina, do not pursue this matter. Speak no more of it – to me or to anyone else.'

'But it was murder, Hapiir. Cold-blooded assassination. Is there no law and order on Sentarion?'

'There is no crime here, Domina,' said Hapiir. 'Everyone knows that.'

'No crime? What do you call Lazlo's death, then?'

'This is a religious matter, Domina, such things are not discussed on Sentarion.'

Bernice felt she was losing her grip on reality.

'Terrific! So if there's a murder you deal with it by refusing to discuss it and then it never happened?'

'Yes, Domina. I mean, no, Domina,' said Hapiir miserably.

Bernice, of course, had refused to let things lie. She stormed out of the Great Library and found her way back to the café on the edge of the desert where Zemar had died, demanding to know what had been done with his body.

Nobody would admit that there had ever been a body.

The grasshopper-like manager said nervously, 'I remember your visit, Domina. You and your companion left us just before we closed. It was almost dawn.'

'What do you mean, we both left? I left. Lazio stayed here in a pool of his own blood, what was left of it. Are you denying he was murdered?'

'I have no such recollection of any such event, Domina, nor have any of my staff.'

'You've already asked them about this non-event?'

'No, Domina, not yet. But I know what they will say if I do.'

And so do I, thought Bernice grimly. She marched onto the terrace and found the table where they had been sitting.

'And what about this?'

She pointed to a faint pink stain in the wood of the

terrace floor. Somebody had tried very hard to mop up Lazlo's blood, but so much had been spilled that faint traces remained.

'Spilt wine,' said the manager, his antennae quivering with terror. 'Your friend knocked over the bottle.'

On most planets it would have been easy to prove him wrong, but Bernice had little faith in the state of forensic science on Sentarion. Something told her that if she ever came back to the café the stain would have disappeared – even if they had to put in a new terrace floor to get rid of it.

Back at the University, Bernice had insisted, against all protocol, on an interview with the Bursar, a high Sentarrii official responsible for university administration.

He had listened to her story with puzzled amusement.

'There must be some error, Domina. Professor Zemar was summoned home on urgent professional business. Some crisis in the administration of his department.'

'He was murdered,' said Bernice. 'I saw him die.'

'Forgive me,' said the Bursar courteously. 'You had been drinking *rekkar*, had you not? It is known to produce nightmares, hallucinations even, in those unused to it.'

'Are you telling me I *dreamed* Zemar's murder?'

'You both returned to the University, together, in the early hours of the morning,' said the Bursar coldly. 'Apparently it was necessary to ask you to make less noise. There are several witnesses. Very early next morning Professor Zemar received an urgent message from his home university. He left by the next available shuttle. You, I understand, slept late.'

'Maybe I did, but the rest of it's just not true. I came back alone last night and tried to report his death but no one would listen to me.'

'There are many witnesses to the truth of what I say, Domina. Servants, officials, even a member of the faculty.'

'What about fellow students? Off-worlders, like me? Did any of them see Lazio alive here last night?'

'Fortunately for your reputation, Domina, they were all asleep.' The Bursar paused. 'This matter has already reached the ears of the Lord Chancellor. He has asked me to deal leniently with you, for the sake of your connection with some old friend of his. Otherwise I should have been forced to ask you to leave us – and to send a formal report to the University of Antares.' And that had been that. After all, she'd get nowhere with her mission if she was expelled from the planet.

Quietly furious, Bernice thanked the Bursar for his help and went back to find Hapiir. He had taken her to her work-station and she had begun her research.

There just didn't seem anything more she could do. She was already branded as an unreliable drunk, prone to seeing things.

Over the next few days, she had asked one or two of her fellow scholars about Zemar. They all seemed to believe he'd been summoned home. One had hinted he'd been suddenly fired for excessive boozing, another had heard that he'd collapsed and been sent home ill.

Classic disinformation, thought Bernice – and a conspiracy that ran from top to bottom, from the Bursar's office to a boozer's bar.

She was willing to bet that some equally convincing story had reached Zemar's home university to explain his non-arrival. A drunken accident, or a bar-room brawl, all best hushed up.

Sentarion was a place where you could just disappear.

Bernice imagined the Doctor arriving to look for her, only to be met with polite surprise and a convincing story of her unexpected departure.

He wouldn't believe it, of course. But there would be nothing he could do.

Her mind came full circle, back to her mission.

She was convinced that if Sentarion did have a secret history it was all on record – somewhere. It was implicit in the nature of the Sentarrii – they were scholars, historians, archivists. Somewhere the information she wanted existed.

But it wouldn't be found anywhere she was allowed to look.

So logically –

'Computer – provide general map of University complex.' The map appeared on the screen.

'Indicate areas forbidden to visiting scholars.'

Several areas became shaded in.

'Focus on area with highest security rating.'

The screen went blank. Words appeared: 'PLEASE STATE PURPOSE OF ENQUIRY.'

'So that high-security area can be avoided,' said Bernice. She waited. No human would fall for it of course. But computers were literal-minded – and trusting.

The map reappeared and then closed in on a large circular area close to the centre of the University. The area was completely blanked out.

'State official designation of high-security area.'

Lettering appeared across the blank area: 'ACCESS DENIED.'

Bernice thought hard. Computers can deny you information, but they don't lie. Zemar's drunken ramblings came back to her.

'Query. Is the forbidden area designated as a Temple?'

'Partially confirmed.'

'Query. Is forbidden area designation "Temple of the Shining Ones"?'

'Confirmed.'

'Gotcha!' said Bernice Summerfield. She leaned forward and began memorising the map. When she was sure that she had it in her head, she shut down her terminal and went off to lunch.

After another unbearably healthy meal of salad and fruit juice, Bernice went back to her room and changed into the clothes she'd arrived in. She ran into Hapiir in the courtyard and he looked at her in surprise.

'I trust you are not leaving us, Domina?'

'Wouldn't dream of it,' said Bernice sweetly. 'But I've spent so much time peering into a terminal my head's getting fuzzy. I've decided to take the afternoon off and go for a walk.'

'I should be honoured to act as your guide.'

'No, no,' said Bernice, a little too hastily.

Hapiir looked hurt. 'But it is my duty to look after your welfare, Domina. I assure you that you would enjoy your walk much more with an informed guide such as myself.'

He sounded genuinely concerned. Was it all an act? Did he plan to lead her into another trap? In any event, she could scarcely set off on a spying mission with Hapiir trailing along, twittering out a commentary on the local beauty spots.

'It's just that I need to think out the next stage of my research,' she said hurriedly. 'Company – even such pleasant company as yours – would only be a distraction.'

Hapiir was mollified. 'I understand, Domina. All scholars need solitude. I hope you will enjoy your walk. There are many pleasant places to be seen in the city. May I suggest you visit the water gardens? Or the Alien Plant Garden?'

She had to listen to a long list of tourist attractions before she could manage to get free. At last they exchanged bows and Bernice went on her way.

She strolled on, apparently at random, through the innumerable courtyards that linked the buildings of the Great Library. Even though Sentarion itself was basically a desert planet, Sentarion City was extensively irrigated and there were fountains everywhere. There were frequent parks and gardens, filled with exotic flowers, some native to Sentarion, others, Bernice guessed, imported from distant planets.

At first fellow-strollers were frequent, and Bernice found herself exchanging bows with a variety of life-forms. But as time went on and she began to approach her goal the lanes and courtyards became silent and deserted and an eerie hush filled the air.

After a long walk through deserted streets and passageways, she came at last to a great crystal arch set into a high stone wall. At the crown of the arch a glowing sphere pulsed with light.

Beyond the arch was a vast paved courtyard, and on the far side of the courtyard rose an enormous dome, with steps rising up to its entrance.

She had found the Temple.

Bernice stopped and looked around her. She had expected Harrubtii guards or electronic defences, but perhaps there was no need for them. The Temple was protected by its own sacred status. No one on Sentarion would dare to invade its secrets.

No one but Bernice Summerfield.

She walked through the crystal arch, passing beneath the glowing sphere and felt an immediate chill. Not just the chill of fear, though that was part of it, but a literal physical chill. On the other side of the arch, the air was cold.

It became colder still as she crossed the vast open courtyard and mounted the steps that led to the arched entrance to the Temple.

Bernice went inside and stood looking about her in awe. She was standing inside an enormous crystal dome, so huge that cloud vapours drifted across its ceiling. In the centre of the dome floated a vast glowing sphere.

All round the walls of the dome there were pictures, elaborate murals that told a continuing story. Bernice followed them round, moving from left to right. As she paused in front of each mural it glowed into life, each picture fading as she moved on and the next came to life.

The story began with savage battles, armies of Sentarrii soldier-ants locked in combat. Then a vast orb appeared, a gateway through which floated glowing spheres.

The Sentarrii bowed down and worshipped them.

In subsequent murals the spheres floated over the Sentarrii, teaching them, changing them. The Sentarrii built cities, developed ornithopters, learned to live in peace.

Finally, after many generations, the shining towers of the Great Library rose high, and beings from other planets came to share their culture with the wise and benevolent Sentarrii.

There were no words, but none were needed. The whole story was there in the pictures. Bernice found herself moved and awed.

She stepped back from the murals and found herself surrounded by the Harrubtii.

They stood around her in a circle, eyes glowing red with hate, black carapaces gleaming, the long thin spikes projecting from their narrow faces. They were thirsting for her blood.

Bernice knew she was as good as dead.

The Harrubtii had killed Lazio Zemar simply for speaking of the Shining Ones. She had profaned their sacred Temple.

One of the Harrubtii launched itself at her, and doomed or not, Bernice instinctively fought back.

She sidestepped, grabbed the creature in mid air and flipped it over. Shrieking furiously it crashed to the ground and spun helplessly on the polished floor like – like a beetle on its back.

But there were more beetles, too many of them. As the Harrubtii closed in again, Bernice knew it was only a matter of time. They would mob her now, and as soon as the long spikes plunged into her flesh, sucking out her life, she would be too weak to struggle.

The Harrubtii poised to spring – and a great voice called, 'Stop!'

The Harrubtii froze and Bernice turned to see the giant form of the Lord Chancellor stalking towards them, his black robe flapping about the segmented insectoid body. An entourage of Faculty members followed behind him.

For a moment the Harrubtii seemed ready to defy him. Their voices made up a chorus of hate.

'She must die, Lord,' one of them hissed. 'She has blasphemed the Holy Place.'

'Would you spill blood, here in the Temple itself?' boomed the Chancellor.

'It is the Temple that she has blasphemed, Lord. It is fitting that her blood should cleanse it.'

'She was a blasphemer from the first,' said another of the Harrubtii. 'We were warned of her coming. We sought to destroy her, but she evaded us with her cunning.'

'When we saw her intention we drew back our guards and

opened the way to the Temple. Now she has condemned herself by her own actions.'

'Give her to us, Lord. She is a blasphemer. She must die.'

The Lord Chancellor's voice boomed out. 'Blasphemer she may be but I choose to grant her the Sanctuary of the Temple. I tell you that here, in the Temple, her blood may not be spilled.'

There were hisses of protest. 'You cannot do this, Lord!'

'I can and I do. The outer precincts of the Temple are in your charge, but the Temple is my domain. Go! I shall deal with her.'

Dragging away their wounded fellow, the Harrubtii retreated.

Bernice drew several deep breaths, and tried to stop herself from shaking.

'I'm sorry,' she said. 'Believe it or not, I can explain.'

'I fear not,' said the deep voice. 'No explanation can possibly justify what you have done.'

'Well, thank you for saving me.'

'I have not saved you, Domina. The Harrubtii are right. You have blasphemed the Temple. You can never leave here alive.'

9
CRISIS

Lisa Deranne stormed into the control room of the solar yacht *Tiger Moth* waving a plasti-paper flimsy.

'Idiot!' she said. 'Stupid, useless, careless, reckless idiot!'

A lean, grizzled old man looked up from a control panel. He had close-cropped grey hair and a scrubby grey moustache, and he wore the khaki coveralls of an engineer.

'What'd I do?' he asked mildly.

His voice retained the slow drawl of New America, his home planet, even though he hadn't seen it for years.

'Not you, Robar, you old fool – Alexi. He's pulled out.' She passed him the sub-space radio message.

Robar read it aloud. '"Greatly regret financial problems associated recent market fluctuations preclude keeping solar racing commitments…"'

'In other words, our brilliant young financial entrepreneur has taken one flyer too many and lost his stake. And he's lost us the Inter-Systems Solar as well. We're one crewman and a quarter of a million credits short.'

'Yup,' said Robar thoughtfully. 'And I guess it's the credits that count!'

Lisa Deranne had done two men's work before and she could do it again, but her Inter-Systems entry was budgeted down to the very last credit.

Lisa threw herself down in the pilot's chair. Even in plain silver space coveralls, her black hair dragged back by her communications headset, she was a strikingly beautiful

125

woman, with high cheekbones and expressive dark eyes. It was a strong, determined face, marred by the worry lines of constant strain.

Lisa Deranne was one of the finest solar yacht captains in the tri-planetary system. But solar racing was an incredibly expensive sport, and Lisa's only resources were her racing skills. Mostly she worked for hire, a professional captain for wealthy owners. She did the work, they got the prizes.

This time was going to be different. She'd put together her own syndicate. Alexi, Zorelle, Mari and Nikos, four wealthy socialites with the necessary cash and a reasonable modicum of racing experience.

With the money they'd put up between them, she'd bought an old space-clipper and converted it for solar racing, rechristening it *Tiger Moth*. Her contribution was her skill, offering the others the chance of a trophy they'd never get near without her.

Up to now. Lisa Deranne had been feeling confident. She had a good ship, and a good enough crew. With her at the helm, *Tiger Moth* could win.

Could have won.

'What about the rest?' suggested Robar. 'Any chance they'll up their stakes?'

Lisa shook her head. 'I've squeezed them till they squeak as it is. Zorelle's already having second thoughts; she'll use this as an excuse to pull out.' She sighed. 'I'm going to drown my sorrows. Coming?'

'When I finish up here.'

'Why bother?'

'You'll come up with something. You always do.'

Lisa went through the open airlock into the repair dock, and made her way along the metal corridors of Space Station Alpha to its bleak and functional bar. Good old

Robar, she thought, he had more faith in her than she had herself. True, she'd squeaked through tight financial situations before. It was the last-minute nature of the let-down that was the problem. Alexi had been due to arrive this very day, bringing his financial contribution with him. She'd been relying on it for last-minute stores, and for the all-important entry fee.

She perched on a stool, dropped the crumpled flimsy on the bar and tried in vain to attract the attention of the barman. He was busy with a party of wealthy tourists awaiting transfer to a space liner, and had no time for hard-up space pilots. Lisa felt as if she had her credit rating tattooed on her forehead.

A voice called, 'Hey, barman. Over here.'

It was a low, rather husky voice, but somehow it caught the barman's attention.

Lisa turned and looked at the man standing beside her. He was middle-aged, medium-sized, sturdy-looking, with a pleasant, weathered face. He raised a hand and crooked his finger, and the barman, a burly four-armed Dravidean, came sulkily over, grumbling all the way.

'Doing my best, it's a busy time, only got two pairs of hands…'

'And I guess you'd like to keep them all in working order,' said the newcomer amiably. 'The lady's waiting to be served.'

The barman opened his mouth, caught the stranger's eye and closed it again. He looked enquiringly at Lisa who stood with her mouth open. She'd been too preoccupied to think about what she wanted to drink.

'Champagne, cold, quick!' said the stranger and the barman hurried away. The man smiled at Lisa, a lazy pleasant smile. 'You look like a lady who needs champagne.

I know the signs. This the trouble?'

Calmly he picked up the flimsy and smoothed it out. He produced a pair of old-fashioned half-moon reading glasses and studied the message.

Lisa Deranne felt control of the situation slipping away from her. It wasn't something she was used to.

'Gentlemen don't read other people's mail,' she said severely.

The stranger peered at her benignly over his glasses. 'They don't?' he said in apparently genuine surprise. He put away the glasses, folded the flimsy neatly and returned it to her.

'Seems like you've been let down. Tough break.'

The barman appeared with the champagne, opened it with the usual flourish, put down two crystal goblets with his other hands, poured the champagne and disappeared down the bar.

The man handed Lisa a glass.

'Maybe I don't like champagne,' said Lisa perversely.

'Of course you do. Everyone likes champagne.'

Lisa drank some champagne. It was ice-cold, fizzy and delicious. 'You're absolutely right.' She took another hearty swig. 'Who the hell are you?'

'Name's Kurt.'

'I'm—'

'You're Lisa Deranne. Saw you winning the Algolian Cup on the holovids. You entering the Inter-Systems?'

'Not any more.'

'Why not?'

Lisa pointed to the flimsy. 'You just saw. My last crew member's just dropped out, taking his financial contribution with him. I could manage without the man at a pinch, but the credits are essential.'

'Maybe I can help.'

'Not unless you're an eccentric millionaire with a gap in his busy schedule and a taste for solar yacht racing.'

'Funny you should say that—'

Lisa finished her champagne and stood up.

'Thanks for the drink and for trying to cheer me up. This is too serious for me to make jokes about.'

'Who's joking?' He nodded along the bar at the group of flashily dressed, noisy tourists. 'I'm booked on a luxury three-planetary tour with those creeps. If I have one more day of them I'll start chucking them out of the airlock. Sooner go with you.'

'Ever done any solar racing?'

'A bit. Amateur stuff, but good class.'

Slowly Lisa sat down. 'You're serious, aren't you?'

'I could be. Who else is in the crew, besides you?'

'There's Robar, my engineer, Zorelle, the designer, and Nikos and Mari.'

'Who are?'

'Couple of the beautiful people, young, rich and madly in love.'

'Sounds like I'll fit in very well.'

'Solar racing's not cheap, you know.'

'I know.' He snapped his fingers for the barman and produced a small gold card. 'What's the deal?'

Lisa's eyes widened. A Galactic Gold Card was valid, without limit, on almost every inhabited planet. It meant serious money.

'Every syndicate member puts in a quarter of a million credits.'

'How soon do you want it?'

'Sooner the better. I've got to pay my entry fee today, and I still need more supplies.'

'How about I pay your entry fee right now, and give the stores a draft for the balance?'

Lisa gulped. 'That will do very nicely.'

'OK.'

He held out his hand and they shook.

'I'll get my gear sent on board. Where are you?'

'Bay Four. Ship's called *Tiger Moth*.'

'What's the programme?'

'We set off for Station Beta as soon as we finish final checks. Just a simple shakedown cruise, shouldn't be any problems.'

'Right. See you back here as soon as it's all sorted. Shouldn't take long.'

Kurt signed for the champagne, added a magnificent tip and moved away. Lisa sat staring into her champagne glass, trying to take in the last-minute reprieve.

Robar came into the bar and sat beside her. She looked up and grinned at him. 'Have some champagne, we're celebrating!'

'I'll take a beer.'

'One beer, coming right up,' said the barman. He seemed anxious to please.

Robar nodded after the departing Kurt. 'How come you were talking to *him*?'

'He's our new crew member.' She told Robar about their meeting and Kurt's offer. 'Talk about luck!'

'You know who he is?'

'He said his name was Kurt. Do you know him?'

'Know of him. Appeared on the scene with a load of credits, did a few very shrewd deals on the commodity market and made a heck of a lot more. Started dabbling in solar yacht racing.'

'So?'

130

'Shady character. Nobody knows who he is, where he comes from. Rumour's he was a smuggler, maybe even a space pirate.'

'I don't care who he is, or what he was,' said Lisa Deranne. 'He can pay and he can sail and he's our new crew member. So finish up that beer, you old soak, round up our crew and tell them to meet me here. I've got news for them. Then get back to the engine room. You've got work to do.'

Amongst the handful of passengers who got off the shuttle from Megerra was one who looked far from well. He was very tall with long silver hair and a neat pointed beard, and he wore expensive-looking silk robes.

He made his way to Station Alpha's travel office and demanded details of all forthcoming departures.

The clerk checked his screen. 'The Tri-Planetary cruise liner has just left. Next one's the return shuttle to Megerra.'

'I do not wish to return to Megerra. What else?'

'Nothing after that until the Canopean Spaceliner, late tomorrow.'

'Nothing? No departures at all?'

'Only the space yacht *Tiger Moth*. She'll be leaving shortly on a shakedown cruise to Station Beta. The captain's Lisa Deranne, you know, she's entering the Inter-Systems Solar...'

'I can book passage on this ship?'

'I'm afraid not, sir, she's a private yacht, they don't carry passengers.'

The traveller staggered a little and the clerk noticed that his face was pale.

'Are you all right, sir? Shall I call the station medical officer?'

'No, it is all right.' The passenger made a ghastly attempt

131

at a smile. 'I have been rather overdoing it recently. Where can I find Captain Deranne?'

When Kurt arrived back in the bar, Lisa was still trying to explain things to her astonished crew.

'I'm sorry it's so sudden, and I realise it's something of a liberty to ask you to sail with someone you don't even know. But at this late date, there's just no alternative.' Zorelle opened her mouth to protest and Lisa said, 'And it does mean I don't have to ask you all to increase your contributions.'

'Just as well, my dear,' said Zorelle acidly. 'I'm practically ruining myself for you as it is. But I'm still concerned that you should accept a man of his somewhat dubious reputation…'

She broke off as Kurt wandered up to the little group. He nodded to Lisa and said, 'All taken care of.'

She gave him a quick, grateful smile.

He glanced round the little group, sizing them up. The older woman, dressed up to the nines, had to be Zorelle, using everything that money could buy in the way of clothes and make-up to fight off the years.

The luscious young beauty in the low-cut sleeveless gown would be Mari, and the handsome young fellow with his arm around her must be Nikos. Love's young dream, and the best of luck to them.

Then there was Lisa. She made the proper introductions and Kurt shook hands all round.

'It's very good of you to save the day for us like this,' said Mari, with an automatically flirtatious smile.

'It's a pleasure and a privilege,' said Kurt. He saw Nikos look hard at him and added, 'It's a privilege for us all to crew for Captain Deranne.'

Lisa gave him a look and said, 'If you'll forgive me, I've still got quite a lot to do. I'll see you all back on board.'

With Lisa gone they all looked a little awkwardly at one another.

'Let's have some champagne and drink to a successful voyage,' said Kurt. He raised his hand for the barman. 'I'd better go over the financial side with you all, my contribution and so on.' He smiled around the still-wary group. 'By the way,' he added casually, 'anybody ever heard of something called a Tontine?'

'I'm sorry,' said Lisa Deranne. 'It's quite out of the question. The *Tiger Moth* doesn't carry passengers.'

The arrangements and formalities were all complete at last, she was eager to be off – and now this tall white-haired stranger had accosted her with his absurd request, just as she was about to go on board.

'If it is a question of credits—'

'No it isn't. I'm not licensed to take paying passengers. Besides, I'm going on a shakedown cruise with a relatively inexperienced crew.'

'But your eventual destination is Station Beta?'

'That's right, but there's no telling when we'll get there. We'll be proceeding under solar sails for some of the way. I'm sorry, but what you ask is impossible.'

The stranger made a last effort to convince her. 'It is really important for me to get a passage from this station as soon as possible. Its atmosphere does not agree with me.' He managed a ghastly smile. 'As you can see, I am not in the best of health.'

'I'm sorry, but I can't help you, I really can't. Believe me, a solar yacht is no place for a sick man. There'll be a liner leaving soon and they have full medical facilities.'

There was a roar of engines and the hull of the *Tiger Moth* vibrated with power.

The stranger looked hungrily at the ship, eyes gleaming. 'You leave at once?'

'Very soon. The crew's on board and my engineer is just running up the drive. If you'll forgive me, I've a lot to do.' The stranger stared fixedly at her.

(Kill? Copy? Negative. Role too difficult to sustain.)

'Are you all right?' asked Lisa. 'Shall I call help?'

'No, forgive me, I am just a little tired.'

Lisa went on board, and the stranger watched her go.

As the entry-lock door closed behind her, the stranger shimmered and blurred, re-forming into a feebly pulsing sphere of light. The sphere hovered for a moment, as if gathering its forces, and then floated towards the rocket vents beneath the ship.

Soon afterwards Bay Four depressurised, the exit doors slid open and the solar yacht *Tiger Moth* moved away from the space station to begin her shakedown cruise.

10
TAKEOVER

After *Tiger Moth* set off on her cruise, life on Space Station Alpha went on as usual – for a time.

The next shuttle from Megerra arrived, disgorging a number of hungover engineers, a small dark angry woman and a large blond cheerful young man, both of whom immediately started asking questions.

They questioned station officials, technical staff, stopping-over space-crew, passengers in transit and anyone else who would talk to them. They were seeking news of a tall silvery-haired man, possibly rather unwell, who had arrived on the previous shuttle from Megerra. They got it too, up to a point – then the trail simply disappeared.

It wasn't easy keeping track of people on a busy space station. All the time space freighters and space liners were making routine arrivals and departures, picking up and setting down goods and passengers, so that the population was constantly changing.

By the time the Doctor arrived, Roz and Chris had followed the trail to a dead end. He found them in the bar, where Roz was trying to persuade Chris to stick to beer rather than try the barman's recommendation, a Dravidean Deathwatch.

'I'd take her advice if I were you,' said the Doctor. 'Three beers, please, barman.'

The barman started to ask him who he thought he was

135

to interfere, caught the look in the cold grey eyes, and went to get the beers.

Chris and Roz greeted the Doctor enthusiastically, though their delight at seeing him soon gave way to despair at what they insisted on seeing as their failure.

'One step behind, that's us,' said Roz gloomily. 'If I were you, Doctor, I'd fire me and hire the Pinks.'

'Nonsense,' said the Doctor firmly. 'I don't know of any other investigators who could have found Karne's trail so quickly and held on to it for so long.'

'Trail is the word,' said Chris. 'As in trailing behind.'

'That's enough breast-beating,' said the Doctor. 'Tell me about what happened on Megerra.'

Interrupting each other as usual, Roz and Chris told him the full story.

The Doctor was particularly interested in the events in the nightclub on their last night on Megerra.

'It sounds to me as if our Rutan friend will be in a pretty feeble state.'

'It was far from feeble in that nightclub,' said Chris.

'It carved up the whole place single-handed,' agreed Roz. 'And most of the occupants as well.'

'Ah, but it was fighting for its life,' said the Doctor. 'Lashing about in a frenzy. And you say it absorbed a good deal of blaster-fire?'

Roz nodded. 'Everyone in the place was blazing away at it.'

'Didn't seem to do it any harm, though,' said Chris.

'It may not have seemed to,' said the Doctor. 'It will have put up an energy shield, you see, absorbed most of the blaster-fire. But to do that must have been a tremendous drain on its power levels. And if the shield faltered it may even have suffered some tissue disruption. It's very hard to kill a Rutan with energy weapons but it can be done.'

'How do you kill them?' asked Roz. 'Could be a very useful piece of information.'

'I dispatched my first one, or rather my friend Leela did – purely in self-defence, mind you – with a rocket-launcher stuffed with bits of old iron, a sort of improvised blunderbuss.'

'An improvised what?' asked Chris.

The Doctor explained. 'In a way, the more primitive the weapon the better. They can shield themselves from energy weapons, and projectile weapons go straight through them without doing much harm. A blunderbuss blows them to bits.' He looked severely at his two companions. 'May I remind you both that we don't want to kill this particular Rutan. We want to persuade it to share some valuable information with us.'

'I might try to get hold of a blunderbuss, though,' said Chris. 'Just in case I need it – purely in self-defence, mind you.'

'The point is,' said the Doctor, 'it sounds as if our Rutan friend – let's keep calling him Karne – may be in a pretty bad way.'

'He was looking pretty feeble when he left the spaceport on Megerra,' said Roz.

'I wonder why he reverted to the Sakis shape?' said Chris. 'You'd expect him to kill again, if only to get a new form.'

'He may not have felt strong enough,' said the Doctor. 'Easier to revert to a form he'd used. You're sure he caught the shuttle before you?'

'Oh yes,' said Roz. 'What's more he arrived here too. Went straight to the transport office and started enquiring about leaving again. They said he looked dreadful, really ill.'

'And where did he go?'

'That's just it, he didn't,' said Chris. 'Not before we arrived anyway, there were no ships leaving. We started hunting for him as soon as we got here, but he'd just disappeared.'

'We searched the whole place,' said Roz. 'Not a sign of him.'

'Then ships started arriving and leaving,' said Chris. 'We checked every departure, but he must have got past us somehow. We thought he must have changed shape again – but from what you say, that's unlikely. And there were no deaths reported, and no more robberies.'

The Doctor stared into his beer. 'But you're sure he was here when you arrived?'

Roz nodded. 'Must have been, there were no departures between the two shuttles.'

'Well, only the space yacht,' said Chris.

'What space yacht?'

'Something called *Tiger Moth*,' said Roz. 'Solar yacht on a shakedown cruise to Station Beta. But they don't take passengers, we checked.'

'I wouldn't mind betting that they took this one,' said the Doctor. 'He knew you were close behind him, he'd have been desperate to get away, *on the first available ship*. If they wouldn't take him as a passenger, he'll have stowed away. Either that or substituted himself for one of the crew.'

'If he did the copying here there'll be a body around,' said Roz. 'We'll have to search for it, then we'll know his new shape.'

'We must get a message to *Tiger Moth* as well,' said Chris. 'Let them know what they're carrying.'

In the communications room of Station Alpha, Ferris, the station manager, a short, stocky, confident type, was congratulating his staff, and himself, on a model work-shift. 'Solar yachts and space freighters, spaceliners and shuttle ferries,' he said eloquently. 'They arrived on time, they departed on schedule, and we handled them all. Well done!'

Dobbs, Ferris's number two, who was tall and thin and nervous, crossed his fingers behind his back. He felt that this kind of talk was tempting fate.

Dobbs was right.

Ten seconds later, a massive alien ship appeared on the main vision screen. It was shaped like a massive wheel, like two wheels, connected by a dome.

'What the hell is that?' demanded Ferris. 'It's not a scheduled arrival!'

A voice blared from their com-unit speakers. 'Station Alpha! This is the Sontaran War Wheel. We are sending a boarding party. Do not resist. To convince you of our seriousness, we shall now fire one warning shot.'

Ferris ran to the com-unit. 'Must let people know what's happening.'

There was a shattering crash, and the whole station shuddered.

In the bar the Doctor, Roz and Chris were still making plans. Roz lowered her voice. 'Can you catch up with *Tiger Moth*, Doctor – in the TARDIS?'

'Well, it's a tricky thing materialising on a ship in flight, but I've done it before – usually when I didn't mean to.'

Their plans were interrupted by the blare of an alarm, followed by a panicky voice over the intercom. 'Everyone, please remain calm. It appears that this station is under attack by an alien military vessel…'

There was a crash of laser-cannon that shook the whole station and the voice cut off.

'Come on,' said the Doctor, heading for the door. Roz and Chris hurried after him.

'Where to?' asked Chris.

'The TARDIS. I checked her in at the storage depot. Whatever's happening here, I want to be somewhere else.'

As they ran along the corridors towards the storage section, they heard the clang of a docking craft somewhere ahead.

They turned a corner and ran into squat dome-headed figures in space armour who covered them with blasters.

'Halt!'

They halted.

One of the figures stepped forward. 'I am Lieutenant Vorn, in command of this Sontaran Assault Group. This station is in our hands. All personnel will assemble in the main refectory hall. Obey and you will not be harmed. Resist and you will die.'

'Blast!' said the Doctor.

They were taken to the refectory, a big brightly lit hall filled with plasti-steel chairs and tables, with a long counter along one end. There were Sontaran sentries on the door. As they arrived, other occupants of the station, both passengers and officials, were being rounded up and herded into the hall. A line of Sontaran troopers, blasters drawn and levelled, stood along the wall. They looked, thought the Doctor ominously, like a firing squad.

At the other end of the hall two Sontaran troopers were setting up a piece of apparatus. It consisted of two parabolic reflectors connected to a small console. A Sontaran officer stood by the console. Under the blasters of the assembled Sontaran assault force, the line of prisoners was made to pass, one by one, between the reflectors.

'What's going on, Doctor?' whispered Roz. 'What shall we do?'

'Just walk through like the others. Whatever happens, don't fuss. Don't draw attention to yourself. And don't call me Doctor!'

The Doctor was the first of their group to walk between the twin reflectors. The process produced a powerful tingling sensation throughout the body.

The Doctor was waved on, and stood waiting for the others.

When Chris went through the apparatus gave a high-pitched buzz. He was stopped, roughly searched, and his vibroknife, cosh and blaster taken away. He was waved on.

Much the same thing happened with Roz.

The three of them stood aside and watched the rest of their fellow captives file through.

Those who were armed had their weapons confiscated without comment.

During the entire procedure, no questions were asked, or answered. Those who protested were ignored. Those who made nuisances of themselves were clubbed into silence.

A burly mining engineer who tried to get tough was killed.

Things ran much more smoothly after that.

Roz was inclined to be indignant at what she saw as very sloppy security work.

'What a way to run a round-up,' she said. 'Even Chris could do better. They didn't ask us who we were or where we were going. They didn't even want to know why we were armed. What's going on?'

'That device is some kind of cellular scanner,' said the Doctor. 'The weapon-detection is just a fringe benefit.'

'But why no questions?'

'At the moment the Sontarans only want to know one thing about you. Are you really the carbon-based life-form you currently appear to be, or are you a cunning simulacrum produced by a mimetic, polymorphic energy-system?'

'Come again?' said Chris.

'A Rutan, dummy,' said Roz. 'Right, Doctor?'

'Right. If you're not a Rutan, the Sontarans don't want to know you. Let's keep it that way, it's a lot healthier.'

'So what do we do?'

'We just lie low and wait.'

Some time later on the Sontaran War Wheel, currently in orbit around Space Station Alpha, Admiral Sarg presided over another planning conference.

With his fellow Sontaran officers, Commander Steg watched as Lieutenant Vorn, newly returned from Station Alpha, marched into the conference room, crashed to attention and saluted.

'I have the honour to report that the capture of Space Station Alpha is complete.'

Typical of Vorn, thought Steg, to make the takeover of an unarmed commercial space station sound as if he'd conquered the Rutans' home planet.

Sarg wasn't impressed either. He came straight to the point.

'Have you captured the Rutan spy?'

'No, Admiral. He is not on board the station.'

Steg sighed gustily. He had wanted to lead the expedition himself, but the High Command felt that this simple but important operation offered Vorn a chance to distinguish himself.

'You are certain of this?' rasped Sarg. 'Rutans are cunning; the spy could be concealed somewhere.'

Lieutenant Vorn was dim, but he was very conscientious. 'Every centimetre of the station has been searched with the tracker, Lord Admiral. Every life-form on the station was detected, rounded up and scanned. Most were humans and similar inferior species. Every life-form has been scanned. The Rutan is not there.'

The Admiral turned to Steg. 'Suggestions, Commander?'

'If our Intelligence agent's report was accurate—' He broke off. 'Have there been any supplementary reports?'

A communications officer said, 'None. We attempted to communicate with the agent to arrange a requested pick-up, but could make no contact.'

Abandoning the question of the vanished agent – now being digested by a number of Wolverines – without further thought, Steg said, 'There are only two possibilities. Either the Rutan spy is still on the space station, or he is not. To cover the first possibility, the search should be renewed. If the Rutan has assumed its dormant condition it may be able to elude the trackers.'

Steg paused. 'If the Rutan left the station, we must discover the means. We need a list of every ship that departed between the spy's estimated arrival and our takeover. Every one of those ships must be overtaken and searched. A task force must be left at the station to prevent the vessels concerned being warned.'

Steg's plan was agreed. A second search of the station proved as fruitless as the first. A rapid and ruthless interrogation of the space station staff produced the list of departures. Very soon a copy was in Steg's hands.

He studied it eagerly.

First name on the list was the solar yacht *Tiger Moth* – bound for Space Station Beta – on a shakedown cruise…

*

143

The Doctor, Chris and Roz sat at a table at the back of the hall, waiting for something to happen. The Doctor was drumming on the table eyeing the ranks of Sontaran troopers, and cursing in very low Gallifreyan.

'What's the matter?' asked Chris.

'It's not like you to get so worked up,' said Roz.

'It's infuriating!' muttered the Doctor.

'What is?'

'I know,' said the Doctor. 'I just know that the Rutan is on board that solar yacht – and there's nothing, *nothing* I can do about it!'

BOOK TWO
SHAKEDOWN

11
ATTACK

Sails furled, the solar yacht *Tiger Moth* moved through space looking oddly ungraceful, like an insect with far too many legs…

Jacket slung carelessly over her shoulder, Lisa Deranne marched grimly along the ship's narrow metal corridors, Robar at her side. The very beginning of the cruise and already there was trouble.

Without speaking, Lisa strode into the control room, tossed her jacket onto a nearby console and threw herself into the command chair. Robar sat beside her in the co-pilot's seat. For the next few minutes Lisa's hands moved expertly over the controls, checking readings.

When she'd finished she looked at Robar. 'It's perfect.'

'Nope,' said Robar stubbornly. 'There's a fault.'

'Nothing shows on the checks. Nothing!'

'Comes and goes. Ever since we left Alpha One.'

'*What* comes and goes?'

'Power. Fluctuations at irregular intervals.'

'Which unit?'

He shrugged. 'Any of 'em. All of 'em.'

Lisa thought for a moment. It was infuriating to have engine trouble so soon, but if Robar said there was a fault…

'All right. Make a full power check, every unit.'

'Aye, aye, Cap'n. Have to shut down the drive, though.'

147

'Then we shut down. I'll give them their first sail drill while you're checking.'

'They'll like that,' said Robar, straight-faced.

Lisa grabbed the ornate uniform jacket and strode out. Robar grinned and started checking the power console.

The crew's quarters on the *Tiger Moth* were little changed from the ship's space-freighter days. There was a dormitory with bunk beds, a recreation area complete with gym bench, and a small automated kitchen. The main crew room was a drab, functional place with bench seats covered in blue plastic, a table and a few chairs.

There were three people in the crew room at the moment, and a certain amount of grumbling was going on.

The source, as usual, was Zorelle.

She was wearing one of her own creations, an exotic black and silver gown that would have looked better in a ballroom. She checked her extravagant eye make-up and lavish lip gloss in the minor and returned to her grievance.

'How much longer?' she said sulkily.

'She'll come when she's ready,' said Mari. For someone who'd been spoiled rotten since birth, she was surprisingly good-natured.

'She treats us like nobodies,' complained Zorelle.

Kurt wandered in from the sleeping quarters and sat down at the long bench-seat.

'She's the best solar yacht captain in the galaxy,' he said, adding infuriatingly, 'To her, you're a nobody.'

Nikos laughed. 'A nobody with money,' he protested lazily.

'Exactly,' said Zorelle. 'We're the ones who bought this ship, we paid for its conversion to a solar yacht, we pay all the racing expenses—'

'All useless without Lisa,' Kurt pointed out placidly.

'If it wasn't for us, she couldn't afford to race, let alone win,' said Zorelle. 'I just don't see what gives her the right to treat us as she does.'

Mari snuggled up to Nikos, who began massaging her bare shoulders. 'That's not fair, Zorelle, she's always polite.'

'On the surface, maybe – we're a necessary evil. But you can see she despises us.'

'Maybe it's because she *earned* her reputation,' suggested Kurt blandly.

Zorelle went off like a rocket. 'I built up my design business until it covered three planets.'

Mari got up and wandered across the room, studying Zorelle's outfit with lazy amusement. 'I know, I know… The kids back home raided their grandmothers' wardrobes and made the House of Zorelle fashionable again – almost!'

Zorelle glanced disparagingly at her. 'My dear, it looks as if your little planet needs every bit of help it can get.'

Mari smiled, well aware that she had nothing to worry about. In her clinging, sleeveless white dress, dark hair curled tight to her head, she was as luscious as a newly ripe peach.

Mari was a constant, and painful, reminder to Zorelle that in competition with youth and beauty, high-fashion clothes and clever make-up have their limitations.

'I hear it's your sister who's the real genius,' said Mari teasingly.

'She's just a designer,' said Zorelle furiously. 'I'm the businesswoman, she'd be nothing without me.'

'You inherited a business,' said Kurt. He grinned at Nikos and Mari. 'The real trick is to start with nothing.'

'How did you make your money, Kurt?' asked Nikos impudently.

'Oh, this and that.'

'What about your early days?' asked Mari. 'One hears such interesting rumours. Space piracy, smuggling…'

Kurt produced his innocent look, the one he always used when he was lying. 'Me?'

Nikos leaned back, stretching luxuriously. 'Well, I expect to inherit half a planet from my dear father.' Mari came back to him and he reached out, enfolding her in his arms. 'And Mari here is a planetary president's daughter,' he said in mock-reverent tones. 'Far too important and too beautiful even to think about work!'

While the *Tiger Moth*'s passengers wrangled, the Sontaran War Wheel rolled remorselessly towards them. The latest addition to the Sontaran Battle Fleet, its name derived from the massive wheel-like structures either side of the huge central dome.

The War Wheel's design incorporated a number of smaller vessels, powerful assault-craft, designed to separate from the mothership at need.

Commander Steg and Lieutenant Vorn were in the control room of one of these sub-ships. Vorn was studying a space radar screen.

'Alien vessel in visual range, Commander.'

For a moment Steg made no reply. He was enjoying the last, fading, ecstatic moments of a power-burn. Reluctantly his three-digited hand plucked the feeder-hose from his probic vent.

'According to our scanners they've cut their power,' reported Vorn.

Steg straightened up, renewed energy flooding through his body. 'Convenient. Select a boarding party. This first target looks the most promising. Tell the admiral, I shall deal with it myself.'

Steg, like the Doctor earlier, had decided that the Rutan would have taken the first possible opportunity of leaving Station Alpha, however inconvenient and inappropriate the vessel might be. And if the Rutan was on board *Tiger Moth*, Steg, and no one else, was going to command the expedition that found it.

Lisa Deranne could hear Zorelle's whining voice even before she reached the crew-room door.

'I even designed her a uniform jacket – and what happens? Half the time she doesn't even deign to wear it.'

Then Kurt's flat voice. 'Fancy jackets don't win races.'

Zorelle again. 'The fact remains that our money, however acquired, bought this ship. We should be giving orders, not taking them. Lisa Deranne may be the captain but she's still only our employee after all…'

With a rueful smile, Lisa took the ornate uniform jacket from her shoulder and slipped it on. She went down the metal ladder that led to the crewroom and went inside.

Ignoring Zorelle's guilty silence, she put a bright, public relations smile onto her face.

'I'm sorry to keep you waiting. There's a problem with the power-drive.'

Kurt looked up from his seat in the corner. 'Major?'

'Very minor. Robar's dealing with it now. We can't go on till it's fixed.'

'Why not?' asked Mari. 'We've still got the solar sails? Isn't that the whole point of this cruise?'

With an effort, Lisa managed to keep her smile in place. 'Solar sails are fragile – the thing they do best is break down. If we lose sail and power we'll just drift.'

'So?'

'Food supplies are limited,' explained Lisa patiently.

'We'd end up eating each other.'

Nikos grabbed Mari. 'I'd start with you!' He nipped her earlobe and she squealed delightedly.

'So what now?' asked Zorelle petulantly. 'More waiting?'

'Solar sail drill,' said Lisa Deranne crisply. 'Sail deck in ten minutes.' Her eyes flicked over Zorelle's silver creation and Mari's white gown. She smiled, genuinely this time. 'Working dress, please!'

When Captain Deranne arrived on the sail deck, she found three-quarters of her crew ready and waiting for her.

Formerly the cargo hold, the sail deck was at the heart of the *Tiger Moth*'s conversion to solar sail. A vast shadowy area, lit by an eerie green glow, it now held a main control console at the centre of a semicircle of virtual reality platforms.

Three of them were already occupied. Mari and Nikos both wore expensive but practical green space coveralls, while Kurt was in his usual black. All three held VR goggles and gloves.

Lisa Deranne stood waiting impatiently at the central console, in the full splendour of her uniform jacket.

After a few moments the jacket's creator entered, or rather, made an entrance. She wore a set of stunningly elaborate, over-decorated green plasti-silk coveralls, a high-fashion version of those worn by the others.

Conscious of everyone's attention, and taking their concealed amusement for awed admiration, Zorelle took her place on the remaining podium, picking up her gloves and goggles.

Lisa Deranne looked round the group.

'Now we're all here – remember this, it's important. In solar yacht racing, the start is everything. Whether we win or lose can all be decided in those first minutes. It's vital that the sails be set to the optimum angle at the maximum speed. In other words, we do it right, and we do it quick. Right, stand by!'

She pulled on her VR gloves and goggles and the others did the same. A holograph sprang to life in the centre of the sail deck, a representation of the *Tiger Moth* as she was now, drifting through space with furled sails.

'Each of you controls one bank of sails,' said Lisa. 'Each of you must obey my orders instantly and accurately. Understood? Right, let's do it!'

She began snapping out commands.

'Set mainsail, full extension.'

Kurt's gauntleted hands moved in the air before him. In reality, he stood on a raised podium on the sail deck. But in virtual reality he was out on the deck of *Tiger Moth*, hauling on the cable that sent the great mainsail bellying out above him.

The *Tiger Moth*'s enormous, shimmering mainsail spread out in space – in reality, in Kurt's virtual reality, and on the hologram in the centre of the sail deck.

'Mainsail set,' he reported.

'Set port sails, full extension,' ordered Lisa.

Working feverishly in his own virtual reality, Nikos called, 'Port sails set.'

'Starboard sails, full extension.'

Now it was Zorelle's turn. Anxious but determined not to be shown up, she hauled on her virtual reality cable, in her virtual reality world. 'Starboard sails set.'

'Set spinnaker, full extension.'

Standing on the deck of a great sailing ship sweeping through space, lost in the wonder of it all, Mari was slow to react. Sharply, Lisa repeated the command.

'Set spinnaker, full extension. Wake up, Mari!'

Adjusting her goggles, Mari fumbled for the cable and the spinnaker rose upwards.

'Spinnaker set!'

Lisa paused for a moment. Now came the need for her own special expertise – the minutely calculated adjustments that made all the difference. Studying the solar wind readings on her console, she gave more orders.

Together in their virtual reality world, wrestling with wheels and cables in the rigging of the great sailing ship as it sailed through space, Nikos, Zorelle, Kurt and Mari obeyed her commands and rapped out their replies.

'Port sails inclination, adjust three degrees starboard.'

'Port sails adjusted.'

'Starboard sails elevate three degrees.'

'Starboard sails elevated.'

'Mainsail inclination elevate five degrees.'

'Mainsail elevation, five degrees.'

'Retract spinnaker, two degrees.'

'Spinnaker retracted.'

Lisa considered for a moment longer and then snapped, 'All sails set. Maintain position. Lock off.'

Transformed from an ungainly insect into a shimmeringly beautiful butterfly, the *Tiger Moth* swept through space, propelled only by the pressure of solar winds on her enormous set of fragile metal-foil sails.

The astonishing sight was reflected in the transformation of the hologram on the sail deck.

Mari pushed up her goggles and studied the glowing holograph with awe. It's beautiful,' she whispered.

The crew removed goggles and gauntlets, returned to the real world, and waited for Lisa's reaction.

She studied her console. She studied the holograph. At last she raised her eyes and surveyed the little group.

'Great!' she said. 'Terrific! Wonderful!'

The crew members looked at each other in pleased surprise. Did she really mean it?

She didn't.

'More like an arthritic Algolian dung beetle than a Tiger Moth. By the time we set off, the other ships in the race would be halfway home. Mari, you *must* be quicker with that spinnaker. Zorelle, your lower starboard sail is two degrees out of line. We'd be going round in circles. Nikos, no problems, well done!'

By this time, Mari was tearful, Zorelle furious, Nikos was looking smug, and Kurt mildly amused.

'I don't know why you're so cheerful, Kurt,' said Lisa. 'I said elevate five degrees, not six!'

Kurt's smile disappeared.

Actually, thought Lisa, they'd done better than she'd expected. Not that she was going to tell them so, not yet. You break them down before you build them up.

She looked around her chastened crew.

'We are going to repeat this and similar manoeuvres until you can do them perfectly, smoothly, swiftly, and if necessary, in your sleep. Is that clear?'

In the control room Robar was listening to Lisa over the intercom. He grinned. It was her standard speech with new crews.

Robar was still searching for the cause of the mysterious power fluctuations. He'd checked the control circuits of all the main power units, establishing, at least, where the trouble wasn't, and was about to go down to the engine room and check the units themselves.

Suddenly an explosion rocked the ship.

Robar scrambled to his feet and went to the command

console. He checked instruments and flipped the intercom switch.

'Engineer to Captain. We are being fired on by an unknown vessel.'

Lisa's voice came back. 'Are we hit?'

'Minor sail damage,' said Robar calmly. 'I think it was a warning shot.'

'On my way.'

Lisa turned to the astonished crew. 'Stay here, all of you!' She turned and ran for the control room, pounding along the ship's metal corridors.

She found Robar peering at the monitor screen. It showed a blurred, indistinct image of the vessel that had attacked them. 'Can you establish a com-link?'

'Picture keeps breaking up,' muttered Robar. He tried again, and a distorted image of a helmeted figure appeared on the screen. 'Best I can do.'

Lisa stared in puzzlement at the menacing shape. 'What the hell is that?'

'Beats me.'

Lisa spoke into the com-unit. 'Who are you? What do you want? Why did you fire on us?'

A gruff, distorted voice came back. 'We are sending a boarding party. Co-operate and you will not be harmed. Resist and you will be destroyed. Stand by for boarding.'

The figure disappeared and the wheel-shaped alien vessel reappeared on the screen.

Lisa peered at it thoughtfully. 'Not very informative.'

'What do we do now?'

Lisa's first thoughts were for her ship.

'I'm going to retract the solar sails on automatic. Whatever happens, I won't risk any more sail damage.'

'I'll go down to the power room and start checking those

drive units,' said Robar. 'May as well keep busy.'

Lisa flicked a switch on the intercom. 'Captain to crew. The vessel that fired on us is an unidentified battle cruiser. They've got us covered with their space cannon and they're sending a boarding party. That's all I can tell you because that's all I know. I'm going to retract the solar sails from here on automatic override. Stay where you are until further instructions. Captain out.'

Switching off before anyone had a chance to argue, Lisa set to work.

An opening appeared in the central dome of the Sontaran War Wheel and a smaller ship emerged, on course for the solar yacht.

In the assault craft's control-room, Steg was listening to Sarg's final message. 'Admiral to Commander. We are now proceeding to the next interception point. The admiral wishes to remind the commander of the supreme importance of this mission.'

The recycling vats for both of them if they failed, thought Steg wryly. He watched the solar yacht growing large on his monitor screen.

With a sudden burst of speed, the War Wheel vanished into the distance.

The *Tiger Moth* hung helplessly in space. One by one, her solar sails began retracting and folding back. Only the damaged sail refused to return to its place.

The Sontaran assault craft was very close now.

With no information beyond Lisa's announcement, the crew was getting restless.

'This is an outrage,' said Zorelle. 'I shall protest in the strongest possible terms.'

Nikos too was in a truculent mood. 'Are we just going to stand still for this?'

'What do you suggest we do?' asked Kurt.

'Fight!' said Nikos heroically. 'I've got a blaster!' He produced it from the pocket of his coveralls.

There was an echoing clang as another ship locked on to them.

'They're here,' said Kurt. 'Whoever they are.'

'I'm going to talk to them,' said Zorelle. 'I shall tell them who we are, demand an explanation.'

'I wouldn't,' said Kurt. 'You heard Lisa.'

'Our captain is more concerned for her precious sails than for our lives.'

'True enough,' agreed Kurt. 'But she told us to stay here.'

'I intend to deal with this matter myself,' said Zorelle. She turned to Nikos. 'Well, are you coming?'

Nikos flourished his blaster. 'I most certainly am!'

Mari gave him an admiring look. 'If you're going, I'm going too.'

Led by Zorelle they all headed for the door. Kurt hesitated for a moment, shrugged and followed them.

A few minutes later they stood waiting in the wide metal corridor by the airlock door.

Nothing happened.

Then slowly, very slowly, the airlock door began to open. Nikos raised his blaster but Kurt put a restraining hand on his arm.

Something came rolling towards them through the gap in the airlock doors. It was small, round, metallic and faintly glowing.

'Run!' yelled Kurt, urging the others before him.

The grenade exploded with a shattering boom, pouring

out clouds of smoke. Caught by the blast, Kurt was flung across the airlock corridor.

The others turned and fled.

Squat armoured figures appeared from the airlock, charging through the drifting smoke, blasters in their hands. Their leader paused to look down at Kurt's body, and spoke into his helmet com-unit. 'One target down,' said Lieutenant Vorn. 'Proceeding.'

Spreading out through the ship's metal corridors, the invaders hunted down the *Tiger Moth*'s crew with ruthless efficiency.

Nikos took Mari's arm, hurrying her along before him. He heard pounding feet close behind him, and swung round and fired. The pursuing Sontaran trooper staggered back – but the Sontaran behind him shot Nikos down.

'Second target down.'

Mari screamed, and the Sontaran shot her down as well. 'Third target down. Proceeding.'

Fuelled by sheer terror Zorelle was running surprisingly fast – so fast that she ran blindly into a dead end. She turned and saw a squat figure blocking the end of the corridor.

It fired and the force flung her back against the bulkhead. She slid slowly to the ground.

'Fourth target down. Search proceeding.'

In the control room, Lisa finished retracting the solar sails and locked off. As she straightened up, she saw a squat, helmeted figure standing in the doorway of the control room.

Lisa was too angry to be afraid. 'Who the hell are you? What are you doing on my ship?'

The figure made no reply. She could see little red eyes studying her through the slits in the helmet.

'I am Lisa Deranne, ship's captain,' she said coldly. 'I demand an explanation.'

There was some kind of blaster in the creature's stubby hand. It raised the weapon almost casually and shot her down.

'Five targets down,' said Lieutenant Vorn into his intercom. He removed his helmet, relaxing in the consciousness of duty done. 'This ship is under Sontaran control.'

12
PRISONERS

Commander Steg sat in Lisa Deranne's command chair in the control room, jabbing at the keyboard of the ship's primitive computer. One by one, names and faces appeared on the screen before him. Steg studied each dossier briefly before passing on to the next. When the list finished he sat back, waiting.

Lieutenant Vorn entered the control room, a Sontaran trooper at his heels. They came to attention and saluted. 'Commander Steg!' said Vorn.

'Ah, Lieutenant Vorn,' replied Steg, with considerably less enthusiasm.

'The ship is secured, Commander.'

Steg pointed to the computer screen. 'Six humans are listed on the ship's crew roll.'

'Commander?'

'There were five human bodies.'

Vorn thought this over for some time, and came up with the correct deduction. 'One human is missing, Commander!'

'Precisely, Lieutenant. Robar, ship's engineer. Find him. Bring him to me alive.'

'I shall go at once, Commander.'

'No, Lieutenant Vorn, you shall send a trooper. Unlikely as it seems, I may have need of you.'

Vorn saluted again. He turned away – and then turned back again. 'Commander? Where shall I send the trooper?'

'To find an engineer?' Steg's voice was thoughtful. 'It's a wild guess, Lieutenant, but you could start with the engine room.'

Vorn saluted yet again, and he and the trooper marched away.

Just for a moment, Steg covered his eyes with his hand.

The engine was a long thin chamber in the centre of the ship, in semi-darkness except for a few dimly glowing working lights.

Robar was screwing the hatch-cover back on one of the power drives. He was talking to himself, or rather to his engines, as he worked. 'Not you, then. Well, one more to go. Damn these conversion jobs.'

He went to the last hatch, unscrewed the locking nuts and swung it open. He looked inside – and saw, to his horror, that something was looking back at him. Something strange, alien, that had no right to be there.

With an effort, Robar started to back away. A stream of light flowed from the hatchway and engulfed him. He tried to scream, but the same something sliced the breath from his throat with a blade of light, and the scream died away in a gurgle choked with blood.

Lisa Deranne opened her eyes and saw a face looking down at her. It was a man's face, not young, not handsome, but strong and dependable. She tried to smile at it but her face muscles felt stiff. Her head was throbbing and her tongue felt like a Sentarion cactus.

A hand held a water-flask to her mouth and she sucked greedily at the long straw. It was flat, recycled water, but it tasted like nectar. She tried to sit up, wincing as pain jabbed through her head.

'You'll have a splitting headache for a while,' said Kurt.

Lisa took another sip of water. She managed to sit up and then tried to stand. Her legs collapsed under her and she sat down again with a jolt.

'Take it easy,' said Kurt.

Lisa looked resentfully at him. 'You seem all right.'

'Experience – I've been stunned before.'

As her head started to clear, Lisa looked around her. She was in the bunk area of the crew room, and the rest of her crew, all apparently unconscious, were scattered on the other bunks.

'Why didn't you revive any of the others?'

'They'll only start moaning.'

As if on cue, Zorelle stirred. She started moaning feebly.

'See?' said Kurt.

Nikos revived too. He saw Mari unconscious on a nearby bunk and began crawling painfully towards her, ignoring Zorelle's increasingly pitiful moans.

He knelt over her bunk, and stroked her face. Mari stirred and moaned. 'You're alive!' croaked Nikos delightedly. He looked at Kurt and Lisa. 'She's alive!'

'Of course she's bloody well alive,' said Kurt wearily.

'What happened?'

'She was shot down with a blaster set on stun. You all were – I copped it from the stun grenade.'

'Why? Who are they? What do they want?' Another moan from Mari interrupted the flow of questions. Nikos looked desperately at Kurt and Lisa. 'We must help her.'

Kurt got stiffly to his feet and made his way to the water dispenser. He grabbed a towel from one of the bunks, poured water on it, and handed towel and flask to Nikos.

'Here. She's got a sore head and a dry mouth. Look after

her.' Zorelle produced another theatrical moan and Kurt added hastily, 'Her too.'

As Nikos began bathing Mari's face, Kurt went back to Lisa, who was finishing her water.

'Feeling better?'

Lisa shook her head and immediately wished she hadn't. 'Not much. What do you reckon this is? Piracy?'

'Did you get a look at their ship?'

'Briefly, on the scanner.'

'What was it like?'

'Massive.'

'I don't think it's piracy,' said Kurt slowly. 'Feels – military.'

'I'm going to find out.' With an effort, Lisa made it to her feet.

Suddenly the door opened, revealing a squat helmeted figure, covering her with a blaster. It glared suspiciously at her for a moment and closed the door.

'See?' said Kurt.

Lisa sat down again. She looked round the room. 'Robar's not here.'

'Where was he?'

'Engine room, checking the power drive. Perhaps they won't find him.'

'Don't worry, they'll find him,' said Kurt.

Vorn's trooper moved cautiously into the darkened engine room. The room appeared empty and the trooper began a methodical search.

A human stepped out from behind the power drive casing, and the trooper matched its appearance to the description he had been given. 'You are Robar, the engineer? You will come with me.'

The human did not move or reply.

The Sontaran trooper had little experience of this particular alien species. Otherwise he might have noticed that its features were impassive, its eyes dead, and that it gave off a curious green glow.

The trooper raised his blaster. 'Move or I fire.'

The human began to move, not towards the door, but straight towards the trooper. Suddenly afraid, the trooper retreated. 'Back!'

The human came on. The Sontaran fired but the blaster had no effect.

Before he could fire again, the human was upon him. Light flowed between their bodies, there was a crackle of power, and the trooper glowed brightly for a moment. Then he fell with a terrible choking death-cry.

Glowing faintly, the human looked impassively down at him.

The crewroom door was flung open and a helmeted invader entered, two troopers behind him.

'I am Lieutenant Vorn,' he announced. 'All rise!'

Nobody seemed impressed, and nobody moved.

'Rise!' ordered Vorn again.

'Why?' asked Lisa wearily.

'I said rise!' screamed Vorn. He stepped aside and the troopers swung their blasters in a menacing arc.

Kurt rose to his feet. He looked down at Lisa. 'Don't get yourself killed.'

Lisa stood up, raising her voice. 'All right, let's humour them. Everybody stand up.'

Zorelle, Mari and Nikos got mutinously to their feet.

'I should like to protest at the brutal way in which we have all been treated,' said Zorelle.

Mari drew herself up with a brave attempt at dignity. 'My father is President of Valeria, one of Earth's major colony planets.'

'And mine is the planet's leading industrialist,' said Nikos. 'When they hear of this—'

Vorn had a simple but convincing answer to all their protests.

'Silence, all of you, or you will be shot! Now move!'

Vorn and the trooper urged the little group of prisoners into the main crewroom area, holding them in a semicircle.

Another of the invaders came down the stairs. He seemed broader, more powerful than the others. He sprang down the last few steps with a cat-like bound, and surveyed his prisoners.

He lifted off his helmet and put it down. Vorn did the same.

The prisoners stared in astonishment at the heavy, brutal features of their captors, at the broad corrugated brows, the lipless mouths and the wicked red eyes.

All except Kurt, who had seen those ogreish features before.

'Sontarans,' he breathed.

The newcomer's head swung round to look at Kurt. 'You know our race?'

Kurt realised that he even knew this particular Sontaran. 'Only by reputation,' he said evasively.

Vorn was flattered. 'Even primitives have heard of the might of the glorious Sontaran Empire!'

'I didn't say what reputation,' muttered Kurt.

Vorn stepped forward threateningly, but the newcomer waved him aside. 'I am Commander Steg of the Sontaran Space Corps.'

I know who you are, thought Kurt, but do you recognise

me? Lucky I got rid of the beard!'

'Why were we shot down the moment you arrived?' demanded Lisa.

'To establish discipline. I am here on a special mission. You must learn that nothing, nothing and no one, will stand in the way of that mission.'

'Why does your mission involve taking over my space yacht?'

In any group there is a natural leader, thought Steg. 'And you are?'

'Lisa Deranne, captain of this ship.'

'Forgive me, Captain,' said Steg. 'All primitives look rather alike to me.'

Kurt exhaled in silent relief.

Steg began firing questions at Lisa. 'What is this vessel's purpose? Why has it been equipped with solar sails?'

'To race.'

'Explain.'

'At an arranged time, this ship and others of its kind, will set off to cross an agreed segment of space, using only solar sails.'

Vorn was clearly baffled. 'Why?'

Zorelle felt she'd been silent for far too long. 'The ship that makes the crossing in the shortest time is the winner.'

'Solar sails are clumsy and inefficient,' objected Steg. 'The crossing would be accomplished more quickly by the use of the power drive.'

'That's not the point,' said Lisa wearily.

'Then what is?'

'To race. To compete. What do you do on your planet to amuse yourself, to test yourself to the limit?'

Red fires glowed deep in Steg's eyes. 'Ah! You mean war.'

*

A glowing sphere, trailing tentacles of light, floated along the corridors of *Tiger Moth*. Heavy footsteps approached, and the sphere blurred, and re-formed as a Sontaran trooper.

Another Sontaran trooper, a real one, came round the corner.

'You have found nothing?'

'Nothing.' The false Sontaran's voice was flat and dull, but Sontaran troopers are not alert to subtleties of expression.

'Continue the search,' ordered the trooper, and moved on.

When the real trooper was out of sight, the imitation glowed brightly for a moment and dissolved into a blur of light.

The glowing sphere floated on its way – searching desperately for a way out.

Commander Steg had finished with his questions, and was addressing his captive audience.

'My purpose is simple. I seek an enemy of my people.'

'A Rutan?' asked Kurt.

'What do you know of the Rutans?'

Kurt was already regretting drawing attention to himself. 'You're at war with them.'

'Why are you so sure that your enemy is on my ship?' asked Lisa.

'I am not sure. It is merely a possibility, one amongst many. Your last port of call was Space Station Alpha?'

Lisa nodded. 'We carried out our final refit there, took on supplies. But we left some time ago.'

'We tracked our enemy to Station Alpha,' said Steg sombrely. 'We arrived in pursuit, took over the station and searched it. Our enemy was no longer there.'

Lisa was beginning to understand. 'Alpha is one of the busiest way-stations in the star system.'

'Precisely. In the period between our enemy's arrival there and our own, many vessels arrived and left.'

Zorelle laughed. 'And I suppose you intend to board and search every one of them?'

'Yes,' said Steg seriously. 'Every single one.'

'That's outrageous,' protested Nikos. 'According to all the laws of the Tri-System Alliance—'

Lieutenant Vorn cut him off. 'Sontarans do not concern themselves with the laws of inferior species.'

Mari was horrified 'But you have no right—'

'We have the power,' said Commander Steg. 'That is all the right we need.'

Lisa was thinking about the implications, for herself, her crew and her ship. 'So what happens now?'

'My troopers are currently searching the ship,' said Steg. 'If we find our enemy we will attempt to capture him alive. If we do not succeed in capturing him, we shall kill him. Then we shall go.'

'So whatever happens, my ship and my crew will not be harmed?'

'That is so.' Steg rose and walked along the line of his captives. 'I have no particular interest in your survival. But I have no reason to harm you. Take care not to give me one.'

He paused before Zorelle, who quivered with fear under his burning gaze. 'You have two species on your planet?'

'She's a woman, Commander,' said Kurt evenly. 'A human female.'

Steg moved on to Mari. 'This one too is female.' The broad three-digited hand touched her hair. 'The hair is finer... the thorax of different construction.'

As the hand moved over Mari's body she looked up at

the horrifying face so close to hers and gave a gasp of terror.

'Leave her alone!' shouted Nikos. He sprang forward and tried to pull Steg away. The Sontaran swatted him aside, with a casual backhanded blow that sent Nikos flying across the room. He crashed into one of the bunks and fell, and Mari ran to his side. Vorn and the trooper raised their blasters.

Kurt stepped out in front of them. He spoke directly to Steg, using the same flat, level voice. 'The other is a young human male, Commander. He is sexually pair-bonded to the young female. It is his instinct to protect her.'

'Interesting,' said Steg. He waved Vorn and the trooper aside, and moved on to Lisa. 'This one too is female?'

Lisa stared back at him.

Steg stroked her dark hair. 'Ah yes, she is female. But she is not afraid.' He swung round on Kurt. 'And you are male, but you are not aggressive in her defence. Are you sexually pair-bonded?'

Kurt glanced at the furious Lisa, and his mouth twitched. 'No,' he said solemnly. 'This particular female can defend herself.'

'She is female – like these others – but she is Captain?' asked Steg curiously.

Kurt nodded. 'We humans vary a great deal.'

'We Sontarans do not,' said Steg dismissively. 'Variation is inefficient.' He addressed the room at large. 'Remain here, all of you, and cause no trouble.'

Steg sprang to the metal ladder and swarmed up it, disappearing from sight. Vorn and the trooper followed.

Kurt put a hand on Lisa's shoulder. 'You all right?'

She brushed his hand aside. 'Sexually pair-bonded! That'll be the day!' She paused. 'Did you believe what he said – about letting us go?'

Kurt glanced across the room, to where Zorelle and Mari were tending the semi-conscious Nikos. He lowered his voice.

'No. When he goes, he'll kill us all.'

13
DEAL

The Sontaran pocket-cruiser and the solar yacht hung together in space like mating insects, linked at the airlock tunnel.

Inside the solar yacht, a trooper stood on guard by the airlock door.

A second trooper approached. His face was expressionless, as Sontaran faces often are, and the faint glow about his body-armour might have come from the corridor lights.

Without speaking, the second trooper began operating the wheel that opened the airlock door.

The sentry trooper swung round in challenge.

'Where are you going?'

'To the assault vessel.'

'I have orders to admit no one.' The sentry came closer. 'I do not know you. Who are you?'

Ignoring him, the newcomer went on opening the door.

The sentry grabbed the trooper's arm, attempting to pull him away. There was a crackle of power and the sentry was hurled back, collapsing against the corridor wall.

The newcomer turned back to the door.

Lieutenant Vorn came round the corner and saw one trooper on the floor, and another opening the airlock.

'What is happening?' he called.

The trooper at the airlock ignored him.

Vorn drew his blaster. 'Stop!'

173

When there was still no response Vorn fired – but his target had disappeared. The trooper dissolved into a blur of light and disappeared down the long corridor. Vorn ran to the remaining trooper and dragged him roughly to his feet. He was shocked, but apparently unharmed. 'Are you functional?'

'Yes, Lieutenant.'

'Guard the airlock. Let no one pass. No one!'

Vorn hurried away.

Commander Steg was alone on the sail deck.

He was studying the holograph and musing on the strange ways of humans. Choosing a slow and difficult means of propulsion, just because it *was* slow and difficult. He reflected on the curious differences between them.

The two females, the young and the older one, and the young male he dismissed as insignificant. But for all his apparent calmness there was something disturbing, and somehow familiar, about the human called Kurt. And the Captain female… Steg remembered how she had met his eyes, challenging and unafraid.

It occurred to Steg that there was something interesting about all this variety. He dismissed the thought immediately as being unsound and un-Sontaran.

He swung round as Lieutenant Vorn hurried onto the sail deck. There was nothing strange or different about Vorn, he thought. He was utterly Sontaran, brave, loyal and stupid.

Vorn seemed strangely agitated. 'Commander!' he gasped.

Steg pulled him up sharply. 'Report in the proper form.'

Vorn came to attention and flung his arm across his chest. 'Lieutenant Vorn reporting, Commander.'

'Has the ship's engineer been found?'

'No, Commander.'

174

'Have the search patrols found our enemy?'

'No, Commander.'

'You do have *something* to report?'

'There has been an attempt to leave the ship. The guard trooper was stunned.'

'An attempt by whom?'

'By what appeared to be one of our troopers. When I fired—'

'It vanished in a blaze of light?'

Vorn gasped at his Commander's amazing prescience. 'Yes, Commander!'

'You are sure you hit it?'

'Yes, Commander.'

'Blaster on maximum charge?'

'Yes, Commander.'

Exultantly Steg's fist smashed down on the holograph console.

'Excellent! Our enemy is here, and it is wounded. Organise a thorough search of the power room. Rip the place to pieces if necessary.'

Vorn hesitated. 'If the power drive is destroyed, the ship will be unable to proceed.'

Steg's mouth twitched in the rare Sontaran smile. 'Vorn, this ship isn't going anywhere. Not any more.'

Vorn saluted and hurried away.

Steg stood alone on the darkened sail deck, his eyes glowing red in triumph. He had made the right deduction. The Rutan was on board *Tiger Moth*. It was here, and it would die here.

Even if the ship had to die with it.

Steg's thick finger stabbed at a control. The glowing holograph of *Tiger Moth* disappeared into darkness.

*

The Rutan entity that called itself Karne drifted along the dark corridors at the core of the ship, heading for the power room. Vorn's shot had caught it unawares, before it had time to throw up an energy shield. The close-range blast had led to cellular disruption and consequent energy leak. Weak and wounded, the Rutan desperately needed more energy.

It picked up the vibrations of heavy, booted footsteps and shrank into a side corridor, its glow dimmed, as a Sontaran trooper marched past on patrol.

When the danger was past, it resumed its journey to the power room. It arrived at last, only to find danger waiting. The thick-set shapes of Sontaran troopers moved about the engine room, dismantling the power drives.

The Rutan retreated into the darkness, awaiting its chance.

Lieutenant Vorn looked on, blaster at the ready, while a trooper removed a hatch from one of the power units.

Suddenly the trooper stepped back. 'Lieutenant, look!'

The trooper stepped aside and Vorn saw something dangling from the open hatchway.

It was the arm of a dead Sontaran trooper.

When the Sontaran sentry made his occasional checks, things seemed peaceful enough in the crewroom. The prisoners were properly subdued, talking quietly amongst themselves. Under the surface, however, quite a lot was going on.

Mari was fussing over Nikos, now pretty much recovered, but enjoying the attention. The fall had done no real damage, but it had left him shaken and bruised. His ego had suffered most of all. His attempt to protect Mari had been contemptuously brushed aside, and it was Kurt who had saved the day.

He glanced across the room to where Kurt and Lisa were deep in conversation. They seemed to be arguing.

Zorelle was hovering between the two groups, straining to hear what Kurt and Lisa were talking about.

'What makes you so sure?' Lisa was saying. 'Steg said himself he had no reason to harm us.'

Kurt sighed, despairing of making her realise the total ruthlessness of the Sontaran mentality.

'Look at it from their point of view,' he said quietly. 'Suppose they don't find this enemy they're looking for?'

Lisa shrugged. 'Maybe they'll decide it's not here.'

'Or maybe they'll decide it is, and they missed it. If they blow up the ship, they're covered either way.'

Lisa was trying to figure every angle. 'And if they do find it?'

'Why leave us all alive to complain? If we just disappear…'

'What about all the other ships they'll be stopping and searching?'

'Same problems, same solution.'

She looked at him unbelievingly. 'They're that ruthless? How do you know so much about them anyway?'

Kurt didn't want to say too much about the circumstances of his meeting with the Doctor, so he changed the name and the place to protect the guilty.

'I met this weird hobo once,' he said vaguely. 'In… in a bar on Metebelis Three. Called himself the Alchemist, or the Dentist or something.'

'Frontier worlds are full of them,' said Lisa impatiently. 'Space-bums wandering about in battered old spaceships. So?'

'He knew a lot about Sontarans. Said they live for

war. Don't value their own lives, let alone anyone else's. Reproduce by cloning, millions of warriors at a time.'

Lisa shuddered, thinking of the squat armoured figures taking over her ship.

'You'd think the galaxy would be overrun with them.'

'War with the Rutans keeps them busy.'

'And they think there's a Rutan on my ship?'

'Apparently.' Kurt paused for a moment. 'All the same, with all these spacecraft to stop and search, the Sontarans are spread pretty thin. There can't be more than a handful of them on this ship.'

'So what do we do?'

'We kill them,' said Kurt. 'Kill them all.'

Lisa looked at him, her eyes widening. Suddenly she saw, in this quiet man, a ruthlessness to match that of the Sontarans.

She drew a deep breath. 'How?'

'Apparently they've got one weakness—'

He broke off as the door opened, revealing not the sentry but Lieutenant Vorn.

Vorn jabbed a finger at Lisa. 'You. Come!'

Lisa looked at Kurt. He shrugged imperceptibly, and she got up and followed Vorn out.

As soon as they were gone Zorelle swung round on Mari and Nikos. 'You heard what they were saying?'

Nikos shook a still-aching head. 'I wasn't paying attention.'

Zorelle pointed a jewelled finger at Kurt. 'He's trying to persuade Lisa to join him in some kind of uprising.'

'Sounds like a good idea.'

'You're a fool, Nikos,' said Zorelle shrilly. 'Our only chance of survival is to give Commander Steg our full co-operation. How far did resistance get you?'

Mari clutched Nikos's arm. 'Perhaps she's right.'

'Of course I'm right,' said Zorelle complacently.

'You're wrong, you stupid fool,' said Kurt wearily. 'They'll kill us all.'

'I warn you, Kurt,' said Zorelle icily. 'Unless you give up this mad plan I shall warn Commander Steg.'

Mari gave her a shocked look. 'You'd really betray him?'

'If Kurt starts trouble, he'll get us all killed,' said Zorelle. 'He can throw away his own worthless life, but he's not going to endanger mine.'

Kurt studied her for a moment. She was utterly sincere. 'Survival at all costs,' he said almost admiringly. 'Is that it, Zorelle?'

'If necessary – yes!'

Vorn marched Lisa into the engine room. A couple of Sontaran troopers were dismantling one of the power units, supervised by Commander Steg.

'What's going on?' demanded Lisa. 'Why are you interfering with my power drive?'

'The interference was not of our doing,' said Steg drily.

He indicated the dead body of the Sontaran trooper laid out in a corner of the engine room. 'Our enemy is on board this ship.'

'*Your* enemy,' said Lisa.

'The Rutan wants two things,' said Steg impassively. 'Access to a power-source, and escape. To obtain them it will kill every living being on this ship, Sontaran or human.'

They were interrupted by Vorn's voice. 'Commander – there is also an obstruction in this power-drive unit.'

'Then remove it!'

Between them Vorn and the trooper dragged the obstruction from the power drive and flung it at Steg's feet.

It was the mutilated, blood-soaked body of Robar.

'No!' said Lisa. She dropped to her knees behind the body. Robar's eyes were open and staring, his face waxy. He had been dead for some time.

Lisa got to her feet. She stepped close to Steg. 'You say the Rutan did this? These – mutilations?'

'Most certainly. It partially dissected the body to study its structure.'

Lisa's eyes held his. 'It wasn't you? Or one of your troopers?'

'Think, Captain. I could have killed your engineer. I could have killed you all the moment I came on board this ship. But why should I trouble to hide the body and bring you here to see it discovered? Why should I kill one of my own troopers?'

The logic was unanswerable. Lisa knelt beside the body, rested a hand on Robar's icy forehead, gently closed the staring eyes.

Steg watched her curiously, struggling to understand emotions he could not share. 'You were sexually pair-bonded to this man?'

'We worked together for a long time.'

'You – cared for him?' persisted Steg. 'You want revenge?'

Lisa sprang to her feet. 'Yes!'

'Then help me find and destroy the Rutan.'

Lisa paused for a moment, struggling to recover from the shock of Robar's death. She'd been hoping against hope that he was still alive, hiding in the recesses of the engine room, biding his time. That hope was dead now.

She pushed back her hair. 'What help do you need?'

Steg spoke to her as one commander to another. 'The Rutan is cunning, my resources are limited. I have lost one trooper, I may lose more. I need you and your crew to help me search the ship.'

'I see,' said Lisa bitterly. 'Cannon fodder!'

'I do not understand.'

'You'd sooner this – thing killed my crew than your troopers?'

'Given a choice, undoubtedly,' said Steg in mild surprise. 'That is not the point. We face a common enemy. Will you help me to destroy it?'

Lisa considered. 'What's in it for me – apart from the sheer satisfaction of it?'

'What more do you require?'

'A guarantee of safety for my ship, myself and my crew.'

'You have it.'

'When we find this thing and kill it, you and your troopers will go, leaving the ship and the crew unharmed?'

'We shall.'

Lisa stepped closer, until they were almost nose to snout. *'On your personal word of honour as a Sontaran officer?'*

'I give my word.'

Lisa's long finger jabbed him hard in the chest. 'I warn you, Commander – if you betray me I'll do my very best to kill you.'

'Naturally,' said Steg.

Lisa considered a moment longer, and then nodded decisively.

'Very well, I accept – but I can't answer for the crew. We'll have to ask them direct.'

'I am sure we can convince them,' said Steg.

Lieutenant Vorn approached and saluted. 'Shall I expel the bodies into space, Commander?'

Lisa rounded on him angrily. 'You can do what you like with your trooper. I want Robar's body taken back to his cabin and decently laid out. I'll have him shipped back to New America.'

'But he is dead,' said Vorn. 'Dead bodies have no value.'

'He was a human being, not a piece of garbage,' said Lisa. 'Don't Sontarans respect their dead?'

'We respect death itself,' said Steg. 'Death in battle. That which remains after death is of little value. However...' He turned to Vorn. 'Do as she says.'

Lisa nodded, satisfied. 'I'll go and talk to the crew.' No longer a prisoner but an ally, Lisa strode away.

Thoughtfully, Steg watched her go. Humans were undoubtedly very strange. But not uninteresting.

'Do you really mean to spare her, Commander?' asked Vorn.

'I wish I could,' said Steg almost regretfully. 'She has the spirit of a Sontaran.'

'You gave your word of honour.'

'Promises made to inferior species have no validity. The honour of a Sontaran officer lies in doing his duty. When our hunt is over and the Rutan destroyed, *all* the humans must die.'

14
THE HUNT

By the time Vorn and Steg reached the crewroom, Lisa was putting Steg's offer to an astonished crew.

'Well, that's it,' she concluded. 'Commander Steg promises freedom and safety if we help him to destroy his enemy.'

Kurt was frankly sceptical. 'He's already promised that.'

'You didn't trust him then.'

'And you do now?'

'He needs our help now,' said Lisa exasperatedly. 'We've got something to bargain with.'

Before Kurt could object further, Zorelle seized her moment. Turning to Steg she said, 'I feel I should warn you, Commander, that before you sent for the Captain, she and this ruffian were plotting to kill you.'

Steg looked at Lisa. 'Is this true?'

Lisa made no reply.

Drawing his blaster, Steg strode over to her. '*Is this true?*'

Still Lisa refused to answer. As Steg levelled his blaster at her, Kurt stepped quickly forward.

'I did all the plotting. I told the Captain we'd got nothing to lose by attacking you.'

Steg was still covering Lisa. 'And what did you say?'

'I was considering it,' said Lisa levelly. 'Then you came up with your offer and I accepted. I'll keep my word – if you keep yours.'

Steg swung the blaster round on Kurt. 'You wish to kill me?'

'It seemed a pretty good idea.'

Astonishingly, Steg reversed the blaster and handed it to Kurt. 'Then do so.'

Kurt raised the blaster, levelling it between Steg's eyes.

'Do it now,' said Steg. 'If you have the courage. You can certainly kill me.' He nodded towards Vorn, who had drawn his blaster and was aiming it at Kurt. 'Perhaps, if you are lucky, you can even kill Lieutenant Vorn before he kills you. Then you will have two blasters, and only a few leaderless troopers to deal with.'

Everyone in the crewroom seemed frozen and the silence was endless.

'Well,' said Steg. 'Why don't you shoot?'

Kurt stared into the burning red eyes. He lowered the blaster.

'I don't like the odds.'

'But I do!' shouted Nikos. Burning to redeem himself, he sprang forward, snatched the blaster from Kurt's hand, aimed point-blank at Steg and fired.

Nothing happened.

Nikos stood there, staring in shock at Steg, who stepped forward and took the blaster from his hand.

'There is a concealed safety-control in the butt. Touch it and the weapon will not fire. Touch it again – and it will,' Steg raised the blaster and shot Nikos down.

The close-range blast to the heart smashed Nikos to the floor, killing him instantly.

Mari ran to the body, and threw herself down beside it. She looked up in horror. 'He's dead,' she sobbed. 'He's dead…'

Steg gave Kurt a contemptuous glance. 'In every group of prisoners, there is one who is dangerous, one who may have to be killed. I did not think it was you.' He holstered the blaster and looked down at the dead Nikos. 'He at least had courage.'

'He died a glorious death,' said Vorn admiringly.

Mari's sobbing became a hysterical shriek. 'You killed him, you monster, you killed him!'

She hurled herself bodily at Steg, who flicked her casually aside. She collapsed by Nikos's body, screaming and sobbing.

'Can this female be quieted?' asked Steg wearily. 'Or must I kill her?' Clearly, it was a perfectly serious question.

Lisa ran to a medical locker, extracted an instant hypo, knelt by Mari and touched it to her arm. Mari slumped back, instantly unconscious.

'Move her!' snapped Lisa.

Kurt picked up Mari's limp body and carried her over to a bunk. Zorelle followed him, settling Mari in the bunk and covering her with a metal-foil blanket.

Returning, Kurt went over to Nikos, hoisted the body over his shoulder, and carried it to a bunk in the inner sleeping area, as far from Mari as possible. Closing the connecting door, he rejoined the others.

'We have wasted enough time,' said Steg. 'We must set to work to find the Rutan – even though our forces are now reduced.'

'You reduced them!' said Lisa Deranne.

Steg's forces were about to be reduced still further. In the dimly lit engine room, a solitary Sontaran trooper stood on guard over the power drive. The body of another trooper, the one found inside the power unit, still lay in the corner.

A faint blur of light drifted into the engine room, and sank into the body of the dead trooper. The dead Sontaran glowed faintly. After a moment, he stirred and rose stiffly to his feet.

The dead trooper lurched across the engine room towards the sentry. In a ghastly, croaking voice he said, 'Go! I will stand watch.'

'My orders are to stay on guard.'

'Go!' repeated the other trooper.

The stiff movements, the strange voice and the faint glow were enough to alert even a Sontaran. He peered at the advancing trooper, and suddenly recognised him. 'No! You are dead! You are dead!'

The second trooper lurched forwards and clamped his hands on the other's shoulders. 'Yes. And so are you.'

There was a sudden crackle of energy. The bodies of both troopers glowed for a moment and then fell to the ground.

After a moment a glowing sphere arose from their bodies and floated towards the power drive.

In the crewroom, Steg was telling his human volunteers about the enemy they faced.

'The Rutan is a polymorph – a shapeshifter. It can take on the form of its victims. It feeds directly on energy. If its power is low, it may simply reanimate a corpse. But at full strength it can take on the shape of the entity it has destroyed – at least for a time.'

Zorelle gave him a horrified look. 'Wait a minute. Are you telling me this thing can look like anyone? Like one of us?'

'Only if it has destroyed the original. It must kill to copy.'

Lisa looked uneasily at her companions. 'But how do we tell if someone's a copy or not?'

'If you encounter the Rutan disguised as one of you – you will know.'

'How?' asked Zorelle uneasily.

'It will kill you.'

There was a moment of thoughtful silence.

Then Lisa said, 'If we do find this thing – disguised or not – what do we do?'

'Retreat towards either the engine room or the airlock, drawing the Rutan after you.'

'Terrific,' muttered Kurt. 'Live bait!'

'Why those places?' asked Lisa.

'That is where my remaining troopers will be concentrated. We shall wait in ambush to destroy the Rutan.'

There was a crackle from the com-unit on Steg's neck-ring and he heard Vorn's voice. 'Commander, there is a message from the trooper sent to relieve the guard on the power units. He found two dead troopers. Nothing else.'

'The creature has re-energised,' snapped Steg. 'We must double the guard upon the airlock. It will try to steal our assault craft and escape.' He turned to the others. 'The Rutan is at its strongest and most dangerous. We must find and destroy it without delay. Come!'

Lisa glanced across at Mari, lying motionless beneath her blanket. 'What about her?'

Kurt shrugged. 'Leave her here. She'll be safer than we will!'

Lisa nodded. 'I'll lock the door.'

They followed Steg out. Lisa went last, closing the door behind her and locking it from the outside.

On her bunk, Mari slept peacefully.

Steg led Vorn, a Sontaran trooper, and Lisa, Kurt and Zorelle to a corridor junction in the centre of the ship. Lit only by dim working lights, the corridors were filled with sinister shadows.

'Lieutenant Vorn will mount guard on the power drive. I

shall join the guard at the airlock. These are the two danger points. The Rutan needs power and it needs to escape. The rest of you will search your assigned sectors.'

Steg went off in one direction, Vorn and the trooper the other. Lisa, Kurt and Zorelle watched them go.

When they were out of sight, Lisa turned angrily to Zorelle. 'If we survive this, I'll deal with you later.'

'Leave it,' said Kurt wearily.

'All right,' said Lisa. 'Let's go.'

They moved away.

Surfacing a little from the narcotic, Mari moaned and stirred in her bunk. A faint glow oozed under the locked door and flowed across the room. It moved across to the door that led to the sleeping area and slid beneath it.

For a moment all was silent. Then the connecting door sprang open revealing Nikos, his face faintly glowing. He stalked across the room, knelt beside Mari's bunk, and bent to kiss her lips. A pulse of light flashed between them and Nikos disappeared.

Mari lay back in her bunk, staring into space, her face and body glowing...

Moving along the dimly lit metal corridors, Lisa, Kurt and Zorelle reached another, larger junction.

Lisa looked round, getting her bearings. 'We're supposed to split up here.'

Suddenly Zorelle said, 'Look, I'm sorry, I can't take any more of this, I really can't. You can go on with this monster hunt if you like. I'm going back to the crewroom. I can look after Mari, she really shouldn't be left.'

Lisa looked hard at her. Zorelle was clearly terrified, and she wouldn't be much use in Lisa's future plans.

'All right. Here, you'll need this.' She handed Zorelle the key-card for the crewroom door.

Zorelle took the card and hurried back the way they had come.

Kurt looked at Lisa. 'Well, do we split up?'

She grinned fiercely at him. 'Do we hell.'

'You don't buy Steg's deal?'

Lisa shook her head. 'About as much as you do.'

'We're not going to hunt the Rutan?'

'Hunt it?' said Lisa. 'We're going to help it!'

Lisa had been over every inch of the ship during its conversion. She knew every connecting ladder, every hatch, every passageway. She moved to a nearby hatch and lifted it, revealing a metal ladder leading downwards.

Kurt followed her along a maze of corridors and walkways and then through another hatchway into a large, darkened area.

'Where are we?' whispered Kurt.

'Back of the engine room. Wait here.'

She slipped silently along the wall until she reached a large control-wheel. Not far away, past the banks of machinery, she could see Lieutenant Vorn and a trooper guarding the power units. She spun the control-wheel to maximum, and hurried back to Kurt. 'Come on!'

'Come where?'

'The front door.'

'What front door?'

'Just come on!' hissed Lisa fiercely, and pushed him back through the hatch.

In the crewroom, Zorelle had changed back into her silvery ball-gown, put on a more than usually elaborate make-up, and was finishing the third of three very large drinks.

189

Tipsily she toasted her image in the mirror. 'If I'm gonna die, then at least I'll do it in style.'

Suddenly she saw someone in the mirror. She turned and was amazed to see Mari advancing towards her. Mari's face had a strange, fixed expression, and her skin was a sickly green.

Zorelle swung round. 'You really don't look yourself, darling! Should you be out of bed?'

Mari didn't reply. She moved slowly closer.

'I said should you be out of bed?' repeated Zorelle.

'I'm not,' whispered Mari.

Zorelle blinked. 'Of course you are,' she said, her voice slurred. 'Don't be ridiculous. Are you still delirious? I know Nikos's death was a shock but you must pull yourself together.'

'Someone's in the bed,' whispered Mari. 'Come and see.' She led Zorelle to a nearby bunk and pulled back the blanket. Zorelle looked down and saw the blood-soaked body of Nikos.

Zorelle gasped and looked back at Mari who was suddenly very close. Her hands reached out and touched Zorelle's face. There was a crackle of energy and light pulsed between them.

With a scream, Zorelle fell back.

15
SHOWDOWN

In the engine room, one of the power units was throbbing alarmingly.

Lieutenant Vorn regarded it with dismay. Clearly something should be done about it – but he lacked the technical knowledge to do it.

The throbbing grew louder.

Vorn was just about to adopt his usual remedy and refer the problem to Commander Steg when the human female who was the ship's captain ran into the engine room.

She stopped and listened to the throbbing. 'What's happening?'

Vorn demonstrated his usual unfailing grasp of the obvious. 'The power drive is malfunctioning.'

'It's the Rutan,' said the Captain. 'It must still be in there. We can trap it. I'll open the inspection hatch.'

Vorn was too excited by the prospect of capturing the Rutan to question her logic.

Drawing his blaster, he watched as she opened a glass-fronted waist-level inspection hatch, revealing a blaze of light.

'It's here, in the heat exchanger,' she called. 'Come and see!'

Slow-thinking as he was, Vorn had a well-developed sense of self-preservation. He turned to the Sontaran trooper.

'Go and check!'

Drawing his blaster in turn, the trooper approached the glowing hatchway.

'Look inside,' urged the Captain.

Something about her eagerness aroused Vorn's suspicion. Was the Rutan really there, or was it some trick? And if the Rutan was there, how was he to deal with it without getting himself killed? Suddenly Vorn saw the perfect answer – a typically Sontaran solution.

'Thrust her into the heat exchanger,' he ordered. 'While the Rutan is killing her we can destroy it!'

Obediently the trooper rushed at the human female. To Vorn's amazement, she met the advance head on, twisted her body, and used the trooper's own momentum to send him hurtling through the blazing hatchway, slamming the door behind him.

There was a terrible sizzling sound and a horrible scream. The writhing trooper appeared on the other side of the safety glass, screaming soundlessly, head and hands already melted into a shapeless blob.

Vorn levelled his blaster. 'You have killed him. Now I shall kill you.'

Before he could fire, the female sprang forward, grabbing the blaster and pushing it upwards. Vorn smiled grimly. No human could hope to match a Sontaran for strength. He began wrenching the blaster from her grasp.

When the weight of another human body thudded into his back, and a human arm curved around his neck, Vorn was still confident of victory. He managed to turn his head a little and caught a glimpse of the strain-distorted face of the human called Kurt.

He would kill them both.

Even as he was desperately trying to throttle Vorn, Kurt knew that the task was hopeless. The Sontaran's neck was too thick, his strength too great. With or without a blaster, Vorn was more than a match for them both.

Locked together, the three bodies crashed into the engine-room wall. Kurt hung on desperately. Once Vorn broke free he could easily kill them both in turn.

Something moved under Kurt's foot and he nearly fell. Looking down he saw Robar's tool kit. Releasing Vorn, Kurt bent and snatched up a long-bladed screwdriver, inserted it into the circular aperture at the base of Vorn's neck and thrust it home with all his strength.

Vorn gave a horrible bubbling scream, went rigid, and crashed to the ground, taking Kurt and Lisa with him.

Slowly and painfully they disentangled themselves, got up and leaned against the wall, totally exhausted.

'How did you do that?' gasped Lisa.

Kurt struggled for breath. 'The – Dentist told me. Probic vent… weakness… screwdriver.' He held up the screwdriver, still dripping with thick, Sontaran blood. 'It works!'

Lisa stared at the screwdriver, eyes wide. 'I'll bear it in mind.' She straightened up, suddenly aware that the throbbing in the air meant that the power drive was approaching danger level. 'I'll close down the drive.'

Commander Steg stood by the open airlock door, a sentry beside him. He touched the com-unit in his neck ring.

'All patrols report in.'

Silence.

'Report!' snarled Steg.

More silence.

Just the faint ping that signified there had been no reply from any of the other Sontarans on the ship.

Steg considered for a moment. Brushing the sentry aside

he stumped down the airlock tunnel towards the door that led to his own ship.

Armed with the blasters of the dead Sontarans, Kurt and Lisa hurried along darkened metal corridors towards the airlock.

A familiar shape stepped out of a narrow doorway ahead of them. It was Robar, face pale, eyes staring. 'Lisa!'

Lisa stared at him unbelievingly.

'Kill him,' said Kurt urgently. '*Kill him!*'

Lisa seemed paralysed as the agonised figure lurched towards them.

'Lisa, my dear, it's me. I'm hurt, help me!'

Instantly Lisa raised her blaster and fired. The Robar-shape dissolved into a glowing sphere and vanished down the corridor.

Lisa caught Kurt's enquiring glance.

'Robar never called me "my dear" in his life,' she said.

They went on their way.

The assault craft's armoury was a circular metal chamber, its walls lined with weapons of every kind. The dim red lighting was reflected in Steg's eyes as he studied the assortment. He selected a semi-transparent metal cylinder packed with complex machinery. His hands moved expertly over the controls set into its base.

Drawing the standard-issue officer's blaster from his belt, Steg put it down. He opened a locker holding a number of smaller weapons.

When all was ready, Steg carried the cylinder out of the armoury and left the ship. Closing the door behind him, he moved along the airlock tunnel and put the cylinder down close to the door at the other end.

He stepped out of the airlock and found himself facing Lisa and Kurt. They were covering the Sontaran sentry with their blasters – as he was covering them.

The sentry glanced at Steg, who was apparently unarmed. 'Commander?'

'Kill them!' roared Steg.

The sentry fired, just as Kurt and Lisa dived apart.

The Sontaran's first shot missed. Kurt blasted him down before he could fire a second.

Without even a glance for the dead sentry, the final casualty of his defeated assault force, Steg backed away towards the airlock door.

'I shall leave now,' he said calmly. 'You and the Rutan have defeated me between you. I leave you to each other.'

Kurt stepped forward, blaster raised. 'Ask me now if I want to kill you.'

Steg raised his hands. 'Would you kill someone who is quite unarmed?'

'You did,' said Lisa.

'I am a Sontaran. Humans have different standards.'

'Don't count on it,' said Kurt grimly. He aimed his blaster – but he hesitated all the same.

It was just that hesitation that Steg had been counting on. 'Surely you will allow a defeated enemy to depart in peace?'

Even as he spoke, Steg's hand flashed to the mini-blaster concealed at the back of his belt. He fired, and this time Kurt didn't dodge quite quickly enough. The blast took him across the top of the shoulder, smashing him to the ground.

Before Steg could fire again, Lisa shot him down.

He staggered back, slammed into the wall beside the airlock door and slid slowly to the ground.

He raised his head, looking up at Lisa. 'I was wrong,' he said feebly. 'It was you I should have killed.' His arm moved painfully across his chest. 'I salute you, Captain Deranne. You were a worthy... enemy...'

Steg's eyes closed and his head slumped forward.

A glowing sphere drifted along the corridor, transforming suddenly into Zorelle – but not the Zorelle they had known. Her body glowed with power and she looked taller, statelier, more beautiful than ever before.

When she spoke her voice had a remote, alien quality. 'Is he dead?'

'They're all dead,' said Lisa bitterly. 'All the Sontarans and most of my crew. I take it Mari and the real Zorelle are dead as well?'

'Death is inevitable in war,' said the Rutan in Zorelle's form. 'Do not attempt to harm us unless you too wish to die.'

There was a crackle of energy and a tentacle of light sent the blaster in Lisa's hand spinning across the corridor.

Lisa rubbed her tingling hand. 'I shouldn't dream of it.'

'We could kill you now with ease, but we share a common enemy,' said the Rutan. 'We shall spare you. We go now, in our enemy's ship, with the secret that will save our people – and in our natural form.'

The Zorelle shape blurred and vanished, and a glowing sphere of light, trailing fiery tentacles, hovered before her. It floated away down the airlock.

Suddenly Lisa heard a faint voice. 'Destructor bomb... airlock tunnel...'

It was Steg.

Without conscious thought, Lisa hurled herself into the tunnel. She snatched up the cylinder from its place inside the door and ran to the far end of the tunnel where the door to the Sontaran ship was just closing.

She thrust the cylinder through the gap and ran back down the tunnel. The door at the far end was closing too.

Short as the distance was, Lisa saw that the door would close before she could get through. She would be trapped in the airlock tunnel – which was just about to depressurise.

She flung herself at the fast-closing gap, knowing that she was already too late. A massive three-digited hand curled round the edge of the door, holding it back for a few vital seconds.

Lisa squeezed herself through the gap, Steg released his grip, and the door closed.

On the other side, Steg looked up at the closed door, eyes blazing with triumph. 'I win, Rutan. I win!'

His head slumped forward, as if the effort had been his last.

Lisa went over to Kurt who was beginning to revive. 'Quick. We must see the end.'

With Lisa's help, Kurt managed to get to his feet and make his way to the control-room. There, on the monitor screen, they watched the Sontaran assault craft curve away from their ship.

Moments later it blew up.

It was some time later. Kurt was in Robar's seat, Lisa in her command chair. She was spraying plasti-skin onto the deep groove burned into Kurt's shoulder. It stung, and Kurt yelled in protest.

'It's only a fringe-burn,' said Lisa dismissively.

Kurt grunted, shrugging back into his coveralls.

'Told you Steg would try to blow up the ship.'

'All the same,' said Lisa, 'he saved my life.' She sighed. 'Some shakedown cruise. A damaged ship and a dead crew.

That's the end of the Inter-Systems Solar for me.'

'Not necessarily.'

'With a ship full of dead bodies to explain?'

Official enquiries held few terrors for Kurt.

'You worry too much. There'll be an enquiry, sure. We'll come out of it heroes.'

'Maybe so – but I'm still out of the race. I'll never get a new owners' syndicate together in time.'

'You're looking at it,' said Kurt complacently. 'I persuaded the others to make the syndicate a tontine.'

'A how much?'

'Anyone died, the rest shared the money.' He tapped his chest. 'Sole survivor, sole—'

'Owner!' concluded Lisa. She smiled at him. 'This could be the beginning of a beautiful friendship.'

'When we get to Station Beta we'll have a full refit, hire a professional crew and sail the socks off every other space yacht in the system!'

Lisa's face lit up with hope. 'If we can only be ready in time…'

'Call up Beta and get things moving.'

Lisa flicked a switch on the sub-space com-unit. 'Solar Yacht *Tiger Moth* to Space Station Beta. *Tiger Moth* to Beta…'

Slumped back in his chair, Kurt looked affectionately at her eager face. He reached out and touched her gently on the cheek.

Lisa gave him a wary look. 'This is just a solar racing partnership. It doesn't mean we're sexually pair-bonded.'

Kurt put on his innocent face – the one he always used when he was lying. 'Never entered my head.'

Lisa turned back to the com-unit. '*Tiger Moth* to Space Station Beta. *Tiger Moth* to Beta. This is Lisa Deranne…'

*

Battered and bruised, but undefeated, still a contender, the solar yacht *Tiger Moth* moved on through space, heading for Space Station Beta.

BOOK THREE
AFTERMATH

16
BREAKOUT

'Right,' said the Doctor. 'Here's my plan.'

Two pairs of eyes gazed hopefully at him.

'Well?' said Roz.

'What plan?' asked Chris.

The Doctor sighed. 'Joke!'

'Nothing to laugh about,' muttered Roz. 'How much longer do we have to take this?'

'Not long,' said the Doctor.

They were still imprisoned in the refectory of Space Station Alpha. It was as good a location as any to be held prisoner in, with food, drink and sanitary facilities all readily available. Half a dozen Sontaran sentries stood guard over them.

'So what are we going to do?' demanded Chris.

'I keep telling you,' said the Doctor testily. 'We wait.'

'For what?' asked Chris.

'For events to take their course.'

'What course?'

The Doctor sighed. Sometimes working with Chris was like dealing with a seven-foot toddler, full of insatiable curiosity.

'The Sontarans came here after Karne,' he said, 'just as you did. As a species, they're not the greatest brains in the galaxy, but they're single-minded and extraordinarily thorough. So – what do they do first?'

'They round up everyone on the station and check them

out,' said Chris. 'Like they just did.'

'As they just did,' agreed the Doctor. 'If they don't find him – and somehow I don't think they will – then what?'

'They'll search the space station in case he's hiding somewhere,' said Roz.

'Exactly,' said the Doctor.

'And if they still don't find him?'

'They'll search again. As a matter of fact, I rather think that's what they're doing now. And if that doesn't produce any results, they'll conclude, just as you did, that he left on one of the ships that came and went between his arrival and theirs.'

'So they're stuck, just like we were,' said Chris.

The Doctor shook his head. 'Brilliant as we undoubtedly are, there are only three of us. A full-scale military expedition has rather more resources. They'll get a list of the ships concerned, go after them, and stop, board and search every one.'

'That's a pretty formidable undertaking,' said Roz.

'The Sontarans are a pretty formidable species.'

'So we sit here and wait for them to go away?' said Chris. His expression made it clear he thought it a pretty feeble plan.

'We wait for most of them to go away,' corrected the Doctor. 'This space station is swarming with Sontarans at the moment. Far too many for us to tackle with any hope of success. When they've convinced themselves the Rutan's gone, they'll go too. But I think they'll leave a small crew just in case it turns up somewhere – and to make sure we don't send out any warnings.'

'Wouldn't it be simpler just to blow up the station?' asked Roz.

'It would,' said the Doctor calmly. 'They may still do

it. But there are diplomatic reasons against it. They can probably get away with a few missing ships, especially if there's no real proof. Accidents happen in space. Missing space stations are rather harder to explain away.'

Since then they had waited – and waited.

Considerable numbers of Sontarans had come and gone. Occasionally members of the space-station staff were taken off for interrogation. Some returned in a shaken state, others didn't return at all.

They'd eaten several tasteless prepackaged meals, and Chris had tried every drink and snack in the dispenser. Their fellow prisoners sat around listlessly, some brooding alone, others muttering in groups. Roz and Chris both found the waiting hard going, and even the Doctor seemed affected by the monotony.

He wandered over to an ornamental stand in the corner, lifted down an elaborate steel sculpture of a solar yacht, and carried it over to their table. Fishing out a pocket-knife with every imaginable gadget on it, he began taking the model to pieces.

Chris watched him in puzzlement. 'What are you doing, Doctor?'

'Deconstructing a solar yacht,' said the Doctor.

Chris gave up.

They heard the sound of some kind of craft taking off from the landing bay.

'Gone back to report failure,' said the Doctor, still busy with his model. He was assembling the different steel pieces into a weird-looking metal framework. 'There must be some kind of mothership close by. Won't be too long now.'

Some time later they heard the ship return. Soon afterwards, a Sontaran officer appeared in the doorway.

'You will be held prisoner here for a short time longer. As soon as this operation is concluded, you will be released. Meanwhile, remain here quietly, obey all Sontaran orders, and you will not be harmed. The sentries have orders to shoot any troublemakers.'

There were no questions. The Sontaran didn't expect any. He turned and marched out, leaving only two sentries on the door. Before long they heard the sound of a ship taking off.

'All right,' said the Doctor quietly. 'I think most of the Sontarans must have gone. Stand by to move when I say "Now!"'

'When will that be?' asked Roz.

'As soon as I've finished this piece of artwork.'

The Doctor went on working on his metal frame.

Roz looked at him worriedly, wondering if he was cracking up.

'What's it supposed to be, Doctor?' asked Chris, in the soothing tones of someone humouring a hopeless case.

'It's an abstract,' said the Doctor. 'I think I'll call it "Sudden Death".'

Chris studied the contraption in puzzlement. The Doctor had used the steel wire of the model solar yacht's cables to put several of its metal masts under tension. Now he was turning an improvised handle to wind in the cables and bend the masts, increasing the tension still further.

One of the Sontaran sentries made occasional patrols of the room, leaving the other to guard the door.

'Look out, Doctor, he's coming round again,' warned Roz.

'Let him,' said the Doctor.

The Sontaran came nearer – and paused by the Doctor's device.

'What is this?'

'Abstract sculpture,' said the Doctor proudly.

'What is its purpose?'

'It's a work of art,' said the Doctor. 'It has no purpose.'

He tightened the cables another notch, and inserted a steel rod, formerly the model yacht's mainmast, into a groove in the centre of the contraption.

'If it has no purpose, why make it?' asked the Sontaran.

'To express myself,' said the Doctor loftily.

Obviously feeling himself in the presence of some obscure alien ritual, the Sontaran moved away.

'Now!' whispered the Doctor. He hunched over his model, sighted along it and touched a lever. There was a metallic twang and the steel rod shot from the device, thudding home into the departing Sontaran's probic vent.

The sentry stiffened and fell forwards with a bubbling scream.

The second sentry ran from the door, blaster in hand. 'What has happened?'

'I think he must have fainted,' said the Doctor.

'Sontarans do not faint!' The sentry looked down and saw the steel rod projecting from the back of the dead trooper's neck.

'You have killed him!'

He aimed his blaster at the Doctor, but before he could fire, Chris shoulder-charged him, knocking him off his feet.

They rolled over and over, struggling furiously, sending chairs and tables flying. Their fellow prisoners – passengers and technicians – gathered round, cheering Chris on but powerless to help.

Chris was exceptionally strong and for a time he actually held his own. For one glorious moment he found himself sitting on the Sontaran's barrel chest and thumping its head on the floor.

It couldn't last. Sontaran muscles can exert incredible strength, far beyond that of any human. All too soon, positions were reversed. Chris found the immense weight of the Sontaran pinning him down, while two huge hands tightened about his neck. A roaring blackness started swallowing him up, and the last thing he was aware of was the red glare of the Sontaran's eyes, staring down into his own.

Suddenly the Sontaran screamed. Its body convulsed and the huge hands released their grip.

Chris scrambled from beneath the crushing weight and saw the steel rod projecting from the Sontaran's probic vent. He looked up and saw Roz beaming down at him.

'It worked once, so I thought it might work again,' she said. Chris realised she must have snatched a second rod from the Doctor's model and rammed it home. He scrambled to his feet.

'Thanks!' He looked at the model, which had now collapsed into its component parts. 'What is that thing, Doctor?'

'Oh, it's nothing really,' said the Doctor modestly. 'I just reinvented the crossbow!'

'You might have given us a bit more warning,' protested Roz.

'Sorry. I had to fire as soon as I realised I had him in my sights. You only get one shot with this thing, and it takes hours to reload.'

The Doctor took the blasters from the dead Sontarans, and handed them to Chris and Roz. Their fellow prisoners gathered round, all talking excitedly.

'Well done,' shouted one of the technicians. 'What do we do now?'

'I'd advise you all to stay here for the moment.'

'Come on, can't we all join in? We're dying to take a crack at them.'

The Doctor shook his head. 'There are probably a few more Sontarans still on the station and they won't be too happy about all this.'

'So what are you going to do?'

'Oh, we'll just go and mop them up,' said the Doctor confidently. 'I know you mean well, but please don't try and help. My friends are professionals, and you'd only get in their way.'

'Thanks for the vote of confidence,' said Roz, as they headed for the door. 'Personally, I'll take all the help I can get.'

'There won't be many more,' said the Doctor reassuringly. 'No point in getting innocent people killed. Now, the communications room is this way, I think.'

The Doctor led them along bare metal corridors to a set of open double doors. A shaky voice came from inside.

'This is an all channels announcement from Space Station Alpha. We have had an accident in the power area and we are leaking dangerous amounts of radiation. We can accept no further dockings until the situation is under control. All vessels are requested to divert to Stations Beta, Gamma or Delta.'

A Sontaran voice said, 'Excellent. Continue to transmit this announcement at frequent intervals.'

'That won't be necessary,' said the Doctor, strolling casually into the communications room. He saw a Sontaran officer standing over a tall, thin and terrified technician. Another technician lay dead in the corner.

'I'm happy to tell you that the invasion's over,' said the Doctor. 'Normal service will be resumed as soon as possible.' He turned to the Sontaran. 'I don't suppose you'd care to do anything sensible – like surrendering?'

The Sontaran officer drew the blaster in his belt.

'No, I thought not,' said the Doctor regretfully. He leaped nimbly aside and the Sontaran fired at him and missed. The technician snatched up a chair and hurled it at the Sontaran. It did no damage at all, but it distracted him while Chris and Roz came through the doors, blasters in their hands. At this range even Roz couldn't miss, and they caught the Sontaran neatly in a crossfire.

Roz nodded to the technician as the dead Sontaran crashed to the ground. 'Thanks.'

'You take some chances, Doctor,' said Chris. 'How did you know we'd be ready to back you up?'

'Because we're professionals,' said Roz. She booted the Sontaran's body, making sure he was dead. 'Any more, Doctor?'

'I doubt it,' said the Doctor. He turned to the technician. 'Are there?'

'They only left three behind,' said the shaken technician. 'Two guarding the prisoners in the refectory, and this one here.' He gave the Doctor an anguished look. 'That's Ferris in the corner there, Station Manager. That Sontaran told him to transmit a fake message, to keep people away. He refused, so the Sontaran killed him and then asked me. I transmitted it all right, over and over again.' He began to shake.

'Very sensible too,' said the Doctor. 'There's never much point in arguing with Sontarans.'

'We did,' said Roz.

'I know,' said Chris. 'But we talk their language.' He grinned reassuringly at the trembling technician. 'No need to worry any more. They're all dead.'

'We've got to get this place working normally again,' said the Doctor. 'Who's second in command?'

'I am, I suppose.' The technician looked down at himself, as if surprised to find himself still there. 'My name's Dobbs.'

'Well, Mr Dobbs, now you're in charge.'

'Me?' said Dobbs worriedly. 'Forget it, I'm an administrator, not a leader. Ferris was the one with leadership qualities, and look where it got him. You take over, you seem to know what you're doing.'

'We've done our bit,' said Roz. 'We've seen off the Sontarans for you.'

'And you helped,' said Chris, giving the technician a slap on the back that made him stagger. 'If you hadn't been so handy with that chair, he might have got one of us.'

'We haven't the time or the training to run your space station for you,' said the Doctor. 'All you've got to do is get your staff together and get this place working normally again. Come along to the refectory and we'll give them the good news.'

'It's old Dobbsy,' shouted one of the technicians as they re-entered the refectory. 'Where's Ferris, Dobbsy?'

'Dead,' whispered Dobbs. 'They killed him.' He started shaking again.

The Doctor raised his voice. 'The Sontaran who killed Mr Ferris is dead – Mr Dobbs knocked him down with a chair and my friends finished him off.'

There were cheers and someone shouted, 'Good old Dobbsy! Well done!'

'Mr Dobbs will be taking over command of the station,' said the Doctor. 'Mr Dobbs?'

For a moment Dobbs seemed unable to speak. Then he swallowed and said, 'All communications staff back to the com-room. We've got to get a considerable number of warning messages out.' His voice grew stronger.

'Maintenance and technical staff get back to your station. I want damage reports right away.'

A wealthy-looking passenger said, 'What about us? It's disgraceful the way we've been treated!'

By now Dobbs was into his stride. 'The management apologises for any inconvenience which, I think you must admit, was caused by circumstances beyond our control.'

There was some rueful laughter. Encouraged, Dobbs went on, 'Our aim is to get this station back working normally again so we can get you on your way.'

In fact, it was going to be some considerable time before Space Station Alpha returned to anything like normality. There were wounded to be cared for, dead to be gathered up and decently bestowed, damage to be assessed.

Messages had to be sent to Stations Beta, Gamma and Delta, to Valeria and the other planets in the system. Warning messages telling of the Sontaran attack, and others asking for reinforcements, for supplies and repair crews.

And of course there were stranded passengers, demanding to know when their delayed connections would arrive.

Much as they tried to avoid it, the Doctor, Roz and Chris were everyone's heroes, praised, congratulated and thanked over and over again.

The nervous Dobbs was still inclined to refer every decision to the Doctor, who tried hard to get him to take charge himself.

It was quite a while before things were sufficiently sorted out for the Doctor, Roz and Chris to slip away. The Doctor led them in the direction of the storage area.

'First thing to do is get back inside the TARDIS,' he said briskly. 'I can think there. We must try to track down that solar yacht, *Tiger Moth*, somehow – if it's not too late. And there's Bernice on Sentarion to be considered.'

They reached the end of a corridor and found their way barred by sealed doors. A maintenance technician was putting up a sign.

'DANGER – NO ADMITTANCE.'

'Excuse me,' said the Doctor firmly. 'We have to get through here.'

'I wouldn't advise it, sir,' said the technician cheerfully. 'Not unless you fancy a space walk without a suit.'

'I have to recover some extremely valuable property from your storage section,' said the Doctor.

'Sorry to hear that, sir,' said the technician. But he didn't sound sorry. He sounded like a man hugging a secret joke.

The Doctor forced himself to be patient. 'Surely that's the way to the storage section?'

'It was – when the storage section was still there.'

'All right, that's enough mystification,' said the Doctor sharply. 'You've had your fun, now explain – briefly and clearly, please!'

'When those aliens attacked us they fired off a warning blast from their space cannon. It hit a junction point and sheared the storage section clean away. Automatic sealing system worked, so we didn't lose pressure. But the entire storage section floated off into space.'

It was the first time Roz had seen the Doctor totally at a loss. He stood staring helplessly at the technician, eyes and mouth wide open.

'This storage section,' said Chris. 'Will they be able to get it back?'

'Oh, they'll get it back all right,' said the technician. 'I mean, it's not going anywhere, is it? Just drifting.'

The Doctor swallowed. 'When?' he asked. 'When will they get it back?'

'Soon as the repair ships arrive from Valeria. Soon as they locate it, tow it back and weld it on again.'

'How long?' asked Roz.

'Could be days, could be weeks.'

With a mighty effort, the Doctor recovered his poise. 'Well, it's extremely inconvenient, but I suppose it can't be helped. Come along, you two!'

He led them back along the corridor.

'Now what?' asked Roz.

'Well,' said the Doctor. 'Here's my plan!'

17
FLIGHT

'You made it all sound so bloody easy,' said Lisa Deranne. Mockingly she mimicked his words. '"When we get to Station Beta we'll have a full refit, hire a professional crew and sail the socks off every other space yacht in the system!" You and your promises!'

It was unfair to blame Kurt, she knew it was unfair, and she didn't care. It had all gone wrong, and she was both angry and bitterly disappointed. 'You know how many spacedock technicians they can spare to work on *Tiger Moth*? One!'

'So we hit a few snags,' said Kurt. 'Why don't you stop being a prima donna and we'll try to work out some solutions?'

She threw a punch at him that would have bloodied his nose. Kurt caught her hard fist in one big hand and held it. Lisa tried to break free and found she couldn't move. She gave him the hard stare that had paralysed racing crew and officials all over the Tri-planetary System.

'Don't talk to me like that.'

'Time someone did,' said Kurt. He let go of her hand. 'Now, do we go on providing free cabaret for the rest of the bar, or do we have some more champagne and talk about what to do?'

Lisa looked round the bar and found everyone's eyes on her. She returned the stares and everyone hurriedly looked away. She looked back at Kurt and grinned reluctantly. 'All right, blast you! But what can we do?'

It was all the fault of the Sontarans, she knew that really. *Tiger Moth* had limped into Space Station Beta to find the place in uproar. Rumours had been coming in of mysterious spaceship disappearances, of anguished Mayday calls followed by sinister silence. It had been followed by a report of a terrible accident on Station Alpha – then by further reports that the accident story had been a fake and the station had been taken over by Sontarans, but was now free again.

The arrival of *Tiger Moth* with its story of Sontaran attack had only stirred things up even more.

Kurt had insisted that they report straight to station security, but the story had soon leaked out. A cargo of corpses is a difficult thing to conceal.

As an inevitable result of all this, nothing was running normally. All available stores and spares had been dispatched to Station Alpha for emergency repairs, and most of the engineering technicians had gone with them. Refitting a solar yacht with damaged sails and a dodgy power drive came very low on the station workshop's priority list.

Meanwhile, the starting date for the Inter-Systems Solar Yacht Race was coming ever closer.

To make matters worse, every able-bodied spaceman was at work on various rescue and repair missions. Wealthy amateurs, like her former crew, were keeping well away until the danger was past. At the moment, chances of finding a new crew were non-existent.

Lisa shivered at the thought of Robar, Nikos, Mari and Zorelle, now occupying steel shelves in the station morgue – with a squad of dead Sontarans for company.

She looked across the little table at Kurt, happily drinking champagne, and felt another surge of irritation.

'Nothing really bothers you, does it?'

'Listen,' said Kurt seriously. 'If I've learned one thing in a long and dodgy career, it's that the universe operates according to Sod's Law – what can go wrong, will! As the Great Buddha said, "Life is suffering." Once you realise that, things don't seem so bad!' He sat back and grinned cheerfully at her.

Lisa gave him a sceptical look. 'I didn't figure you for a religious philosopher.'

'I once shared, er, accommodation with a fake fakir. He was a swindling old rogue but he taught me a lot.'

Rather resentfully – she enjoyed a good sulk – Lisa found that she was feeling better – and that it was because of Kurt. With a sense of shock, Lisa realised she was no longer alone.

But she'd always been alone. Alone, and in charge. That was the way she liked it.

It was a situation that called for a lot more thought.

Putting that particular problem aside, she returned to matters at hand. 'So what do we *do*?'

Kurt sighed. 'You're acting as if you're the only one affected by the situation.'

'So who else is?'

'Everybody!' said Kurt explosively. 'The race organisers, other solar yacht racers… Do you really think they're going to hold a yacht race in the middle of a potential war zone? If they do, we'll be the only entrants. At least we'd be sure of a win!'

'You think they'll cancel?'

'Nope. It's too important for that. But they'll postpone.'

'You can't be sure of that.'

'I can't be sure that if I drink enough of this stuff I'll fall off my chair – but it's overwhelmingly likely all the same. All we can do is act according to instinct guided by experience.'

'That's enough philosophy,' said Lisa, jumping up impatiently. 'I'll check with the com-office, see if they've heard anything.'

An announcement came over the public address system.

'The delayed shuttle from Space Station Alpha is about to dock in Bay Three.' There was a general exodus from the bar.

Kurt stood up. 'Com-office will be busy with the docking for a while. Let's go and see the shuttle arrive; maybe we can pick up some fresh information.'

The first passengers were coming down the ramp as they arrived, and the landing area was crowded with people waiting to meet them and to hear their news.

One particular group seemed to be the centre of attention. It consisted of a small man in a crumpled white suit and a battered old hat, flanked by a big fair-haired man and a smaller dark-skinned woman.

'It's the Doctor!' said Kurt in astonishment. He grabbed Lisa's arm and bustled her over to the group. 'Doctor! I might have known you'd be mixed up in all this!'

'I didn't know you were,' said the Doctor. 'What are you doing here?' He looked at Lisa, took off his hat and bowed. 'Do forgive me, Kurt and I are old friends. I'm the Doctor, and these are my colleagues, Roslyn Forrester and Christopher Cwej.'

Lisa nodded in acknowledgement. 'I'm Lisa Deranne.'

'*Captain* Lisa Deranne? Of the solar yacht *Tiger Moth*?' Chris was staring at Lisa in admiration.

'That's right. Captain of a beat-up yacht without a crew.'

'You won the Algolian cup just recently! I've always wanted to try solar racing.'

'Autographs later, Chris,' said the Doctor impatiently. He turned to Lisa. 'Were you stopped by the Sontarans? Did they find what they were looking for? How did you manage to survive?'

'We were and they did,' said Kurt.

'We survived, they didn't,' said Lisa. 'Nor did what they were looking for.'

The Doctor looked at Kurt. 'You mean you were on board as well? What an amazing piece of serendipity, our meeting like this. We must talk, I think we've got a lot to tell each other.'

The telling was done over more champagne at a large corner table in the bar. The Doctor and Kurt apart, it was an uneasy group.

Roz and Lisa sized each other up, and declared a truce.

Cop instincts aroused, Chris viewed Kurt with deep suspicion. He was already quite convinced the man wasn't good enough for Lisa Deranne. She needed a different type altogether.

Kurt and the Doctor were talking animatedly.

'So how did things work out on Jekkar, Doctor?' asked Kurt.

'Surprisingly well. When the Sontarans pulled out, the Earth colonists pulled out too – just in case the Sontarans changed their minds and came back again!'

'So the Jekkari are happily back up their trees?'

'Oh yes. The forests are almost completely re-established. I'm not too sure about the jekkarta weed crop, though.'

'Shame on you, Doctor. Don't you know that stuff's illegal?'

The Doctor turned to Lisa. 'Do forgive us, nothing worse than other people's reminiscences of places you've never been. It's your adventures I really want to know about. Please tell me.'

Lisa, although inclined to be suspicious of strangers on principle, found herself responding to the Doctor's charm.

Skilfully, he drew out of them the full story of the events on the *Tiger Moth*'s shakedown cruise.

'You're sure the Rutan was killed?' asked the Doctor.

Kurt shrugged. 'It was in the assault craft.'

'And so was the bomb,' said Lisa. 'I put it there.'

'And we both saw the assault craft go up,' concluded Kurt.

'Rutans can survive almost anywhere,' said the Doctor. 'Even in space if they have to. But in a small craft in close proximity to a large bomb…'

'There'd have been other explosives on the ship as well,' said Kurt. 'That ship went nova. Believe me, that Rutan got scattered all over deep space.'

'It's a pity,' said the Doctor. 'A very great pity.'

'Come on, Doctor,' protested Roz. 'That thing was a killer. It left a trail of corpses over a dozen planets.'

'It killed my engineer, Robar,' said Lisa. 'And most of my crew as well. How can you be sorry that it's dead?'

'I know,' said the Doctor. 'I know.' He looked around the group. 'Maybe it's time I told you all what this is about.'

'Don't mind us, Doctor,' said Roz sourly. 'We'll just go on dodging the blasters and collecting the corpses.'

The Doctor winced. 'I'm sorry, I know I've asked you to take a great deal on trust. It all begins with a Rutan spy, their greatest spy of all, operating behind Sontaran lines in Sontaran form. At that time he called himself Karne…'

There was a moment of silence when the Doctor finished his long and complicated story.

Then Kurt said, 'Let me see if I've got this straight. The Sontarans have learned some great Rutan secret – a secret they could use to win the war. This Rutan spy, Karne, found that the Sontarans knew—'

'That they were on the track of the secret at least,' corrected the Doctor. 'But that's near enough.'

'The spy gets blown up in a battle with the Sontarans,' continued Kurt. 'But somehow he survives.'

The Doctor nodded. 'Weak, wounded, and possibly partly amnesiac as well. But the memories revived, and he became obsessed with one overriding mission. To get back to his people and warn them that the great secret is in danger.'

'And where do you come into all this?'

'I was involved in that battle myself,' said the Doctor. 'It was a long time ago – it almost seems like another life. But I didn't really become concerned until some time later, when I picked up some partial information from a damaged Sontaran computer system on Jekkar. Then I got a report from – from my own people. They drop me little titbits of information from time to time – when it suits them. They know I can never resist sticking my nose in.'

'You'll lose it one day,' said Roz.

Lisa was staring hard at the Doctor. 'Who are you?' she asked. '*What* are you?'

'Just a wandering scholar,' said the Doctor hurriedly. 'Anyway, my people informed me that Karne had survived, that he was on the move, and that the Sontarans were on his trail. So I thought I'd better get after him as well.'

Lisa frowned. 'I don't understand. You wanted to stop him?'

'Oh no,' said the Doctor. 'I wanted to make absolutely sure he survived to complete his mission.'

'Why?' said Lisa angrily. 'What does it matter if the Sontarans wipe out the Rutans? I'd say it was good riddance.'

221

The Doctor leaned forward, fixing her with his cool grey eyes. Lisa felt the full impact of his mind and his personality.

'It's hard to see past the death of a friend,' he said. 'Believe me, I know, I've lost too many friends myself. It always sounds cold and calculating to say look at the broad picture.' The Doctor smiled ruefully. 'But – look at the broad picture.'

'What broad picture?'

'You've seen something of the Sontarans and their methods by now. Did it ever occur to you to wonder why they're not better known? Why they've always been distant bogeymen, somewhere on the far fringes of the galaxy?'

'Rutans,' said Kurt.

'Exactly,' said the Doctor. 'They've been fighting a war with the Rutans for hundreds of years. It takes up all their energies and all their resources, and it's an utter deadlock, no one wins, no one loses. But what do you think will happen if the Sontarans do win? If they achieve a decisive victory?'

'They'll look round for someone else to fight,' said Kurt. 'It's all they know how to do.'

The Doctor nodded. 'Their whole society is one vast war machine. They won't turn it off, they don't know how. They don't even want to. Believe me, if the Rutans ever lose, we'll all be seeing a lot more of the Sontarans.' The Doctor stared into space, as if seeing a galaxy swarming with Sontaran troopers. 'Where was I?' He nodded towards Roz and Chris. 'My two friends here had relevant experience, so I put them on Karne's trail. They nearly caught up with him too.'

'Nearly,' said Chris.

'He was planet-hopping,' said Roz. 'Killing to provide himself with resources and cover. We were right behind him on Alpha.'

'Then he smuggled himself onto your ship,' said Chris, giving Lisa his best smile. 'And you blew him up for us!'

'Sorry,' said Lisa, not sounding sorry at all. 'It seemed a good idea at the time.'

'I don't blame you in the least,' said the Doctor. 'Unfortunately, it means I've failed.'

'Can't you warn the Rutans yourself?'

'I tried,' said the Doctor sadly. 'Unfortunately, the Rutans are paranoid, they only talk to other Rutans. Well, they're all the same Rutan really – they only talk to themselves. They'd believe Karne, but they won't listen to me.'

'What about Benny?' asked Roz.

'I was forgetting poor Benny,' said the Doctor guiltily.

'I'm getting confused again,' said Kurt. 'Who's Benny?'

'I have another colleague, an archaeologist called Bernice Summerfield. I sent her to Sentarion, the Library planet, to research the Rutan-Sontaran war – and to see if she could get a line on the secret. I don't suppose she found anything out, it was more of a holiday for her really. When I get the TARDIS back we must go and pick her up.'

The thin, fair young man was called Rye, and he was a steward on the space liner *Hyperion*. He had an hour to kill before take-off time and he decided to go to Bay Seven and visit the solar yacht *Tiger Moth*. Everyone was talking about Lisa Deranne's epic battle with the Sontarans, and it would make a good story to tell the passengers.

Bay Seven was empty when he arrived. He studied the little ship for a moment, noticing the shattered solar sail, still projecting fin-like from the hull. Then he saw that the airlock door was open. The ship was being checked over, prior to eventual refitting and the workman had been careless.

Rye hesitated for a moment, but the temptation was too great. Actually to have been on board would make an even better story. He went up the ramp.

Excitedly he moved along the ship's dimly lit metal corridors, imagining the thrilling scenes that had taken place. He made his way to the power room, the very place where the Rutan had been found lurking.

The faint glow from the power drive didn't alarm him, not at first. He simply assumed the drive had been left on. Curiously he approached – and a glowing sphere surged out of the power drive and engulfed him. He tried to scream, but it was far too late.

The sphere hovered about the body for a very long time, as if somehow unaccustomed to its grisly task. But the necessary dissection was completed at last, the information stored.

The sphere blurred, solidified – and a pale-faced version of Rye appeared beside the body. Moving stiffly at first, the figure made its way along the corridors and out of the airlock.

Not long afterwards, the spacedock technician returned from his break. He slipped as he entered the engine room, bruising himself against the machinery.

Then he saw what he'd slipped on, and started to scream.

The spaceport security man came into the bar, looked round and spotted the party at the corner table. He handed Lisa a sealed message flimsy and stood waiting.

Lisa tore open the seal and read the message. Her face tightened. 'They've found a dead body – in the power room of our ship. Apparently it was – mutilated. Partially dissected.'

'Come on,' said Kurt. They jumped up and headed for

the exit. It seemed quite natural for the Doctor and his friends to come with them.

In the power room, the appalled little group stood looking down at the blood-soaked body.

Roz knelt to examine it. After a moment she straightened up.

'Rutan work.'

'You're sure?' asked the security man.

'We've seen it before,' said Chris. 'Too often.'

'We've all seen it,' said Kurt.

'The Rutan's dead,' whispered Lisa. 'We both saw it die.'

The Doctor looked at the body, at the pale face and the lank blond hair. 'Do we know who he is?'

'Name's Rye,' said the security man. 'Steward on space liner *Hyperion*.'

'Where's the ship now?'

'En route for Sentarion. Only…'

'Only what? Speak up, man!'

'We contacted the ship.'

'And?'

'They said no one was missing from their crew.'

'Send them another message,' snapped the Doctor. 'Tell them—' He broke off, shaking his head. 'No, don't tell them anything, they'll be safer if they leave it alone.'

'Can't send any more messages anyway,' said the security man. 'They'll be in hyperdrive by now. Can we remove the body?'

The Doctor nodded and a security team gathered up the body and took it away. The Doctor stood staring into nothingness.

Kurt studied his face for a moment. 'You know what happened, don't you?'

'There's only one possibility,' said the Doctor. 'Can I have some more light?'

Lisa took a heavy torch from a locker and handed it to him. The Doctor shone the powerful beam into every corner of the power room. Suddenly he stopped. 'Aha! I thought so.' He shone the beam into a narrow space under one of the power units, revealing a pool of gelatinous slime.

'What is it?' asked Lisa.

'You might call it afterbirth,' said the Doctor. 'Rutans reproduce by binary fission, just like the humble amoeba on Earth. Before it made its break for freedom, the Rutan reproduced itself.'

Lisa looked at him in amazement. 'At a time like that? Why?'

'Insurance!' said the Doctor. 'Don't you see? All Rutans are in effect the same Rutan. Karne was handing on the mission. This new Karne will have all the same memories. It isn't over after all! We must set off for Sentarion at once.'

He looked hopefully at Lisa, as if he expected her to start up the power drive right away.

'What's all this "we" business, Doctor?' said Lisa. 'I've got a solar yacht race to think about.'

'You mustn't worry about that,' said the Doctor impatiently. 'It'll probably be postponed anyway. I'm having a little local difficulty with my own transport, you see. It's – gone adrift.' He bowed to Lisa and said grandly, 'Captain Deranne, I wish to charter your yacht!'

18
REVIVAL

The space yacht *Tiger Moth*, now under special charter, was en route for Sentarion.

It hadn't been that easy, of course. At first Lisa had turned down the Doctor's charter proposition flat. They'd adjourned to the station bar, where the argument had raged for hours.

'For one thing, the ship's not ready,' said Lisa. 'The power drive still needs work, and there's not an engineer to be had.'

'That's where you're wrong,' said the Doctor. 'I can offer you the services, entirely without charge, of one of the finest engineers in the cosmos.'

'Who?'

The Doctor tapped his own chest. 'Me!'

'You're qualified in space engineering?'

'I'm qualified in practically everything.'

In the end it had taken all the Doctor's charm, a fortunately timed official message from the Solar Racing Authority announcing the postponement of the Tri-Systems Solar, and a personal appeal from Kurt to persuade Lisa to go.

It was Kurt who had finally won her over.

'Listen, Lisa,' he said quietly, 'I'm not even going to mention that I own the ship. You're Captain, and what you say goes. But I owe the Doctor, big. He saved my life when the Sontarans were going to execute me. Wasn't for him, I'd be in an unknown grave on a nowhere planet.'

'That still doesn't mean I have to hazard my ship, or our lives on—'

Kurt interrupted her. 'The fact that I turned up on Alpha and joined your crew, that we ever met, is all down to the Doctor.'

Lisa looked hard at him for a moment. 'Then I suppose I owe him too.' She turned to the Doctor. 'All right, I'll go. But it'll cost you.'

'Name your terms,' said the Doctor grandly.

Lisa thought of her usual charter rate and then tripled it.

The Doctor looked surprised. 'But surely that's—'

'Take it or leave it. That's my price, and it's non-negotiable.'

'Then I'll take it.'

'Oh, come on, Lisa,' protested Kurt. 'You're robbing him. I'll pay the charter fee, Doctor.'

'My dear chap, I wouldn't think of it. Believe it or not, I do have perfectly adequate – resources.'

Roz Forrester had been listening to the wrangle with quiet amusement. Not for the first time, she wondered exactly what the Doctor's resources were and where they came from. They were certainly adequate all right. Wherever he needed to go, wherever he needed to send his unfortunate assistants, the necessary funds were available, immediately, and without fuss.

She leaned across to Lisa. 'Soak him for all you can get,' she advised. 'If you work for the Doctor, you'll be lucky to come out with your life, let alone your ship.'

'Nonsense,' said the Doctor cheerfully. 'This is going to be a perfectly straightforward trip. We go to Sentarion, pick up Bernice, and see if she's turned anything up in her researches, which she probably won't have. We'll also see if

228

there's any trace of our Rutan friend, which there probably won't be either. He'll have moved on by now. Then we come back here, Captain Deranne and Kurt prepare for their race, while we go back to Station Alpha. By then they'll have recovered my transport. Nothing to it. There shouldn't be any danger at all.'

'Where have I heard that before?' mused Roz.

The Doctor jumped up. 'Now everything's settled, I'll just go and tell the station authorities about our plans.'

He hurried away.

Chris smiled happily around the thoughtful little group. 'Oh well, that's all right, then!'

'What is?' asked Roz.

'The Doctor says there won't be any danger.'

Roz looked wonderingly at the others.

'Do you know,' she said, 'I think he actually believes him!'

There were objections from the space station authorities when the Doctor announced their departure and asked to be allowed to purchase the necessary supplies. It was felt that *Tiger Moth* and its surviving crew should stay for the enquiry.

'I couldn't possibly allow any of you to leave at the moment,' said Malic, the station manager. He was a plump, sleek-haired man who liked to see things done properly. 'Captain Deranne must face an enquiry into the deaths of her crew – and indeed into the deaths of a large number of Sontaran nationals currently occupying the station morgue. And I understand, Doctor, that you and your companions were very much concerned in the liberation of Station Alpha.' He studied his screen. 'I see you have a claim against Station Alpha for the loss of certain property

– described here simply as "a blue box". Antique, was it?'

'Depends how you look at it. Some people call it an antique. Others would say it was ultra-modern.'

'And what was its value?'

'Priceless. Anyway, I'm not interested in compensation; I just want it returned. It has great sentimental value.'

'Well, we shall see,' said Malic. 'I'm sure my colleagues on Alpha will do their best to recover it. But you must understand that with all these matters still pending, I cannot possibly allow either you or Captain Deranne to depart.'

'Well, if you say so,' said the Doctor. 'I should like to say how much I admire your courage.'

'I don't follow, Doctor. Courage has nothing to do with it. It's simply a matter of principle.'

'But it's extremely brave of you to stick to your principles so firmly – especially in the face of such great danger to yourself and your station.'

Malic was looking agitated. 'What danger is that, Doctor?'

The Doctor leaned forward confidentially.

'You know what happened on Station Alpha – the attack, the damage, the terrible loss of life?'

'Yes, of course I do. But I fail to see the relevance—'

Sadly the Doctor shook his head. 'The Sontarans executed poor Ferris, the station manager, you know, simply for questioning one of their orders. He was a man of principle too – very much like yourself, come to think of it. I'm sure you won't stand any nonsense from the Sontarans – even if it costs you your life.'

Malic shuddered. 'What exactly are you trying to tell me, Doctor? Why should the Sontarans come here?'

'Well, the attack on Alpha happened because, for reasons

of their own, the Sontarans were after *Tiger Moth*. As we know, they didn't get it. But they probably know where it was heading.' The Doctor sighed. 'I'm afraid they're rather angry with me as well. I'm very grateful to you for insisting on giving me your protection. The Sontarans would probably regard any association with me as a crime carrying the death penalty in itself.'

'I see,' said Malic thoughtfully. He paused for a moment. 'These supplies, Doctor – exactly what do you need?'

'Couldn't do enough to speed our departure,' the Doctor told Lisa later, when they were finally under way. They were in the control room, where the Doctor was checking the results of his emergency repairs on the instrument consoles.

He was sitting in Robar's place, next to Lisa. Somewhat to her surprise, she found she didn't resent it in the least.

'Do you really think the Sontarans will come after us?'

'I'm afraid it's a possibility. They seem obsessed with capturing your Rutan passenger – and they don't know the Rutan's dead. They'll be waiting for reports from the commander of their assault team – and of course, he's dead as well. So when they don't hear anything from him—'

'His name was Steg,' said Lisa. 'Commander Steg.'

She remembered the red glare of triumph in the Sontaran's eyes as he fell dying by the airlock. She remembered his last defiant whisper. 'I win, Rutan. I win!'

And she remembered the way he'd saved her life.

'Steg?' said the Doctor. 'Really? Kurt and I met him once, you know.'

'You met Steg? What happened?'

'We didn't really hit it off,' said the Doctor regretfully. 'As a matter of fact, he condemned us both to death.'

He gave her a brief account of their adventure.

'He didn't seem to recognise Kurt when they took over the ship.'

'I think they find humans pretty well indistinguishable.'

Lisa nodded. 'That's what he told me when we first met.' She imitated the Sontaran's guttural voice. '"Forgive me, Captain. All primitives look rather alike to me."'

'Besides,' said the Doctor, 'Kurt wasn't looking his prosperous self in those days. Clean clothes and no stubble make a big difference.'

'I wonder why Kurt didn't tell me about it.' Lisa sounded a little hurt. 'He didn't really tell me about you, either.'

The Doctor went on checking dials. 'We talked a bit when we were sharing that cell. Kurt's had a pretty tough life. I imagine he's used to keeping his own counsel, trusting no one, relying on nobody but himself.'

'That's something I know a lot about.'

'It's hard when you have to learn to do that,' said the Doctor. 'Of course, *un*learning it's harder still. But if you don't – you might meet someone you could trust and not know how to deal with them.' He tapped a quivering dial. 'There you are. Steady power-flow from all drives. Guaranteed no Rutans.'

'You're quite a fixer, aren't you, Doctor?'

'Sometimes I think I'm just a meddler who does more harm than good. But I have to try.'

'Why?'

'Good question.' The Doctor paused, grey eyes staring somewhere very far away in space and time.

'I was brought up with an ideal of service. In time I learned that the system I served was hopelessly corrupt. But somehow the ideal stayed on. You could call it the Gallifreyan work ethic!'

Lisa gave him a baffled look and the Doctor smiled.

In a deep, actorish voice he boomed:

'The time is out of joint. Ah, cursed spite

That ever I was born to set it right.'

'What's that?'

'Just something my pal Will knocked off, between pints at the Mermaid Tavern.'

Lisa looked around the control room, remembering all that had happened. 'It's funny but I still half-regret killing Steg – not that he didn't deserve it. But he did save my life.'

In the crewroom, Roz and Chris and Kurt were stretched out on the long benches, trying to relax and waiting for the voyage to end. Chris was very curious about Kurt, though he didn't like to ask direct questions.

'So you and the Doctor have met before?' he said casually.

Kurt nodded. 'We were in jail together.'

'What for?' asked Roz.

'Smuggling for me. I suppose it was more like politics for the Doctor. He was helping the local life-form to rebel against Earth colonists. When the Sontarans turned up he just sort of transferred the rebellion to them.'

'Sounds like the Doctor, all right,' said Roz.

'So you're a smuggler?' said Chris, studying Kurt hungrily. He looked as if he was getting ready to issue a caution, inform Kurt of his rights and make an arrest.

'Ex-smuggler,' corrected Kurt. 'And you're some kind of cop.'

'Ex-cop,' said Roz.

'Well, there you are,' said Kurt. 'It just goes to show anyone can overcome their early disadvantages if they really try.'

'What's your interest in all this?' asked Roz.

Kurt shrugged. 'When the Doctor and I were in that jail, the Sontarans were going to shoot us at dawn. The Doctor got me out – so I owe him.'

'Honour amongst thieves?' said Chris.

Kurt leaned forward. 'Look, sonny, some crooks are people, believe it or not – just like some cops. Now, if you want to try to take me when this is over, you're welcome to try your luck. Meanwhile, suppose you try to remember that for the moment we're on the same side?'

Chris blushed. 'Sorry. Old habits—'

'Sure,' said Kurt easily. 'How about a game of cards to pass the time?'

Roz shook her head. 'Not me. Think I'll catch up on some sleep.' She chose one of the many spare bunks and stretched out.

'I wouldn't mind a game,' said Chris. 'We can play two-handed.'

Kurt took a pack of cards from a shelf. 'Don't know much about cards myself. I seem to remember there's some old game called – poker, is it?'

'I know that,' said Chris eagerly. 'We used to play it in recruit school at the Academy.'

'Fine,' said Kurt. 'You can teach me how to play.'

Ah well, thought Roz. Everyone has to learn...

Business was booming in the morgue on Space Station Beta. Usually it had only one or two occupants: some unfortunate space technician caught in an accident, an overfed cruise passenger who'd paid the price for too many good dinners.

But now there was a full house. The unfortunate crew of the *Tiger Moth*. All their Sontaran attackers. And now they'd found this other poor devil on *Tiger Moth*. Talk about a death ship.

Kraal, the morgue attendant, found it was getting him down. He was a conscientious soul and it worried him having so many corpses to look after. He found himself checking and rechecking them all the time. Silly, really. After all, they weren't going anywhere.

Or were they? On his latest check, Kraal seemed to be one dead Sontaran short.

He counted and recounted, and he just couldn't make the numbers come out right. He even knew which one was missing. The one in the fancy uniform, the Commander. Kraal counted again. 'Come on, Commander,' he muttered. 'Where are you?'

A dreadful voice behind him said, 'I am here.'

Kraal whirled round and saw a massive form looming over him. He tried to scream but two hands clamped around his throat. He saw two little red eyes glaring into his own.

It was the last thing he saw.

Minutes later, Kraal was one of his own customers, neatly laid out on a slab.

Steg looked round the room and discovered that the dead Sontarans' weapons had been neatly stacked on a shelf. Seizing a blaster, Steg was about to set off when something caught his eye. It was a body on a slab – the body of a slight, fair-haired young man. The body had been extensively mutilated in a fashion that Steg found very familiar. His mind flashed back to the body of the engineer on *Tiger Moth*.

Like Robar, this human had been killed by a Rutan – a Rutan who was probably now wearing that human's shape. But where had it come from?

Steg lurched out into the corridor in search of some answers.

The first to know of his revival, apart from the unfortunate Kraal, were the communication technicians of Space Station Beta.

Steg marched into the communications room and barked, 'Your attention! I am Commander Steg of the Sontaran Space Corps. I need information and a certain amount of assistance. Give me what I require and no one need be harmed.'

The duty security man tried to draw his blaster. Immediately, Steg shot him dead.

'I said no one *need* be harmed. That is up to you. If you make it necessary, I will kill you all.'

'You're one of the Sontarans they brought in on *Tiger Moth*,' said Malic shakily. 'You were dead. They were all dead. We saw the bodies.'

'The report of my death was greatly exaggerated. Where is the *Tiger Moth* now?'

'On the way to Sentarion.'

'*Sentarion?*'

'Yes, you know the Library Planet—'

'I know of Sentarion. Why is *Tiger Moth* going there?'

'She's under charter—'

'To whom?'

'To a Doctor John Smith.'

'Describe this Doctor.'

'There's nothing special about him—'

'*Describe him!*'

'Smallish, grey eyes, rumpled clothes – very ordinary looking. Got a way with him though—'

Steg held up his hand. 'Enough!'

Doctor John Smith. General Smith! The one who had deceived and defeated him on Jekkar. The Doctor. The old enemy of the Sontaran people, interfering once more. Interfering, it seemed, in the most important operation in Sontaran history. Then there was the Rutan. He resumed his questioning.

'There is the mutilated body of a young human in your mortuary. Where did it come from?'

'It was found on board *Tiger Moth*…'

Prodded by Steg's urgent questions, Malic told the strange story of Rye's death – and of the fact that the crew of *Hyperion* seemed to think he was still on board after his death.

'This spaceliner – where is it bound?'

'Sentarion.'

So the Rutan was heading for Sentarion – with the Doctor in close pursuit. How much did they know?

Watched by the handful of terrified technicians, Steg thought for a moment.

'To an extent, our interests are the same. I wish to leave here. You, I am sure, wish to see me gone. You will send a message for me to our War Wheel, and it will come and remove me. Here is the message.'

Steg dictated a stream of guttural syllables, the secret battle-code of the Sontarans, only employed in the greatest military emergencies.

Obediently Malic transmitted the message.

'What now?'

'We wait,' said Steg. 'Continue with your normal duties, making no reference to my presence. Conceal the body of your colleague. And I warn you, do not copy his rashness. It will do you no good to attack me. Even if you succeed, you will die. Now that the message has been sent, the War

Wheel will come. If I am not here, waiting, when it arrives, this space station will be destroyed.'

Hunched into a corner, blaster in hand, Steg settled down to wait.

19
SANCTUARY

Bernice Summerfield was going mad.

It wasn't that the conditions of her imprisonment were so unbearable, especially for an archaeologist. The Temple, after all, was an outstandingly beautiful place, filled with fascinating works of art. She had free access to all sorts of historical material that no scholar outside of the Sentarrii themselves had ever been allowed to see.

'Your name's made if you manage to survive and publish, Benny,' she said to herself. (She was talking to herself quite a lot these days.) But of course, she was never going to publish. It was by no means certain that she was going to survive.

Physically she was comfortable enough. Her room in the inner part of the Temple was much like her room at the University.

Three times a day, a university servant brought her simple nourishing food, with unlimited fresh water and fruit juice to wash it down. No alcohol of course. Her requests for a bottle of Eridanean brandy had simply been ignored.

Bernice Summerfield had never felt so disgustingly fit and healthy in her life. She hated it.

The trouble was that imprisonment, however comfortable, was still imprisonment.

At first Bernice had thought that the Lord Chancellor himself was condemning her to death. 'You can never leave here alive,' he had said. Then she realised that, as so often with the Sentarrii, his words were to be taken absolutely literally.

Here in the Temple she was safe. If she left, she was dead.

It was a sentence of life imprisonment – with no remission.

Once she realised what he really meant, Bernice had pleaded with the Lord Chancellor to let her go. She had sworn perpetual secrecy, she had reminded him of his friendship with the Doctor, she had appealed to every moral principle in the cosmos, from common decency to the inalienable rights of sentient life-forms.

The Lord Chancellor had been polite, courteous and implacable.

'No doubt there is much in what you say, Domina, but the facts cannot be altered. By entering the Temple, you have incurred the sentence of death. I could not lift that sentence, even if I wished to do so. All I can do is what I have done. For the Doctor's sake, and yours, I commanded the Harrubtii that blood may not be spilled in the sacred temple precincts. I think they will obey my authority in that – but in that alone. If you leave the Temple, they will kill you. Even if you succeed in evading them here and escape from the Temple they will follow you and kill you – anywhere on the planet. Even if you manage to leave Sentarion, their emissaries will follow you and track you down. Only one place in the cosmos is safe for you – and that is here.'

And the Harrubtii, Bernice soon realised, were all around, watching and waiting. She caught glimpses of their shining carapaces in the gardens around the Temple. She felt their fierce black eyes following her every movement.

Day followed day, until she began to feel herself losing

track of time. She saw herself growing old here, going mad from boredom and finally fading away.

Of course, the Doctor would eventually turn up to look for her. No doubt they would have a cover story ready to explain her disappearance, just as they had with poor old Lazio. There would be a faked message for the Doctor saying she'd had no luck with her researches and had gone off to another university on some distant planet. The Doctor would be disappointed. When she didn't reappear, he'd assume she'd just got bored or chickened out. Never very reliable, poor old Benny. No doubt he'd miss her – for a while.

No, she told herself fiercely. The Doctor trusted her. He wouldn't be fobbed off, he'd know they were lying. He'd come looking for her. Determinedly, she hung on to the thought. At the moment it appeared to be her only hope.

Meanwhile, she did the only other thing she could. In her pocket was a silver sphere with an inset button. It was called a SPATAB. A Spatio-Temporal Alarm Beacon – otherwise known as a Panic Button. It would tell the Doctor she was in trouble and guide him to her when he came to find her.

She took it out of her pocket, and pressed the button.

Meanwhile, so as to have something to tell him when he arrived and to help pass the endless hours, Bernice carried on with her researches. She studied the murals and frescos in the Temple itself and scanned its archives. She began forming a theory about the beginnings of Sentarrii civilisation.

Luckily for Bernice, she wasn't entirely confined to the interior of the Temple. On the far side was a huge formal garden. It was filled with beds of exotic alien plants, fountains and ornamental pools, and overgrown with lush green vegetation. At its centre was a huge statue of a shapeless, shrouded form, before which myriad different insectoid life-forms bowed down in worship.

The Lord Chancellor had assured Bernice that the Inner Garden was sacred, a part of the Temple itself. Here too she was safe – at least, so she thought.

She was strolling past a bank of flowering bushes, brooding over her theory, when dark shapes sprang out at her, bearing her to the ground. A filthy cloth was jammed over her face, covering her nose and mouth. Within seconds she was fighting for breath.

Bernice struggled wildly, thrashing about with her arms and legs. With a desperate heave she managed to break free of her attackers and scramble to her feet. She found herself surrounded by a circle of Harrubtii, several of them clutching cloaks.

'What do you think you're doing?' gasped Bernice. 'This garden is part of the Temple. Don't you obey your Chancellor any more?'

'We do not disobey,' hissed one of the Harrubtii.

'You were told it was forbidden to spill blood.'

'We spill no blood,' said another Harrubti. 'We mean only to stop your breath.'

'It's the same thing,' yelled Bernice indignantly. 'I'll be just as dead, won't I?'

'We spill no blood,' repeated the Harrubti obstinately and the circle closed in on her.

Bernice struggled to break free of the grasping claws. She was helped by the fact that the Harrubtii could not use their blood-sucking spikes, but she was still badly outnumbered. The Harrubtii bore her to the ground by sheer weight of numbers and soon the choking cloth was over her face once more.

Weakened by lack of oxygen, Bernice felt her struggles becoming feebler. There was a roaring in her ears, a red mist before her eyes...

'*Stop!*'

The deep voice penetrated the roaring. Suddenly the pressure was released, the cloth fell away. Bernice drew in great sobbing gasps of the warm scented air.

Gasping, she struggled to her feet and saw the tall robed form of the Lord Chancellor towering over the Harrubtii, his entourage hovering around him.

He looked sternly down at the Harrubtii.

'Did I not command you to spill no blood here?'

'We spill no blood, Lord. We seek only to stop the blasphemer's breath.'

Bernice expected the argument to be dismissed at once. But to her horror, she heard the Lord Chancellor say, 'The point is an interesting one. I must consider.'

The tall insectoid form was frozen in thought. The Harrubtii gathered round, waiting eagerly for a decision. The more optimistic ones were already folding their cloaks into pads.

'Hang on,' yelled Bernice. 'I refuse to be murdered on a technicality.'

The Lord Chancellor's great head with its glowing eyes swung round to face her. 'You wish to contribute to this debate, Domina?'

Suddenly Bernice realised she was talking for her life. It's not easy to be calm when the question under discussion is whether or not you are to be killed. Nevertheless, she forced herself to speak calmly, as if discussing some abstract point of philosophical jurisprudence.

'Surely, Lord Chancellor, your ruling was expressed metaphorically? You spoke of blood to the Harrubtii because they deal in blood. The true meaning of your order was that *I was not to be killed in the precincts of the Temple*. That meaning must not be evaded by trickery. Laws must be obeyed in spirit as well as in letter.'

There was another long silence. Then the Lord Chancellor's voice boomed, 'Such was my meaning. The Domina Bernice has attained sanctuary in the Temple. Within its precincts, she may not be harmed – in any way!'

Disappointed, the Harrubtii moved away, disappearing into the bushes. The Lord Chancellor turned to Bernice.

'You argue well, Domina. It was an interesting point of doctrine, was it not?'

'Fascinating,' said Bernice. 'Glad we got it cleared up.'

They began strolling through the gardens, his entourage following at a respectful distance.

The Lord Chancellor's regular visits were one of the high spots of Bernice's captivity. Having condemned her to spend the rest of her life as his unwilling guest, he seemed to feel a responsibility for her. Despite the rather strange nature of their relationship, a curious kind of friendship had grown up between them.

Bernice felt faintly ashamed of the fact that she was abusing it. There were still some Sentarrii secrets known only to the Lord Chancellor himself.

'Lord Chancellor,' she began, 'we were talking on your last visit of the Sacred Texts. I asked if I might see them.'

'I fear it is not possible, Domina. Doctrine states that only the eyes of the Sentarrii may behold them.'

'Does it say anything about their *hearing* them?'

'I do not understand.'

'I'm sure you know the Sacred Texts well, Lord Chancellor. Suppose you were to *tell* me what's in them – recite them to me – would that be forbidden?'

By now they had come to the statue in the centre of the gardens. The Lord Chancellor bowed his head, considering. 'Nowhere is it written that this is forbidden.'

'To hear you recite the Sacred Texts would be a great honour, Lord Chancellor,' said Bernice, blessing the literal nature of the Sentarrii mind.

The Lord Chancellor began to speak in a low, chanting voice.

'In the dark time the Sentarrii, the Harrubtii and all the other species that dwelt upon Sentarion were as savage beasts, thinking only of war and slaughter…'

There followed a long recital of generations of Sentarrii warfare, of soldiers slaughtered and nests destroyed. Bernice could feel her head nodding, but she made herself listen with an air of keen attention. Then, at last, came the bit she'd been waiting for.

'But then, upon the Sacred Day of Revelation, the sky darkened above the Holy Place. The vessels of the Shining Ones appeared, great glistening nests in which burned sacred fires. The ships landed and the Shining Ones emerged. They were shapeless yet they were all shapes, they were formless yet masters of every form.

'The Shining Ones dwelt amongst the Sentarrii for a time, altering their bodies and their minds, and giving them great knowledge. The cruel and ferocious Harrubtii they changed also, and from this time the Harrubtii became the fiercest and most loyal of their servants, the appointed Guardians of the Faith.

'But it came to pass that the work of the Shining Ones was done, and they returned to their own place. Before they left, they made the Great Compact with the Sentarrii. If the Compact is upheld, a day will come when the Shining Ones return, bringing all power and all knowledge to their servants, the Sentarrii. And the Temple was built upon this holy place, against that day.'

As the chant concluded, Bernice was thinking furiously. It was just as Lazio had said, the classic myth found on so many planets.

The gods came from the stars, conferred great benefits on their humble worshippers, and then went back to whatever heaven they had come from – usually promising to return some day if their worshippers kept the faith.

They left behind them a group of fanatical devotees, waiting for the great day, fiercely intolerant of anyone who questioned the faith.

Some scientists had come up with the theory that the gods of these curiously common myths were in fact space-travelling aliens, landing upon still primitive planets and accelerating the development of native species, possibly by genetic manipulation. The hypothesis had originated long ago on Old Earth, where it was sometimes known as the Von Daniken Myth, or the Quatermass theory, after the long-forgotten scholars who had originated it.

Bernice remembered Lazlo's words in the tavern, just before the Harrubtii had killed him.

'Suppose it really happened, right here on Sentarion? *Suppose it's still going on?* There's a secret temple, somewhere in the city…'

Lazio had been brutally murdered just for expressing such thoughts in public. She herself had been almost killed, and condemned to perpetual imprisonment, for investigating the Temple. She was well aware that the Lord Chancellor was speaking so freely only because of his certainty that she could never pass on her knowledge.

The Doctor had been right after all, decided Bernice. Some great secret was hidden here – and it wasn't just the story of Sentarion's old-time religion.

'This Great Compact the scrolls speak of,' she began – and broke off when she saw that the Lord Chancellor was staring upwards. She followed his gaze and saw a winged shape high in the sky overhead.

'That is very strange,' said the Lord Chancellor.

'What is?'

'Nobody on Sentarion would fly an ornithopter above the Temple. The area of sky directly above is called the Gateway of the Gods. It is fully as sacred as the Temple itself.'

'Some stranger, like me, who doesn't know the rules?' suggested Bernice.

'It is forbidden for anyone not native to the planet to fly an ornithopter,' said the Lord Chancellor. 'If he lands here, the Harrubtii will certainly kill him. Unless I save him as I saved you. It may be that you will have a companion in exile.'

Perhaps it's the Doctor, thought Bernice, flying in on some mad rescue mission. Will I lose my immunity if I try to leave? If he lands will we survive to take off together?

Bernice and the Lord Chancellor watched intently as the ornithopter circled downwards.

The service staff of the space liner *Hyperion* were very worried about their young colleague Rye. Since the stopover on Station Beta he simply hadn't been himself at all.

Usually cheerful, bustling and efficient, he had become vague and hopeless, scarcely able to carry out the simplest of his duties. The general opinion was that he must be ill.

Then there was the strange message from Beta just before they entered hyperspace. Some nonsense about

Rye being killed. All the time there he was, large as life, dropping plates in the first-class passenger saloon.

Rye's condition had degenerated so badly by the time they made the jump to hyperspace that the chief purser had ordered him confined to the sick bay. There he had remained, refusing food, drink and medical attention, until they emerged from hyperspace and prepared for planetfall on Sentarion.

When the chief purser visited him, all Rye would say was, 'I must land on Sentarion.'

The chief purser looked at the slim, fair-haired figure sitting motionless on the bunk. He turned to the ship's doctor.

'What do you think?'

'Perhaps it would be for the best. I can't help him here. He refuses all medication, won't even let me examine him. He's in some kind of hypermanic state. My nurse swears he gave her an electric shock when she tried to bathe his face. Besides...'

'Besides what?'

The ship's doctor shrugged. 'Sometimes the patient really does know best. Perhaps he's developed an allergy to something about space travel itself. The hyper-jumps or the anti-grav field. Who knows? Maybe he'll do better planet-side. There are good medical facilities at the University on Sentarion.'

'I think something happened to him on Beta,' said the chief purser. 'Something so horrible that it affected his mind. When we get back to Beta, I'm going to try to find out what it was.'

(Much later he looked at Rye's mutilated body in the morgue on Beta, and wondered what he had carried to Sentarion.)

The ship's doctor said, 'Listen, Rye, we'll drop you off on Sentarion if that's what you really want. We're landing to pick up a couple of homegoing scientists from the University. I'll hand you over to one of the University staff, I'm sure they'll look after you.'

Rye stared straight ahead. 'I must land on Sentarion.'

And so he did. When farewells had been made and the scientists were safely aboard, the ship's doctor explained Rye's case to the University official who had been in charge of them.

The official, a spindly grasshopper-like creature called Hapiir, couldn't have been more helpful.

'Of course, we will be glad to help. I have my 'thopter here, I will fly him to our medical facility myself. Poor young man.'

Rye was led down the ramp and handed over to Hapiir. As the liner prepared for blast-off, Hapiir led him across the little spaceport to the 'thopter, helped him into one of the passenger seats and climbed into the cockpit.

They waited until *Hyperion* blasted off. Then with a clumsy flapping of its wings the ornithopter rose slowly into the sky.

As they approached Sentarion City, Hapiir heard a flat, dead voice from behind him. 'Take me to the Temple.'

'That is not possible,' said Hapiir. 'I see that you do not know our ways. It is forbidden even to speak of such things.'

'Take me to the Temple.'

'Please, this is most discourteous. You are not well, you do not know what you are saying. I will take you to our medical complex where you will be cared for.'

A palm slapped down onto Hapiir's carapace. Before he could so much as protest, five thousand volts seared through his body.

Hapiir screamed thinly, once, and then died.

Rye scrambled into the cockpit and hurled Hapiir's charred corpse from the 'thopter. The controls were unfamiliar, but seemed simple enough. He flew on over the city, flying in great sweeping circles until at last the Temple appeared below him.

He began to descend.

The Lord Chancellor watched the descending craft with increasing indignation.

'If he lands here, I shall let the Harrubtii kill him. You, at least, came reverently, as a scholar, but this intrusion is sheer insolence.'

Directly overhead now, the 'thopter suddenly went into a descending spiral, clearly out of control. Bernice and the Lord Chancellor retreated to the bushes as the 'thopter crashed to the ground before the central statue, disintegrating with the impact.

'I do not think the Harrubtii will be needed,' said the Lord Chancellor grimly. 'No one could have survived such a crash.'

The Harrubtii were there all the same, though. Appearing with their usual mysterious suddenness, they gathered menacingly about the wreck.

A light flared briefly inside the wrecked 'thopter and for a moment Bernice thought it was going to burst into flames. The light faded and a slender young man climbed from the wreckage, apparently quite unhurt.

He looked at Bernice and the Lord Chancellor without surprise and said, 'Take me to the Temple.'

'I shall do no such thing,' said the Lord Chancellor and gestured towards the waiting Harrubtii. 'Kill him!'

'No!' shouted Bernice. She tried to move forward but the

Lord Chancellor's claw held her back.

As the Harrubtii advanced, the slender young man blurred, and changed. Suddenly, in his place, there was a hovering globe of light, trailing fiery tentacles.

The Lord Chancellor released Bernice's arm and threw himself to the ground. The Harrubtii too prostrated themselves.

Bernice looked at the hovering sphere. It was the shape that was on the murals in the Temple, and on the statue before her.

The Shining Ones – or one of them at least – had returned to Sentarion.

20
REVELATION

Commander Steg's head fell forward onto his chest, and he slumped back against the wall of the communications room. With a mighty effort he forced himself back to wakefulness. If he slept now, he would die – and he *would not die*! Not until his mission was complete.

He glanced around the room and saw the humans watching him eagerly, waiting for him to succumb to the rising tide of weakness.

'Not yet,' he rasped. 'Not yet.' He swept the muzzle of his blaster in an arc around the room.

Suddenly one of the technicians called, 'Mr Malic – look!'

Steg looked too, and saw, with enormous relief, the War Wheel looming up on the main monitor screen.

A Sontaran voice blared out over the com-unit. 'War Wheel to Commander Steg. Respond!'

Steg lurched forward. 'Commander Steg to War Wheel. Request immediate pick-up. I repeat, immediate! Top priority.'

'Stand by.'

Steg stood by. He stood by until he heard the clang of a docking assault craft, until a Sontaran lieutenant and a squad of troopers marched into the room.

The lieutenant saluted. 'Commander Steg.'

'Return me to the War Wheel immediately,' ordered Steg.

'Shall we kill the humans?'

Steg looked round the room, at the terrified humans who had been waiting for him to die, who had seen his weakness.

The one called Malic whispered, 'You promised. You promised we wouldn't be harmed if we co-operated.'

As if that meant anything, thought Steg. It would to a human, of course. Humans had different standards. For some reason the words reminded him of the captain of *Tiger Moth*, the human female. Lisa – Lisa Deranne…

Shaking his head to clear it he ordered, 'Destroy the communications equipment. Do not harm the humans.'

He straightened up and with an immense effort marched steadily from the room.

Admiral Sarg's suite on the War Wheel was a dark, metal-walled chamber, devoid of all luxury.

Commander Steg marched in, freshly uniformed and immaculate, and saluted, a little stiffly.

Sitting behind a massive war-desk, the admiral raised his grizzled head and regarded him steadily for a moment. As if satisfied by what he saw, he said, 'Report.'

'My assault craft captured the solar yacht *Tiger Moth* as ordered. We conducted a search, and evidence was discovered suggesting that the Rutan was indeed on board.'

'What kind of evidence?'

'Partially dissected dead bodies – human and Sontaran.'

'Continue.'

'I organised a search and the Rutan was located in the power room. It escaped, killing a number of my troopers and several of the human crew. Since my forces were already much reduced, I entered into a pact with the surviving human prisoners, promising them freedom in return for their aid in trapping the Rutan.'

The admiral looked mildly surprised. 'Did you intend to honour this agreement?'

'Naturally not, Admiral. Once the Rutan had been destroyed, any surviving humans would have been killed to preserve the secrecy of this operation.'

Reassured that Steg had not given way to undue sentiment, the admiral nodded. 'Go on.'

'Unfortunately, the humans acted first. Led by their captain, they revolted against us, killing another of my troopers and Lieutenant Vorn.'

'Did Vorn die well?'

'He fell honourably in battle, Admiral.'

The admiral made a note. 'His clan will be so informed.'

'With only one trooper surviving,' said Steg, 'I judged it best to destroy the human ship – and the Rutan with it. I armed a destructor bomb, set the timer and placed it in the airlock between our two ships.' Steg paused, recalling the last desperate flurry of events. 'The human captain and her last surviving crew member ambushed us. My trooper and myself were both shot down. The Rutan appeared in the shape of one of the dead humans then reverted to its own form. It departed through the airlock, with the intention of escaping in our assault craft.'

'A difficult situation, Commander,' said the Admiral drily. 'And then?'

'I recovered sufficiently to inform the captain of the presence of the destructor bomb in the airlock tunnel. She succeeded in putting it through the door of the assault craft just as it closed.'

'Why should this human captain wish to aid you?'

'It is rather that she wished to destroy the Rutan. It had killed an older human with which she had formed some kind of emotional relationship. Humans do this.'

Steg did not feel it necessary to inform the admiral that he himself had held back the airlock door, saving the human female's life. The admiral would have wanted to know his reason for this extraordinary action, and Steg had none to give him.

He hurried on. 'At this point, I collapsed from my wound and went into anabolic coma.'

(A badly wounded Sontaran automatically shuts down all systems, falling into a protective coma. Usually, this condition ends in death. More rarely, anabiosis occurs and the subject returns from the brink – as had happened with Steg.)

'So your mission was successful?' said the admiral. 'The assault craft blew up and the Rutan was destroyed?'

'Such was my belief, Admiral.'

'*Was?*'

'I recovered consciousness in the morgue on Station Beta. There was a body there, a human, which had clearly been killed by a Rutan. I took control of the communications room. Interrogation of the humans present revealed that the dead body had been killed on the solar yacht – after its arrival on Beta.'

'Explanation?'

'A second Rutan must have been concealed on the ship.'

'Or the first reproduced,' said the admiral, 'passing on all its knowledge.'

'My interrogation also revealed that the Rutan, wearing, no doubt, the shape of the dead human, had taken ship for Sentarion.'

The admiral's fist crashed down on the desk. 'You bring me disturbing news, Commander Steg. Is this operation compromised or not? I must know.'

'There is worse news still,' said Steg. '*Tiger Moth* is also en route for Sentarion – chartered by the Doctor.'

The admiral sat quite still for a moment, absorbing the news.

'The Doctor has a habit of appearing when there is a crisis in Sontaran affairs. Always he interferes, never to our benefit. Suggestions, Commander Steg?'

'Compromised or not, the Sentarion project must go on – we are committed now. Give me a new assault craft and a new crew and I will go to Sentarion at full speed and investigate the situation. The War Wheel can follow close behind me.'

Steg waited while the admiral considered. His own reputation as well as Steg's was now at stake. Success would mean immortal glory, past failures forgotten. Failure meant death, and worse still, disgrace.

Steg was a veteran with valuable experience of this mission – but his success had been qualified. Would the admiral gamble on him once again, or appoint some new commander?

He became aware that the admiral was studying him closely.

'Are you functional, Commander Steg?'

'The medical team has given me a full efficiency check. At my own request I have been given the maximum emergency power burn, regardless of the possibilities of permanent damage.'

'Present health status?'

'Currently there is slight impairment of motor function, extensive tissue damage and some discomfort. But I am still capable of functioning at peak efficiency for the duration of this mission.'

Admiral Sarg studied him for a few moments longer. 'Very well. We shall proceed as you suggest. I shall give you our fastest assault craft and a crack assault team. Try not to lose them this time, Commander Steg.'

Steg saluted. He turned and, lurching only slightly, marched from the room.

Lisa Deranne entered the control room of *Tiger Moth* and found the Doctor busy at the scanner.

'Nearly there,' she said. 'Soon be time to come off automatic. What are you doing?'

'Well, you know I'm going to Sentarion, to pick up Bernice Summerfield? First I'll have to find her.'

'One woman on a whole planet?'

The Doctor smiled. He had a very nice smile, thought Lisa, and dismissed the thought as irrelevant. This odd little man was a customer not a friend.

'Exactly – but it's not quite as bad as it sounds. She'll be somewhere near the University. And if she's in trouble, which she probably is by now, I can locate her with this.' He produced something that looked like an old-fashioned pocket watch and opened it. A light pulsed steadily. 'Yes, she's already signalling,' said the Doctor. 'I've succeeded in programming your scanner to receive her signal on the same frequency. We can establish her general location with the scanner, and track her down precisely with this once we've landed.'

Lisa took her place in the command chair and flicked the com-switch. 'All crew stand by. We are about to leave hyperspace.'

'If I might assist?' murmured the Doctor, and slipped in the seat beside her.

'I take it you're a fully qualified space-navigator, Doctor—' She broke off. 'I know, you're a fully qualified everything.

'We are leaving hyperspace – now!'

Her hands moved over the controls, correcting and stabilising, with the Doctor checking instruments at her side.

Reality blurred, and she had the usual feeling that every cell in her body had turned inside out.

Tiger Moth flicked into existence in orbit around Sentarion.

The Doctor hurried to the scanner. It showed a stylised map, with, at its centre, the spires of Sentarion City.

'An excellent piece of navigation, Doctor,' said Lisa.

'Well, it is the only city on the planet!' The Doctor adjusted controls and a light pulsed in the very centre of the city.

'There's Bernice,' murmured the Doctor. 'In the middle of things as usual. I'll set the course, Captain, if you'll steer. Three degrees north…'

Lisa's hands moved over the controls. On the scanner, Sentarion City swam steadily nearer. They moved closer, and found themselves over a great shining dome.

'She appears to be in the Temple itself,' said the Doctor. 'Which means that she really is in trouble. Captain Deranne, can you land us in that garden beyond the Temple? Not too close to the Temple itself, but not too far either?'

'All part of the service, Doctor.' Lisa's hands moved surely over the controls.

'Then let's go down and see what she's up to!'

Minutes later the ship touched down.

The Doctor and the others gathered by the airlock.

'I must warn you,' said the Doctor, 'the fact that we've landed in the Temple grounds means that we'll be going into considerable danger.'

'What's all this we?' said Lisa Deranne. 'You may be going into danger, Doctor. I'm staying with my ship. I got you here, and if you survive I'll take you back, but the charter fee doesn't cover heroics.'

'I wouldn't expect it to,' said the Doctor. He turned to Kurt. 'What about you?'

Kurt hesitated for a moment. Finally, he made a sweeping gesture that took in both Lisa and the ship. 'Sorry, Doctor. Got to protect my investment!'

'Come on, Doctor,' said Roz Forrester impatiently. 'Let's go and get Benny. Ready, Chris?'

'Born ready,' said Chris.

'See you soon, I hope,' said the Doctor. He led Roz and Chris from the ship.

Lisa and Kurt looked at each other for a moment.

'Let's go to the control room and get ready for instant blast-off,' said Kurt. 'If I know the Doctor, they'll be back with half the planet on their tails.'

As they walked along the corridors towards the control room, Lisa said, 'You wanted to go with them.'

Kurt shrugged. 'I wanted to go with them and help the Doctor find his friend. I wanted to stay here and look after you. I can't do both – I chose you.'

Lisa stopped. 'You can still go.'

'No,' said Kurt. 'I can't. Let's go to the control room.'

The Doctor, Roz and Chris moved cautiously through the lush tropical gardens.

'Be on your guard,' warned the Doctor. 'These gardens are part of the Temple itself – sacred ground. We could be killed just for being here.'

'What else is new?' growled Roz.

Suddenly a shiny black shape hurled itself through the

260

air at them, shrieking fiercely. Chris and Roz both fired when it was still in the air, and the creature was dead when it hit the ground.

The Doctor bent to examine the body, noting the long sharp proboscis protruding from the narrow head.

Roz looked down and shuddered. 'What the hell is that?'

'Bloodsucker beetle,' said the Doctor. 'I imagine they act as temple guards.'

'You mean they're intelligent?' said Chris.

'Oh yes,' said the Doctor. He bent down and pulled at the cloak wrapped around the insect's body. 'It's an insectoid civilisation here on Sentarion.' He looked round. 'I'm surprised there aren't more of these things about. Maybe something's distracting them.'

'I do hope so,' said Roz.

'These aren't the dominant species, though,' said the Doctor, as they moved on. 'There are some intermediate insects, but the real rulers are the Sentarrii – giant soldier ants.'

'Terrific,' said Roz.

'Don't worry,' said the Doctor. 'They're dedicated to peace and scholarship – unless something's stirred them up, of course.'

They forced their way through a clump of towering ferns and came out into a little clearing. There before them arose a vast shining dome.

'There it is,' said the Doctor. 'The Temple. Whatever's happening, it'll be happening there. Come on.'

They moved steadily forwards.

Bernice Summerfield was at the centre of things at last.

She was close to the heart of Sentarion's most sacred

secret. Now she was wondering how long she could survive there.

After its dramatic transformation, the glowing sphere had addressed its terrified worshippers in a strange burbling voice.

'Take me to the Sanctum.'

It had floated towards the Temple, followed reverently by the Lord Chancellor and his attendants. The Harrubtii, clearly overawed, had fallen back.

No one took the slightest notice of Bernice. She supposed that when a god returns, the odd blasphemer is neither here nor there. She felt that she could have walked free from the Temple without anyone even noticing. But where could she go? And how could she miss the final revelation – whatever it was?

Unable to resist her curiosity, she hurried after the Lord Chancellor.

When she reached the Temple, she found the Lord Chancellor and his attendants by the entrance to the great dome, gathered reverently about the glowing sphere.

'Reveal the Sanctum,' ordered the glowing sphere.

The Lord Chancellor slid back a hidden panel and his two forelegs moved over the controls. For a moment nothing happened.

Then, with a faint rumbling, a vast section of the wall of the great dome slid back in two halves, revealing a space filled with glowing alien machinery.

Bernice stared into the vast shining cavern with a feeling of total awe. The machinery seemed to be made of spun crystal, with elaborate whorls and loops, complex structures and pillars and towers. Here and there light ebbed and flowed, and there were pulses of power. There was no noise, nothing moved, all was cool and silent. The control room – she supposed it must be a control room – was beautiful.

The Lord Chancellor bowed to the glowing sphere.

'Shall you open the gateway? Will the rest of the Shining Ones return now?'

'No!' said the burbling voice fiercely. 'The gateway must never be opened now. It must close for ever. I came here only to send a warning—' Suddenly it noticed Bernice, standing by the entrance. 'What is that?'

'It is a human, Great One, a scholar who entered the Temple. I have granted her sanctuary.'

'Kill it!'

The Lord Chancellor's body quivered in distress. 'Great One, I promised her sanctuary—'

'Kill it. It has seen the Great Secret and it must die.'

Bernice turned to run but one of the Chancellor's aides was suddenly at her side, gripping her arm with its powerful foreclaw.

'Summon the Harrubtii and give her to them,' said the Lord Chancellor sadly.

'You promised sanctuary,' said Bernice. 'You gave your word.'

There was grief in every line of the Lord Chancellor's body.

'That is so, Domina. But when a god commands…'

'Rubbish!' said a familiar voice. 'That thing's not a god – it's a Rutan.'

21
ASSAULT

'Doctor!' cried Bernice joyfully. Wrenching free from the claw of the Sentarrii aide, she ran to join him. 'Am I glad to see you!' She looked at Chris and Roz, looking grim and efficient with their drawn blasters. 'You too!' She took the Doctor's arm. 'Doctor, look!' She pointed to the glowing crystal control room.

'I'm looking,' said the Doctor, genuinely impressed. He bowed to the glowing sphere. 'Rutan workmanship at its finest. I congratulate you.' He went up to the Lord Chancellor, grasping him warmly by the foreclaw. 'And how are you, old friend?'

'Doctor,' said the Lord Chancellor, in very different tones from Bernice, 'this is not fitting. You intrude on our most sacred moment.'

'Nonsense,' said the Doctor firmly. 'Important, yes, momentous even. But sacred – no!'

'Kill them,' burbled the Rutan in its eerie fluting voice. 'Kill them all!'

'Now don't start that again,' said the Doctor firmly. 'I hate violence myself, and my two friends here hate it even more. So if you threaten us again they'll blast you into glowing gobbets!'

The Rutan crackled angrily; the Sentarrii wailed in horror. 'Doctor,' said the Chancellor in anguished tones, 'you threaten our god!'

'If it were a god there'd be precious little point in

threatening it,' pointed out the Doctor. 'But it isn't. It's a Rutan, a member of a highly evolved species from the other side of the galaxy. They have a number of interesting attributes, including polymorphism and group consciousness, but I assure you, divinity isn't amongst them.'

'Doctor, you do not understand,' whispered the Lord Chancellor. 'The Rutans *are* our gods.'

In the control room of *Tiger Moth*, Lisa and Kurt sat looking at each other.

'We're doing the right thing,' said Lisa.

'Absolutely,' said Kurt. 'Only—'

'Only what?'

'Only it doesn't feel right.'

Kurt fiddled with the scanner controls, changing the field from the earth below to the skies above. Suddenly he tensed. 'Lisa, look!'

She came to join him. There on the screen was a blunt, dreadfully familiar shape.

'Sontarans!' said Kurt. 'It's another assault craft.' He took a blaster from a wall-locker and headed for the door. 'I've got to warn the Doctor.'

Lisa snatched up a blaster and followed him.

He paused. 'What do you think you're doing?'

'Protecting my investment. Come on!'

They ran towards the airlock.

In the Temple, the Lord Chancellor was desperately defending his creed. 'The Rutans *are* the Shining Ones. Long, long ago the Shining Ones came to us from on high, bringing us truth and knowledge…'

'They made contact with you at a time when you were

still at a primitive stage and they were already highly evolved,' said the Doctor. 'They gave you knowledge, certainly, though for purposes of their own. But they fed you lies as well. They encouraged you to worship them as gods.'

The Lord Chancellor gestured up at the soaring dome.

'But they gave us all this, the Temple, the University!'

'You gave them the Temple, in mistaken adoration,' said the Doctor. 'The University, the Great Library, you achieved yourselves. They gave you your start, but you have outstripped them in achievement. The Sentarrii are honoured as scholars on all civilised worlds. Who has heard of the Rutans?'

The Rutan crackled with rage. 'The whole galaxy shall hear of us once the Sontarans are destroyed!'

Kurt and Lisa ran into the Temple.

'Let's get your friend and go, Doctor!' shouted Kurt. 'The Sontarans are here!'

The warning came too late. In a roar of retro-rockets, the Sontaran assault craft slammed to the ground, directly in front of the Temple. A ramp sprang out and squat armoured figures ran down it, heavy blasters in their hands.

'This is where I came in,' muttered Kurt.

With the Temple and all its occupants covered by Sontaran blasters, a strangely familiar figure limped down the ramp.

'I don't believe it,' whispered Lisa. 'It's Steg!'

Steg made his way up the Temple steps and paused in the doorway. 'Those of you who are armed can see how you are outgunned. Some of us would die, but not one of you would survive. Put down your weapons – now!'

'Do as he says,' said the Doctor.

Reluctantly, Kurt, Lisa, Roz and Chris obeyed.

At a sign from Steg, a Sontaran trooper gathered up the weapons, stacking them against the wall.

Steg looked swiftly around the dome, scanning its occupants one by one, ending with Lisa.

'Greetings, Captain Deranne.'

Lisa sighed. 'How many times do I have to kill you, Steg?'

'More than once, it seems. We Sontarans are hard to kill. As indeed, are you, Doctor. And you, Kurt, my smuggling friend. Yes, I recognise you now. Seeing you with the Doctor brings it all back. I may yet carry out my death sentence on you both!'

Steg moved closer to the Rutan, studying it curiously. 'And you, I take it, are Karne?'

'We were Karne,' said the strange warbling voice. 'We were many others. We are Rutan. We learned of your plan and came here to frustrate it.'

'And instead you have helped us,' said Steg. 'I take it you planned to send a message through the gateway? How?'

'We thought of all possibilities. Even this one. Passenger units are provided for such emergencies. We shall pass through the Gate, travel the Way and take a message of warning.'

'Not now,' said Steg. 'Instead *we* shall send a message through the Gateway – though not precisely the message you intended. Open the Gate.'

The Rutan made no response.

Steg turned to his troopers. 'You two – cover the human prisoners. The rest of the squad, surround the Rutan.'

In seconds, the Rutan was ringed with Sontaran blasters.

'Hear me, Rutan,' said Steg. 'If I give my troopers the command to fire, you will be disintegrated, blasted to fragments of your filthy primal slime. No shielding can protect you from so many blasters at such close range. Open the Gate – or you die.'

'Give the order if you wish, Sontaran,' said the cold clear voice. 'You understand nothing. We are Rutan, we cannot die. Why should we obey you? This fragment of our consciousness has no importance. You achieve nothing by destroying it.'

'Something of a dilemma for you, Commander Steg,' said the Doctor unhelpfully. 'The lack of an individual consciousness removes the terror from the threat of death – renders it meaningless in fact.'

Steg swung round at the sound of the Doctor's voice. The Doctor ignored him, giving all his attention to the great crystal control console.

'Do you understand this device, Doctor?'

'Oh, I think so,' said the Doctor confidently. 'It may look like the original mighty Wurlitzer, but basically it's a very simple space-time warping template. Not unlike the one in the TARDIS but about a million times simpler.'

'Excellent. I take it, therefore, that you are able to open the Gateway?'

'Oh yes. But why should I?'

'Please, Doctor,' said Steg wearily. 'You may be a Time Lord, but *you* are not part of a group consciousness. Or even if you are – your friends are not. Death still has some terrors for you – and for them. Must I really utter the usual threats?'

'You mean if I don't open the gate for you, you'll kill all my friends, one by one, in a variety of increasingly messy and unpleasant ways?'

'Something along those lines, yes.'

There was a long pause.

'In that case,' said the Doctor, 'you leave me no choice.'

Chris was horrified by his sudden surrender. 'Doctor!'

'Do you really want to die for the Rutans, Chris?' said the Doctor gently. 'More important, do you want to see Roz and Bernice die? Not to mention Kurt and Lisa?'

Chris hung his head. It felt all wrong – but he could find no reply.

'Don't look so shattered,' said the Doctor. 'What do we care what happens to a faraway planet of which we know little?'

'What about the broad picture?' asked Roz.

Like Chris, she had no answer, but she felt curiously let down.

'I'm losing my taste for the broad picture,' said the Doctor. 'Somehow it never seems quite worth it when you start counting the cost in the bodies of your friends. Anything I have to do to get us out of here alive, I'll do.'

'Then do it, Doctor,' said Steg impatiently. 'Or must I execute one of your friends, simply to convince you I am sincere? Order of least importance would be best. Where shall I begin? This overgrown bug here?' He gestured contemptuously towards the stricken Lord Chancellor. 'Or this petty criminal, Kurt?'

'Not so much of the petty,' said Kurt.

'I thought we agreed there was no need for this,' said the Doctor steadily. 'As you well know, I value all my friends, and I'll do what I must to save them.'

He went over to the console and set to work. Steg watched him as he moved from control to control, touching each glowing projection in turn with his palm.

'How much longer?' rasped Steg impatiently.

'Not long. The effect should be visible quite soon.'

'Fetch me the field transmitter,' ordered Steg. Two troopers appeared carrying a heavy piece of communications equipment.

Steg began talking into it, in low, urgent tones. 'Yes, very soon now, Admiral. I suggest that you take position. Thank you, sir. And good fortune to you.'

Steg went over to the Temple doorway and stood looking upwards. Above him the sky began to darken. On a sudden impulse Steg called, 'Gather the prisoners in the doorway here so they may see our triumph. Kill anyone who tries to escape.'

Herded into the doorway by Sontaran troopers, the mystified captives joined Steg in looking upwards at the sky. The Doctor, his work apparently finished, came to join them.

The sky continued to darken, not all over but in a clearly defined area. Soon there was a great circle of darkness, not unlike the effect produced by an eclipse.

A spaceship appeared, heading for the circle of blackness. The massive wheel-like structures either side of the huge central dome gave it the appearance of a mighty juggernaut, rolling remorselessly through space.

'The War Wheel,' breathed Steg. 'Now watch.'

The War Wheel rolled into the circle of darkness and disappeared. The dark circle faded, and the War Wheel had gone.

Steg turned to the Rutan, hovering in the doorway beneath the menace of Sontaran blasters. 'You have seen the doom of your miserable race, Rutan. Now we wait.'

'Wait for what?' demanded Bernice.

'For the Rutan to die, or to go mad. It will be interesting to see which occurs first.'

Bernice turned to the Doctor and discovered that while everyone, guards included, was staring in fascination at the sky, he had slipped back to the Rutan console and was working at frantic speed. His hands flew over the crystal controls in a series of increasingly complex movements. He finished at last and came back to join the others, his face calm and resigned.

'What's happening, Doctor?' whispered Bernice.

'Well,' said the Doctor, 'it's simple enough, really.'

Steg held up his hand. 'Please, Doctor, allow me my moment of triumph.' He addressed his assembled captives. 'What you have just witnessed is the opening, and closing, of a wormhole – a hyperspace tunnel through normal space. Long ago, the Rutans discovered that the wormhole linked their home world and Sentarion. They saw it as an escape-route – a bolt-hole for their supreme ruler, the Great Mother, repository of the group consciousness that links all Rutans. They forgot that a tunnel runs two ways. The War Wheel will emerge from the wormhole on the Rutans' home planet. There it will destroy the Great Mother – and when the Great Mother dies, every single Rutan will either die or go mad.'

The Rutan gave a great shriek of pain.

Steg laughed. 'We shall attack in force, and the Rutans will be powerless to resist us. The Rutan Empire will be finished. Then we shall bring Sontaran discipline to the rest of the galaxy. Is my exposition correct, Doctor?'

The Doctor said, 'Almost.'

Something in his voice sent a chill of fear through Steg's heart. 'What do you mean – almost?'

'You are assuming that the War Wheel will leave the wormhole.'

'What do you mean? It has entered, it will leave.'

'Hyperspace travel is almost instantaneous,' said the Doctor. 'Shouldn't our Rutan friend be going a bit green by now? How do you feel, Karne – if I can call you that?'

'We feel nothing. Nothing has changed.'

'Nor will it,' said the Doctor. 'The Great Mother is safe. The Sontaran plan has failed.'

Steg thrust his way through troopers and captives until he confronted the Doctor. 'Why has it failed, Doctor?'

'I told you that the Rutan device was a simple warping template? It was a simple matter to reverse the polarity. The worm has swallowed its tail, Steg. Its entrance is now an infinite time from its exit. The War Wheel can never emerge. It will journey on for ever.' He turned to the Rutan. 'There's a price to pay, of course. The wormhole can never be used again. You must find some other way to safeguard your Great Mother. And it's time you stopped playing space-gods with the Sentarrii and allowed them to develop alone.'

There was genuine puzzlement in Steg's voice. 'You did all this, Doctor? You tricked and defied me, knowing that it meant certain death for you, and for all your friends?'

'You know who I am, Steg. Did you really think you could intimidate me?'

'I underestimated you, Doctor,' said Steg in a low voice. 'But perhaps you also underestimated me. Did you perhaps think I should spare you, now that all is lost?'

'Why not? Surely vengeance is pointless now.'

'It is all I have, Doctor. All that you have left me.'

'Then spare my friends. I am the one who defeated you.'

'I am defeated and disgraced,' said Steg. 'But I am a Sontaran, Doctor. I shall play the game out to the end.' He raised his voice in command to his troopers. 'Kill the prisoners. Kill them one by one, the Doctor last. Let him see his friends die.' He pointed to Bernice. 'Begin with this one!'

'No!' bellowed the Lord Chancellor.

Ignoring him, the trooper nearest Bernice raised his blaster.

The Lord Chancellor swooped down from his enormous height, seized the trooper in powerful foreclaws, and bit off his head.

The terrified troopers opened fire and the Chancellor fell.

Immediately the other Sentarrii, the Chancellor's aides, flung themselves on the Sontaran troopers, snapping and rending with savage jaws. The Sentarrii had once been warriors too. More Sentarrii flooded in from the Inner Temple to join the fight. They fought with a dreadful ravening ferocity that chilled the blood. Most of the troopers were literally ripped apart. The survivors panicked and fled into the lush tropical garden. A mass of dark shapes moved in the green foliage.

The Harrubtii were waiting.

As the terrified troopers ran through the dense green foliage, the Harrubtii pounced, pulling them down, one by one.

Kurt made a dive for the stack of blasters, tossing weapons to Chris, Roz and Lisa.

'Back to the ship!' he yelled.

The Doctor grabbed Bernice's hand. 'When I say run – run!'

Fighting their way through the carnage, sliding on the blood-slippery Temple floor, they fled into the tropical garden.

Lisa and Kurt ran ahead, Roz and Chris formed a rearguard. They forced their way through the fringe of the battle, shooting down anything, Sontaran or Harrubtii, in their way.

Lisa saw one of the Harrubtii spring onto the back of a Sontaran trooper, search for a weak point and plunge its long spike deep into the probic vent. The trooper screamed and fell.

'Works even better than a screwdriver,' yelled Kurt.

They reached the ship at last, ran up the ramp and through the open airlock door. Lisa ran to the door controls.

A gentle voice said, 'Wait!'

A slender fair-haired young man stood in the doorway, covering them with a blaster.

'We are sorry,' he said. 'Now you must all die.'

'Who the hell are you?' said Lisa.

'It's the Rutan,' whispered Roz. 'He's changed back.'

Chris couldn't believe such ingratitude.

'The Doctor saved you! Saved all your people.'

'He interfered in our plans. The wormhole can be reestablished, the escape route restored.'

'I assure you that's quite impossible,' said the Doctor.

'Perhaps so,' said the young man. 'But you know too much about us and our secrets. It is best for the Rutan that you die.'

Another shape appeared in the doorway behind the young man. It was Steg, blaster in hand.

The young man raised his blaster to shoot the Doctor.

'No!' shouted Lisa.

She raised her blaster, the young man swung round to shoot her first instead – and Steg blasted him at point-blank range.

The Rutan blurred, collapsing in a gelatinous mass – just as Lisa fired. Her blast passed over the dying Rutan and into Steg.

He staggered back against the corridor wall and slid slowly to the ground, the blaster falling from his hand.

The Doctor looked down at him. 'It seems that I must thank you, Commander Steg.'

'No need, Doctor,' said Steg weakly. 'I came for my

vengeance. As it happened, I could kill you or the Rutan. I chose the Rutan.'

Lisa knelt beside him. 'You saved my life – again.'

Steg looked up at her. The thin Sontaran mouth twitched in an attempt at a smile. 'And you took mine.'

'It was an accident.'

'I have saved you twice, and you have killed me twice,' said Steg. 'It… hardly… seems… fair.'

His head fell back.

Kurt turned to the others. 'Chuck the bodies out and let's blast off before any more of those jumbo beetles turn up.'

'No,' said Lisa. She pointed to the remains of the Rutan. 'You can get a bucket of water and swill that up, but Steg stays. We'll find a way of getting him back to his own people. If they don't want him, I'll bury him myself.'

Kurt looked at her for a moment, and then smiled.

'Just as you like. Bury him by all means. At least that way we'll be sure he's really dead this time.'

Kurt dragged Steg's body away. Lisa sealed the airlock door, and she and the Doctor headed for the control room.

Bernice Summerfield looked at Chris and Roz and went up and hugged them both.

'Is there a drink on this tub?' she asked hopefully.

'If there is, we'll find it,' said Roz. 'Come on!'

Chris started to follow, but Roz put out a hand. She nodded towards the pool of slime, all that remained of the Rutan.

'You heard the Captain. Get a bucket and clear up that mess!'

22
PAYBACK

The solar yacht *Tiger Moth*, currently on special charter, was proceeding under power to Space Station Beta.

The hyper-space jump was completed, the power drive was running smoothly, and the voyage was proceeding under automatic pilot, with nothing to worry about until docking.

Captain, owner, charterer and passengers were socialising in the crewroom, drinking Eridanean brandy and all getting on surprisingly well.

It was explanation time, with the Doctor, as usual, reluctantly fielding most of the questions.

'Surely you know it all by now,' he protested.

'Yes, but only ass-backward, and out of order,' said Kurt. 'Begin at the beginning.'

'It started years ago, when the Rutans first discovered the wormhole,' said the Doctor. 'They popped out close to Sentarion, where the simple insectoid natives treated them as gods. The Rutans decided that the wormhole should serve as a secret escape tunnel if ever the Great Mother should be in danger. They accelerated the development of the Sentarrii and set up a religious cult at the same time. They set up a warping template device so they could close both ends of the wormhole, and open them again at will, and concealed the control mechanism in the Great Temple. Everything was fine until a Rutan spy, then calling himself Karne, accessed some Sontaran data and discovered that the Sontarans were on the trail of the Great Secret.'

'Sort of a "he knew that they knew" deal?' said Kurt.

'Precisely. Karne got blown up in a battle soon afterwards and stranded in space. It was some time before he got himself together again and set off home to warn his fellow Rutans that their secret was in danger. Before long the Sontarans became aware that Karne was still alive, and that he knew that they were close to discovering the secret.'

'So they knew that he knew that they knew!' said Kurt.

Lisa jabbed him in the ribs. 'Shut up. Go on, Doctor.'

'I tried to warn the Rutans, but they wouldn't listen. I also tried to find Karne – I knew they'd believe him. I set Roz and Chris on his trail. But the Sontarans were after him too. Oh, and I also sent Bernice to Sentarion as well to poke around. She did so well she got herself locked up in the Temple.'

'On a diet of fruit juice and salads,' said Bernice.

She poured herself another slug of brandy remembering how long she'd been deprived.

The Doctor nodded at Kurt and Lisa. 'Eventually Karne got to Station Alpha and stowed away on your ship, and Steg came after him. You know what happened then. What you didn't know was that before he made his last break for freedom, Karne divided, and left Karne Two hiding on the ship in case Karne One failed – which thanks to you two, he did!'

'I get the feeling you'd have preferred us to get ourselves killed just so Karne got through with his message,' said Lisa. 'Sorry to cause so much trouble.'

'Not at all,' said the Doctor. 'You weren't to know! Anyway, Karne Two decided it was too dangerous to try to get to the homeworld, so he decided to make for Sentarion and get himself home via the wormhole. We set off after him, so did Steg, and the rest you know!'

'One thing I don't know,' said Kurt, 'or rather don't understand. How could you deliberately sabotage that wormhole, knowing it would get you and all the rest of us killed?'

'I've been thinking about that myself,' said Lisa.

'We were all going to be killed anyway,' said the Doctor. 'Steg would never have let us live. It was a choice between dying for nothing, or going down fighting – and dying for something. You faced a very similar situation yourselves, on this very ship. Besides, there's always a chance something will turn up – and luckily it did.'

'But you couldn't know that,' said Bernice.

'You never do know,' said the Doctor. 'You just keep trying. You don't give up until you're dead.'

'Or even then, if you're Steg,' said Chris.

There was an awkward pause. To bridge it Bernice said, 'What will happen now on Sentarion, Doctor?'

'I imagine they'll go on worshipping their Shining Ones. It's embedded deep in their culture by now. But with any luck, the Rutans will leave them alone from now on.'

Chris looked at Lisa, who was looking grim and determined. 'Cheer up – it's all over now. You'll be rid of us soon.'

'That's right,' said the Doctor. 'When we get back to Beta we'll get the shuttle to Alpha – they'll have retrieved my transport by now – and be off.'

'Oh no you won't,' said Lisa. 'Not till you've paid me back. You still owe me, Doctor.'

'My dear lady,' said the Doctor, 'if you are alluding to your charter fee, I paid that in advance.'

'I told you, Doctor – the fee didn't include heroics. We

left the safety of the ship to warn you the Sontarans were coming. You nearly got us killed.'

'If you're trying to negotiate an increase in your already exorbitant fee—'

'Oh, I want a payback, Doctor,' said Lisa. 'But not in money…'

Two weeks later, the solar yacht *Tiger Moth*, refitted and refurbished to the highest standard, was en route from Space Station Beta to Space Station Alpha – on a shakedown cruise.

When Captain Deranne arrived on the sail deck, she found her crew ready and waiting for her.

A vast shadowy area, lit by an eerie green glow, the sail deck held a main control console at the centre of a semicircle of virtual reality platforms.

All four were occupied. Roz, Chris and Bernice wore inexpensive green space coveralls, while Kurt was in his usual black. All four held VR goggles and gloves.

Lisa Deranne looked round the group.

'Remember this, it's important. In solar yacht racing, the start is everything. Whether we win or lose can all be decided in those first minutes. This new sail rig of the Doctor's we're using is exceptionally tricky. So, we do it right, and we do it quick. Right, stand by!'

The crew pulled on their VR gloves and goggles and the others did the same. A holograph sprang to life in the centre of the sail deck, a representation of the *Tiger Moth* as she was now, drifting through space with furled sails.

Lisa began snapping out commands.

'Set mainsail, full extension.'

Kurt's gauntleted hands moved in the air before him.

The *Tiger Moth*'s enormous, shimmering mainsail spread out in space – in reality, in Kurt's virtual reality, and on the hologram in the centre of the sail deck.

'Mainsail set,' he reported.

'Set port sails, full extension,' ordered Lisa.

Working feverishly in his own virtual reality, Chris called, 'Port sails set.'

'Starboard sails, full extension.'

Now it was Roz Forrester's turn. Anxious – she'd never raced before – but determined not to show it, she hauled determinedly on her virtual reality cable, in her virtual reality world.

'Starboard sails set.'

'Set spinnaker, full extension.'

Standing on the deck of a great sailing ship sweeping through space, lost in the wonder of it all, Bernice was slow to react. Sharply, Lisa repeated the command.

'Set spinnaker, full extension. Wake up, Benny!'

Adjusting her goggles, Bernice fumbled for the cable and the spinnaker rose upwards.

'Spinnaker set!'

Studying the solar wind readings on her console, Lisa gave more orders.

Together in their virtual reality world, wrestling with wheels and cables in the rigging of the great sailing ship as it sailed through space, Chris, Roz, Kurt and Bernice obeyed her commands.

Lisa considered the final result and then snapped, 'All sails set. Maintain position. Lock off.'

Transformed from an ungainly insect into a shimmeringly beautiful butterfly, the *Tiger Moth* swept through space, propelled only by the pressure of solar winds on her enormous set of fragile metal-foil sails.

DOCTOR WHO

The astonishing sight was reflected in the transformation of the hologram on the sail deck.

Bernice pushed up her goggles and studied the glowing holograph with awe. 'It's beautiful,' she whispered.

The crew removed goggles and gauntlets, returned to the real world, and waited for Lisa's reaction.

She studied her console. She studied the holograph. At last she raised her eyes and surveyed the little group.

'Great!' she said. 'Terrific! Wonderful!'

The crew members looked at each other in pleased surprise. Did she really mean it?

She didn't.

'More like an arthritic Algolian dung beetle than a Tiger Moth. By the time we set off, the other ships in the race would be halfway home. Benny, you *must* be quicker with that spinnaker. Roz, your lower starboard sail is a degree out of line. We'd be going round in circles. Chris, no problems, well done!'

By this time, Bernice was red-faced, Roz was furious, Chris was looking smug, and Kurt mildly amused.

'I don't know why you're so cheerful, Kurt,' said Lisa. 'You're still elevating too high, I said five degrees, not six!'

Kurt's smile disappeared.

Actually, thought Lisa, they'd done better than she'd expected. Not that she was going to tell them so, not yet. You break them down before you build them up.

She looked around her chastened crew.

'We are going to repeat this and similar manoeuvres until you can do them perfectly, smoothly, swiftly, and if necessary, in your sleep. Is that clear?'

She turned and marched from the sail deck.

'Well, that was fun!' said Chris brightly.

Bernice ripped off her goggles and gauntlets and

282

SHAKEDOWN

slammed them down on the console. 'Is she always like that?'

'Oh no,' said Kurt mildly. 'Sometimes she gets quite ratty.'

'I'll kill her,' said Bernice. 'Before this shakedown cruise is over, I swear I'll kill her. I need a drink.' She stormed out of the room.

Roz Forrester took off her goggles and gloves and laid them neatly on the console. She thought back to her days in recruit training long ago. The sergeant hadn't been born that could break her. Or the yacht captain either. She ran her fingers through her close-cropped hair and grinned defiantly at Kurt.

'Thinks she's hard, does she? Huh!' she said, and marched out.

Kurt saw that Chris was looking at him curiously. 'What?'

'Am I right in thinking you're rather keen on our Captain?'

Kurt glared up at him. 'What if I am?'

Chris, who was roughly twice his size, held up his hands defensively. 'No offence, Kurt. I just wanted to say how much I admire stark courage in a man. I used to think Roz was tough.'

'I can handle Lisa,' said Kurt confidently. 'She's a pussycat really – when she's not racing, of course.'

'She spends most of her time racing, doesn't she?' asked Chris innocently.

'Oh, belt up,' said Kurt. 'Let's have a brandy before Benny finishes it all.'

Looking rather thoughtful, he followed Chris from the sail deck.

*

283

In the control room the Doctor had been listening to Lisa over the intercom. He grinned at the recollection. It was, he imagined, her standard speech with new crews. He looked at the blue box tucked into a corner of the control room and reflected that there were easier ways to travel.

Lisa Deranne marched into the room and slammed a sheaf of diagrams onto the console.

'I want to go over this new rig you're suggesting, Doctor. There are one or two points I don't understand.'

'We've been over it twice already,' protested the Doctor.

'And we'll go over it again,' said Lisa Deranne. 'We'll go over it until I understand it – and until I like it. And if I don't like it, we won't use it. Is that clear, Doctor?'

'Aye, aye, Captain,' said the Doctor.

He wondered what had happened to mild, gentle, womanly women. Like Ace – and Leela.

Just for a moment he looked longingly at the blue box. Then he picked up the first diagram.

The headline in the *Tri-planetary Times* read

LISA DERANNE TAKES TRI-SYSTEMS
WITH MYSTERY RIG
AND UNKNOWN CREW

The picture beneath the headline showed Lisa Deranne, her face radiant, holding the enormous Inter-Systems Cup.

Grouped around her were one very large fair-haired young man, a thick-set, rather older one, a youngish dark-haired woman, a smaller woman with dark skin and short dark hair, and a small man in a rumpled suit, trying to hide behind the others.

The story beneath it began: 'Our picture shows Captain Lisa Deranne, winner of the Tri-Systems cup – a truly sensational victory. With her are her crew, all newcomers to interplanetary class solar racing.

'The gentleman on the right of the picture is Doctor Smith, designer of the sensational new solar sails rig which swept the *Tiger Moth* to a clear victory.

'He also sailed with the winning crew, doubling as ship's engineer. Asked if he intended to remain actively involved in solar yacht racing, Doctor Smith said it was unlikely. He was a simple scholar who preferred a quiet life, and the excitements and stresses of solar yacht racing were just too much for him.

'The rest of the crew were unavailable for comment.'

Also available in the Doctor Who Monster Collection*:*

PRISONER OF THE DALEKS
TREVOR BAXENDALE
ISBN 978 1 849 90755 2

The Daleks are advancing, their empire constantly expanding.
The battles rage on across countless solar systems – and the
Doctor finds himself stranded on board a starship near the
frontline with a group of ruthless bounty hunters. Earth
Command will pay these hunters for every Dalek they kill,
every eyestalk they bring back as proof.

With the Doctor's help, the bounty hunters achieve the
ultimate prize: a Dalek prisoner – intact, powerless, and
ready for interrogation. But with the Daleks, nothing is what
it seems, and no one is safe. Before long the tables will be
turned, and how will the Doctor survive when he becomes
a prisoner of the Daleks?

An adventure featuring the Tenth Doctor, as played by David Tennant

Also available in the Doctor Who Monster Collection:

TOUCHED BY AN ANGEL
JONATHAN MORRIS
ISBN 978 1 849 90756 9

'The past is like a foreign country. Nice to visit, but you really wouldn't want to live there.'

In 2003, Rebecca Whitaker died in a road accident. Her husband Mark is still grieving. He receives a battered envelope, posted eight years earlier, containing a set of instructions with a simple message: 'You can save her.'

As Mark is given the chance to save Rebecca, it's up to the Doctor, Amy and Rory to save the whole world. Because this time the Weeping Angels are using history itself as a weapon.

An adventure featuring the Eleventh Doctor, as played by Matt Smith, and his companions Amy and Rory

Also available in the Doctor Who *Monster Collection:*

ILLEGAL ALIEN

MIKE TUCKER AND ROBERT PERRY

ISBN 978 1 849 90757 6

The Blitz is at its height. As the Luftwaffe bomb London, Cody McBride, ex-pat American private eye, sees a sinister silver sphere crash-land. He glimpses something emerging from within. The military dismiss his account of events – the sphere must be a new German secret weapon that has malfunctioned in some way. What else could it be?

Arriving amid the chaos, the Doctor and Ace embark on a trail that brings them face to face with hidden Nazi agents, and encounter some very old enemies…

An adventure featuring the Seventh Doctor, as played by Sylvester McCoy, and his companion Ace

THE SCALES OF INJUSTICE
GARY RUSSELL

ISBN 978 1 849 90780 4

When a boy goes missing and a policewoman starts drawing
cave paintings, the Doctor suspects the Silurians are back.
With the Brigadier distracted by questions about UNIT
funding and problems at home, the Doctor swears his
assistant Liz Shaw to secrecy and investigates alone.

But Liz has enquiries of her own, teaming up with a
journalist to track down people who don't exist. What is
the mysterious Glasshouse, and why is it so secret?

As the Silurians wake from their ancient slumber, the
Doctor, Liz and the Brigadier are caught up in a conspiracy
to exploit UNIT's achievements – a conspiracy that reaches
deep into the heart of the British Government.

*An adventure featuring the Third Doctor, as played by Jon Pertwee,
his companion Liz Shaw and UNIT*

Also available in the Doctor Who Monster Collection:

STING OF THE ZYGONS
STEPHEN COLE
ISBN 978 1 849 90754 5

The TARDIS lands the Doctor and Martha in the Lake District in 1909, where a small village has been terrorised by a giant, scaly monster. The search is on for the elusive 'Beast of Westmorland', and explorers, naturalists and hunters from across the country are descending on the fells. King Edward VII himself is on his way to join the search, with a knighthood for whoever finds the Beast.

But there is a more sinister presence at work in the Lakes than a mere monster on the rampage, and the Doctor is soon embroiled in the plans of an old and terrifying enemy. And as the hunters become the hunted, a desperate battle of wits begins – with the future of the entire world at stake…

An adventure featuring the Tenth Doctor, as played by David Tennant, and his companion Martha

Also available in the Doctor Who Monster Collection:

Corpse Marker
Chris Boucher

ISBN 978 1 849 90759 0

The Doctor and Leela arrive on the planet Kaldor, where they find a society dependent on benign and obedient robots. But they have faced these robots before, on a huge Sandminer in the Kaldor desert, and know they are not always harmless servants…

The only other people who know the truth are the three survivors from that Sandminer – and now they are being picked off one by one. The twisted genius behind that massacre is dead, but someone is developing a new, deadlier breed of robots. This time, unless the Doctor and Leela can stop them, they really will destroy the world…

An adventure featuring the Fourth Doctor, as played by Tom Baker, and his companion Leela

Also available in the Doctor Who Monster Collection:

The Sands of Time
Justin Richards
ISBN 978 1 849 90767 5

The Doctor is in Victorian London with Nyssa and Tegan – a city shrouded in mystery. When Nyssa is kidnapped in the British Museum, the Doctor and Tegan have to unlock the answers to a series of ancient questions.

Their quest leads them across continents and time as an ancient Egyptian prophecy threatens future England. To save Nyssa, the Doctor must foil the plans of the mysterious Sadan Rassul. But as mummies stalk the night, an ancient terror stirs in its tomb.

An adventure featuring the Fifth Doctor, as played by Peter Davison, and his companions Nyssa and Tegan